101 WAYS TO BUG YOUR FRIENDS and ENEMIES

by Lee Wardlaw

SCHOLASTIC INC.
New York Toronto London Auckland
Sydney Mexico City New Delhi Hong Kong

For my newest friend,
Jennifer Sagran,
who kept me sane and laughing during grad school...
...And for my dear friends and fellow fAiRy gOdSiStErS
Thalia Chaltas, Mary Hershey, Valerie Hobbs,
and Robin La Fevers,
who kept my seat warm at home.

ISBN 978-0-545-48369-8

12 11 10 9 8 7 6 5 4 3 2 1   12 13 14 15 16 17/0

Printed in the U.S.A.   40

First Scholastic printing, September 2012

Book design by Jasmin Rubero
Text set in Caslon Book BE

" . . . great love and great achievements involve great risk."   —Dalai Lama

"And the day came when the risk to remain tight in a bud was more painful than the risk it took to blossom."   —Anaïs Nin

Chapter One

"Stephen J. Wyatt: You're not *peeking*, are you?" Hayley's guiding hand became a boa constrictor squeeze.

"Ow!" I said, rubbing my arm. "You're kidding me, right?"

"Are. You. Peeking." I could feel her infamous SOS (Squint of Suspicion) searing through the blindfold, searching for guilt in my eyes.

"No! Honest!" I half laughed, half gasped. "Goldie tied this blindfold so tight it's imbedded in my corneas." *And scraping my chapped nose like a cheese grater,* I ached to whimper. But there's only so much wimpyness a guy likes to admit. Especially in front of G-I-R-L-S.

Goldie's words dripped with sly glee. "Just a little something I learned at Spy Camp. I call it *Goldie's Knot.*"

"Goldie's not what?" I heard Ace say, his voice filled with Yawn.

"Goldie's *not* able to untie it, that's what," warned my best friend Hiccup. "Especially if it's similar to the Gordian Knot of Macedonia. Legends tell of a knot no one could loosen until Alexander the Great—"

"Zat eez so *not* eenteresting," Pierre said in his phony French accent.

It was early September, and the six of us—me, Hayley Barker, Hiccup Denardo, Goldie Laux, Pierre Noel, and Ace (who is too cool to have a last name)—were all crammed inside the hot, musty office at Gadabout Golf, the funky miniature golf course Hayley's dad owns. I work part-time as their mechanic—when I'm not busy inventing, attending class at Jefferson Middle School, or away on vacation, that is.

After road-tripping across California with my parents all summer, this was my first day home. My first *half hour* home. No sooner had I finished lugging our suitcases into the house than the kitchen phone rang.

"*Sneeze.*" Hayley stated my nickname in her businesslike tone. "It's an emergency. Get to Gadabout. *Now.*"

Hayley's my Number Two best friend *and* my boss. So when she says *now,* I know she really means *Get here in twenty minutes or You. Are. Fired.* That would be the equivalent of surgically removing my soul with a golf club. So I dropped the receiver, clipped on my tool belt, hollered a hasty good-bye to Mom and Dad, and sped off on my bike—with visions of the Leaning Tower of Pisa (Hole #17) ker-splashing in my head.

Rats! Pisa must've toppled into King Arthur's Moat. I warned Mr. Barker weeks ago that it needed propping, but did he listen . . . ?

Nineteen minutes and thirty-two seconds later, I skidded

to a stop at Gadabout's rusty gates and hustled through the office door.

That's when I'd been jumped from behind—

"Hey!"

blindfolded—

"Ow!"

spun thrice—

"Whoa!"

and painfully accused of peeking.

"C'mon, guys," I pleaded now. "What's going on?"

Pierre snickered through his nose. "*Oh-ho-ho-HO!* Pleeze to keep on zee—'ow do you say eet?—pantaloons.*"

"You'll find out soon enough!" Goldie said, spinning me again.

I half laughed, half hurled.

"Easy does it," Hiccup fussed. "Vertigo may induce vomiting."

"Oh, *gag*," Goldie said.

"Exactly," Hiccup agreed.

Hayley tested the knot knuckling my skull. "Not so fast, Sneeze. If you're not peeking, how did you know Goldie tied your blindfold? She snuck up on you from behind!"

"Elementary, my dear Ms. Barker," I said, trying to sound Sherlockian. I have a tenuous reputation for being a genius (as well as a whiz-kid inventor), and never miss the opportunity to strengthen that rep among the nonbelievers (meaning Goldie and Pierre). "First, I deduced Hiccup was standing to my left, by the cash register, because he wheezes whenever he's close to—"

"You're allergic to *cash registers*?" Goldie asked him.

"Don't be ridiculous," Hic replied.

"—that box of golf pencils," I finished.

"You're allergic to *pencils*?"

"Pencil *shavings*. They emit an aroma similar to wood smoke. My respiratory system is *particularly* sensitive to *particulate* pollution." Hic chuckled. "No pun intended."

"No pun taken," Ace said.

"Oh," said Goldie, "you're allergic to *camping*."

"'Oo could blame 'im?" Pierre gave an audible shudder. "Camping food eez so ickee! You Americanz 'ave zee culinary skills of zee caveman."

Hayley snorted. "This from a guy born in Oklahoma, where the official state vegetable is fried okra."

Pierre is desperate to become a world-famous French chef. That's why he speaks wis zat fake accent. Pierre would pour wine on his Cheerios and tattoo the entire musical score of the Blue Danube Waltz on his butt if he thought it would make him more *français*. (And yes, the Blue Danube is actually German, but no one cares enough to enlighten him.)

A whoosh of air sliced past my face. "Oklahoma—bah!" Pierre spat. "Eye 'ave been eensulted! Eye challenge you to zee duel!"

"Give me that," Hayley instructed. "Sword fighting with the clubs is not tolerated at Gadabout."

"Second!" I continued. "I knew Pierre was here because I smelled escargot on his breath."

"What is ess-car-go?" Goldie asked. "A fancy gasoline?"

"A fancy word for 'snail,'" Hiccup explained.

"Oh, *gag.*"

"Indeed. Snail Fever is highly infectious, and may surpass malaria—"

Hayley interrupted: "Pierre needing a breath mint doesn't explain how Sneeze knew Goldie was here."

"I was getting to that." I cleared my throat for the grand finale. "Third, Pierre hates miniature golf and Hic has a moat phobia—"

"Moats plus mosquitoes equals malaria," Hiccup put in.

"—therefore the two of them never come to Gadabout unless something important is afoot. And if something's afoot, Goldie can't be tiptoeing far behind. She's the Snoop with the Scoop, right?"

"*Ooo!* Gotta jot *that* down!" I heard her grope for her ever-present notepad. "I've been *dying* to change the name of my *Goldie's Gossip* column for the school newspaper. How's this? *Goldie Laux: The Snoop with the Scoop!*"

Hayley expressed her opinion of Goldie and Goldie's chosen profession with a murmured, "Even better: *The Snoop with the Poop.*"

Goldie stamped a foot and cuss-sputtered in what might've been a Klingon dialect complete with indignant spit.

"Swearing is also not tolerated at Gadabout," Hayley said

coolly. That's two of the reasons I admire her: She's adamant about running a "safe, family-friendly" fun center; *and* she's too smart to be intimidated by the incoherent profanities of a Hollywood wannabe who thinks stamping a hoof like a petulant pony will send people galloping in mortal fear.

Hayley's hand clasped mine for two whole warm seconds. "I'm sorry, Steve." As she let go, the raspy callous on her right index finger (from years of playing mini-golf) snag-tickled my palm. "I guess this wasn't much of a surprise after all."

"No. Yes. I mean, Ness!" My hand felt *stunned.* "What I mean is, I'm surprised I was supposed to be surprised. On the phone you said 'emergency.' Which is different from a surprise. Although, emergencies can be surprising." *Gaaaa, I'm dithering!* "But Ace was one hundred percent. A surprise, that is. I didn't know he was here till he yawned."

Ace yawned again for effect.

"Of course he's here," Hayley said. "He wouldn't miss your party, would he?"

Debatable. Ace is cool. So cool he probably doesn't even attend his own—

"*That's* what this is about?" I asked. "A *party*—for . . . *me?*"

"Well, duh," Goldie said, and with a yank that gave my sore nose carpet burn, the blindfold fell to my feet.

"*Surprise!*" everyone (except Ace, who is too cool) shouted.

I blinked. My sight shifted from blind to blurry, taking in the familiar "sweetness" of Gadabout's office, which is built with fake lollipops, gumdrops, and graham crackers to resemble the witch's gingerbread cottage from Hansel and Gretel.

Despite my nose being clogged with allergy goo (I'm allergic to practically everything except water and air), I managed to snork up the beloved smells of my home away from home: the lemony tang of golf ball washing solution; the oily metal of putters; lily pads fermenting in King Arthur's murky moat; the plastic putting greens, sepia-scorched from the blazing Southern California sun.

Aaaaaah. It felt great to be home, back to my job, my sanctuary . . .

The Gordian Knot of Disappointment that had twisted my innards the past two weeks began to fray. Until—

"Surprise," Hayley repeated, softer this time so only I could hear.

My vision sharpened crystal crisp.

Streamers dangled from the Tootsie Roll rafters. A balloon bouquet bobbed in the listless breeze of the ceiling fan. On a card table, arranged with festive forks, plates, and napkins, stood a cake.

Oh, what a cake! It was baked in the shape of my most ingenious invention: the Nice Alarm, a clock that awakens you *not* with an annoying bell or buzzer, but with two *nice* taps on the shoulder. Above it hung a banner, declaring in Hayley's bold, no-nonsense hand, the same message spelled on the cake in squares of sugar letters:

IT'S TIME TO WISH SNEEZE CONGRATULATIONS!

Rats. They don't know.

Well, duh, Sneeze, I thought, à la Goldie. *Of course they don't know. You haven't told them yet.*

At that, my nose started to tickle.

And tingle.

And itch.

I tried to hold back. Honest, I did. I wince-pinched my tender nostrils and sucked in a breath so hard I practically inhaled a streamer, but—

"AHHHH-*CHOOEY!*"

A sneeze of titanic proportions typhooned across the Nice Alarm cake.

Chapter Two

"Mon Dieu!" The wail wrenched from Pierre's mouth.

Goldie pouted. "I am so *not* eating *that.*"

Hot embarrassment flooded my cheeks. "Sorry, sorry!" I mopped my nose with a wad of tissues.

"You ee-dee-ot! 'Ave you no self-control?" Pierre looked ready to strangle me. "My cake—she eez ruined!"

Ace glanced over his sunglasses. "Shipwrecked, to be exact."

Most of the meringue frosting had blown overboard. A few letters clung for dear life to a chocolatey edge. The others, strewn like flotsam and jetsam, now spelled TROUT LASAGNA ZONE.

"Disgust-o-*rama!*" Goldie whipped out her camera and, paparazzi-style, snapped a few photos. I had the sinking suspicion they'd soon appear in her column with the headline: *Sneeze's Supersonic Snot Scuttles Celebratory Snack.*

"Oh, for goodness golf tees!" Hayley's dangly golf ball earrings quivered. "You two are the rudest, most exasperating, insensitive . . ."

She snatched a cake server and troweled meringue off

9

the table. "This. Is. Salvageable," she announced, ready to re-slather frosting like mortar. "It might not look pretty, but it'll taste fine."

"An unwise decision," Hiccup warned. "A sternutation of that magnitude travels one hundred miles per hour, expelling forty thousand infectious droplets of—"

"Sacré bleu!" Pierre whispered, clutching his beret at the horror of it all.

Ace arced a dark eyebrow and lounged against Mr. Barker's desk. "Pierre is *snot* interested," he said.

"I'm *sorry*," I said. "My allergies are out of control this week. I'm sneezing triple my daily quota."

Hiccup sprinted to my side like Medicine Man (MM), the caped superhero who stars in the graphic novels he draws. "Did you say *triple*?" he asked, grasping my wrist for a pulse.

"Is that serious?"

"I smell world record!" Goldie's gossipy fingers inched toward her notepad.

Hiccup shook his head. "The World's Longest Sneezing Fit was set by twelve-year-old Donna Griffiths of Great Britain. Her sneezes came at one-to five-minute intervals for nine hundred seventy-eight consecutive days."

Ace released a long, low whistle.

Goldie made a frownie face, struggling to compute Donna's grand total.

Mine wasn't even close to Donna's—yet. My only "record" was for how many packets of travel tissue I'd wedged into my tool belt. Fortunately, I hadn't needed my tools since the Invention Convention®. Unfortunately, after what happened there, I might never need them again . . .

"*Serious* is an understatement." Hiccup's worried, freckled gaze examined me from shaggy hair to straggly sneakers, searching for I-don't-know-what and I-was-afraid-to-ask. Crusty barnacles? Oozing pustules?

Goldie and Pierre peered at me with morbid fascination.

"'Eez nose! Eet eez even more grotesque than evaire!"

"*Ooo*, maybe it's *leprosy!*"

"Hanson's Disease," Hiccup corrected.

"It's neither," I snapped. "My schnoz is just chapped from blowing it so much. Now get out of my face, all of you!"

Hic was not deterred. "You passed the moat on your way in. Were you bit by a mosquito? Think, man! Your symptoms could reveal the onset of West Nile virus, posing dangers to pregnant women!"

"As opposed to pregnant men?" Ace asked.

"Get a grip, Hic. Mom is fine. We're all fine. Honest."

Hiccup has a crush on my mother. When he learned my parents were expecting a baby in December, his puppy love grew into a protective Doberman. Way weird, right? But to a hypochondriac who suspects he's contracted every disorder from Maple Syrup Urine Disease (after gobbling three dozen pancakes) to *Hippopotomonstrosesquippedaliophobia* (the fear of ultra-long words), swooning over my mother-the-scientist isn't weird at all. Especially since Mom saved him last spring from a terminal case of hiccups. (But that's another story.)

"*Whoop-pee-doo.*" Pierre flicked his beret into the air.

"Everyone at zee Wyatt 'ouse eez fine. Let us not concern ourselves wis such minor zings as *zee cake*. Zee cake zat eez now not even fit for Heecup's dogs!"

Goldie rolled her eyes. "*Puh-LEEZ*! The Dynamic Duo of Doggy Garbage Disposals? Pierre, you've been *so* AWOL lately, you haven't heard what they gobbled *this* time." She tossed her mane of golden hair and sent Hic a smug smile. "I'm sure *Sneeze* hasn't heard yet either. *Has he, Hiccup?*"

Hic's freckles blanched. "Ahem, alas, D and D continue to deserve their omnivorous reputation. Yesterday, Dasher dined on the pink pom-poms of our toilet seat cover—"

"That's *not* what I—"

"—and Dancer discovered the *D* section of my Disease Encyclopedia, gnawing from *Diaper Rash* to *Dumdum Fever*."

"That's *not* what I—wait, is that a dunce disease?" Goldie asked.

Ace plucked an invisible hair from his shirt. "You would know."

Goldie stomped another hoof.

"*Dumdum Fever*," Hiccup quoted. "*A parasitic infection, transmitted by sandfly, that—*"

Hayley pulled me aside. "Are you sure you're okay?" she asked. Her eyes searched mine, but the SOS had softened. "That was an impressive sneeze. I've never seen one of yours do *that* before." She pointed with the cake server. A dollop of meringue plopped onto my shoe. "Argh!"

"No worries." I took the stack of napkins she thrust at me. We bent to wipe—

CLUNK.

"Ow!"

"Ow!"

She clutched her forehead. I clutched my nose. It hurt like crazy. But it also felt . . . *nice*. Not the clunking part. Her skin on mine.

My cheeks flooded hot again.

"Sorry about this," Hayley muttered, gesturing at my shoe, then at the Bickersons. "The party was supposed to be just you, me, and Hic. I took extra precautions to keep it secret. But as always, Goldie found out—I swear she learned wiretapping at camp!—and she blabbed to Pierre, who blabbed to Ace—" She sighed. "Sorry. I'm not very good at throwing parties."

"And I'm not very good at *going* to parties."

"Huh," she said, but flinched a smile.

"Anyway, I don't mind *them*," I went on. "Much."

Yeah, Goldie and Pierre bug the boogers out of me sometimes. Ha. Most times. We'd been thrown together last year for a couple of school projects, so now they assumed we were comrades-in-arms. More like comrades-in-calamity. But Ace was cool. (Despite a disquieting habit of appearing and disappearing without reason or warning.) And you couldn't find a truer, bluer pal than Hiccup. He'd been my best bud since toddler-hood. (Okay, my only bud till I met Hayley.) I was used to his eccentricities. He was used to mine.

Besides, the longer everyone bickered, the longer it would take them to remember the Invention Convention®.

"Sneeze, I'm *dying* to get the scoop on the Invention Convention®!"

Pen poised, Goldie perched on the desk a mere millimeter from where Ace lounged. He observed her with a detached annoyance she pretended not to see. "You promised me an *exclusive* interview, so spill it! I want . . . *information.*"

"Uh . . ." I said.

"How much *moola* will you get for the Nice Alarm? Will it be for sale in time for Christmas? Will you share any profits with your *loyal supporters?*"

"Uh . . ."

I glanced at Hayley. Huge mistake. Her SOS powered up. Locked on target.

Uh-oh.

She *knew.* I *knew* that she knew. Just like she always knows when something with me is Not. Quite. Right.

Goldie tapped her foot. Goldie tapped her pen. Goldie tapped her foot *and* her pen. She's a one-woman percussion band, that Goldie.

"WELL?" she demanded.

"Cake!" Hayley said. "Time to eat cake!" She shot Goldie a *you-weren't-even-invited-so-don't-argue-with-me* look, then hacked out a huge hunk of Pierre's former masterpiece and plunged in her fork.

Goldie gagged. Hiccup choked. Ace shrugged. Pierre whispered, "*You are zee cray-zee woman!*"

Hayley eyed them with defiance and shoveled the mess into her mouth. Crumbs avalanched down her chin.

"Dee-licious!" she said, smacking her lips.

I'd known Hayley for more than a year. We'd been through a lot together. But in that instant, I *saw* her as if for the First Time: the bobbed, blond hair curled in a C behind one ear. The ice-cream-cold blue eyes. Her smooth skin, brown-sugary from a summer of sun. And her expression: It was a dare. A challenge. A choice that declared: *I know who I am. I like who I am. Even if you don't.*

My heart raced the fifty-yard dash—in flip-flops. It slapped against my ribs. Stumbled into my lungs.

"Sneeze?" *Hic's voice.* "Are you unwell?"

I couldn't breathe. My legs felt wobbly. My toes and fingers, numb.

"He *can't* be sick." *Goldie.* "He didn't eat any cake!"

Pierre. "Zen why dust 'ee look like zat?"

Hayley gripped my arm. "What's wrong? Do you know what's wrong?"

I nodded. I knew. I knew as I watched her chew.

It was love at first bite.

Chapter Three

A white meteor whizzed through the open window, streaked past my face, and plunked dead center into the Nice Alarm cake.

I jolted from my trance. *"What the—?"*

Hayley reached into the chocolatey crater and dug out . . .

. . . a golf ball.

"Fore!" someone shouted from outside, followed by raucous laughter.

Fists clenched, Hayley strode from the office. Goldie trailed her, singsonging: "This is gon-na be *goo-ood*!"

No, this was gon-na be mes-sy. Hayley has a take-no-prisoners attitude when it comes to "hoodlum horseplay" at Gadabout.

Pierre and I thundered after them.

"Shall I fetch the first aid kit?" Hiccup yelled.

"Find Mr. Barker," I hollered over my shoulder. "Hurry!"

He nodded and darted out the back.

We spotted Hayley standing atop Hole #1, the North Pole. Her SOS swept the course like a prison spotlight, searching for The Culprit.

My breath caught. My heart galumphed. My brain swirled upward with the candy cane stripes of the barber pole.

Hayley was . . . beautiful. The late-afternoon sun hung behind her, reflecting off the "snow," shooting dazzling sword-rays at us. She stood straight and proud like Joan of Arc in a painting I'd seen once.

She stretched out an arm. Her fist uncurled and she displayed on her open palm the chocolate golf ball. "Who. Is. Responsible," she asked.

No answer.

A moat frog burped. The revolving vanes on the Windmill squeaked.

Hayley's penetrating SOS moved from one group of Gadabout players to the next. I was tempted to spill my guts about the Invention Convention® right then and there. Her SOS has that effect.

Then she spotted them: four guys, all lanky, blond, and bronzed; all hacking balls from beneath a canopy of fake ferns at Hole #8, The Bungled Jungle.

Goldie gaped. "*Omigosh*, do you know who they *are*?"

"Quadruplets?" mused Ace, meandering over to join us.

Goldie rolled her eyes, but he could've been right. They wore identical, burgundy-colored short-sleeved knit shirts (with collars), belted khaki slacks (perfectly creased), and matching burgundy caps (emblazoned *PHHSVGT*).

"*Wow*," Goldie breathed. "I wonder what *they're* doing *here*."

"Let me take a stab," Ace said. "Playing mini-golf?"

"Not unless they're *slumming.* That's the *Patrick Henry High School Varsity Golf Team*! But I wonder where *he* is."

'Ee 'oo?" Pierre asked.

Hayley, her chin tipped in anger, advanced toward the team.

Rats. No sign yet of her dad or Hiccup.

"C'mon," I said, tugging Pierre's sleeve. "I know a short-cut."

I led them through the Enchanted Forest. We skirted Little Red Riding Hood and huffed and puffed past the Big Bad Wolf, then trekked a steep, mossy knoll, halting behind Hayley just as she demanded, "Did you guys hit this?"

The blondest guy, whose sun-bleached hair poked from beneath his cap like scarecrow straw, didn't bother to look at her. "What is it?"

His teammates cracked up.

Hayley snorted. "What do you think it is?"

"A mutant Milk Dud?"

More cracking.

"Huh. That's because you hit it through Gadabout's office window and it landed in a *cake.*"

Scarecrow high-fived his buds. "Hole-in-one! What do I win?"

Hayley's SOS narrowed. "A one-way ticket out of here."

"I don't think so. We still have nine lame-o holes to play." Scarecrow teed up another ball. *Swooop.* It ricocheted off Big Ben with a *BOIINNNG.*

Now *my* fists clenched. Last spring I spent two tedious

hours untangling a Medusa-like rat nest from inside Ben's head.

Sic 'em, Hayley. Sic 'em good.

"Surrender your clubs now," she demanded. "Or else—"

"Eh, brah." From within the camouflage of vines emerged the imposing shadow of a god. When it stepped into full sun, I saw it belonged to an imposing god-like guy. He wore a loose tank top, baggy shorts, and flip-flops, and in one massive hand he twirled a golf club as easily as a majorette's baton. "Dis game *pau*," he said. "We go, eh?"

"Holy aloha!" Goldie jabbed me with a sharp elbow. "It's *him*."

"'Im 'oo?" Pierre said.

"Cullen Fu Hanson!"

Had her voice *blushed*?

"He transferred this summer from Punahou High," Goldie whispered. "That's in Honolulu. You know, Honolulu, *Hawaii*."

"I've heard of Hawaii, Goldie," I muttered.

"With *him* on the team, they'll make it to the state championship *for sure*. The scoop is he's the next Tiger Woods!"

More like Grizzly Woods. The guy reared big as a bear. He obviously spent a lot of hours hoisting weights—or palm trees. The only dainty part of him was a triangle of black whiskers sprouting beneath his lower lip. Around his neck dangled a shark's tooth—or maybe his own tooth. No matter. It was pointy.

Goldie gushed: "The high school girls call him Cullen Fu *Handsome*. Isn't he a *dreamsicle*?"

Ace studied his fingernails. "What flavor?"

"What's your hurry, Cull?" Scarecrow was saying. "I thought you were still on island time."

Another *swoooop*. The ball rocketed into the beak of a plastic toucan.

"Bless my Froot Loops," Scarecrow shouted. "A birdie!"

The team hooted and crowed.

Cullen the Bear shrugged. Pecs, triceps, and abs rippled. Man, even his earlobes had muscles.

"It's your *okole*," he said. "But I stay *pau* with dis game of jungle ball."

Jungle ball!

Goldie sucked a gasp. Ace swallowed a yawn.

"Shee will let zem 'ave eet now, oui?" Pierre asked.

"Definitely oui," I said, and waited.

But Hayley didn't. She just stood there, eyes wide, glazed.

Glazed with . . . what? I'd seen that expression before—but on whom and why? Was it apprehension? Fear? Had Hayley finally met her match?

A strange force surged inside my chest. I felt powerful. Invincible. I knew what I must do.

Protect Hayley. Protect Gadabout.

My feet sloshed across the swamp. My hands karate-chopped vines. I stalked toward Scarecrow and Cullen and glared up, up, up into their faces, and said, "Um . . . cut it out, you guys, okay?"

Scarecrow and his three look-alikes examined me—up and down and up again. Then they burst out laughing.

"What if we don't *cut it out*?" Scarecrow taunted. "You gonna fight us, Little Big Nose?"

"Yeah." I snatched a putter from the nearest crony and brandished it.

"Yeah?" His putter clashed sword-like against mine with a hard *clank*.

I lashed my arm the opposite way. So did he. Club met club again. And again. *Clash, clank. Clash, clank.*

"Don't!" Hayley cried.

"Oooo!" Goldie squealed, scribbling into her notepad. *"Do!"*

Ace intoned, "Stephen. *Use your brain.*"

Yikes! He was right. (*Clash. Clank.*) What was I doing? I was no swashbuckler. No musketeer. Plus, there were five of these guys. Seven, actually, because Cullen counted as three.

"On second thought"—the putter went limp in my hands— "I don't care to fight after all."

"Didn't think so." With the toe of his club, Scarecrow beeped my sore schnoz. The pressure made it tickle.

And tingle.

And itch.

"AH-*CHOOO!*"

Scarecrow eyed the string of goo dangling from his putter. With a sneer of disgust, he scraped it off on the grass. "You're all nose, kid," he said. "No guts. No glory. Just—snot."

The team laughed again. Not Cullen. He stood twirling his club, watching me. Waiting. Waiting for what?

Scarecrow teed up again, aiming for—

NoOhNoOhNo. Not Pisa! One whack and it would belly flop for sure . . .

I had to distract him. Stop him.

But how?

Not with "swords." Not even with boogers . . .

"Excuse me, Mr. Golf Guy!" I hollered. "Is that the best you can do?"

He glanced at Pisa. Glanced at the ball. "Whaddya mean?"

"If you're going to insult my body parts, why not do it with style. Wit. *Intelligence.* Oh, I forgot! Those are the exact qualities you're lacking."

"OoooOOOOOoooo!" his team chorused.

Cullen smothered a grin.

Scarecrow straightened, face red. He pointed his club at me. "Now look here, you little snot—"

"There you go again." I shook my head. "Wasting a great opportunity."

"You could do better, punk?"

"Absolutely!"

"Prove it."

"Certainly! Here's what you could've said about my nose."

I mused a moment. Stroked my chin. Began to circle him slowly and said:

"*Superstitious*: If I walk under it, am I cursed with seven years bad luck?

"*Countrified*: I grew one o' them zucchini back in '86. Won first prize at the county fair!

22

"*Descriptive*: It's a cave! A cavern! Studded with boogers like stalactites and stalagmites!

"*Anthropological*: Behold—the sarcophagus of King Tut!

"*Friendly*: I play trombone in the marching band too. Want to practice together sometime?

"*Disappointed*: '*Oh, Pinocchio,*' wailed the Blue Fairy. '*You've been telling lies again.*'"

Goldie giggled. Someone choked on a chortle. I circled Scarecrow faster and faster as my words and confidence flowed.

"*Educational*: Students, rising before you stands Mount Vesuvius, the volcano that destroyed the ancient Roman city Pompeii.

"*Festive*: A few antlers here, a bell or two there, and presto! Rudolph's understudy!

"*Mythical*: Fee, fie, foe, fum! Does it smell the blood of an Englishman?

"*Rude*: Disneyland called. They want their Matterhorn back.

"*Horrified*: My God! Elephant Man lives!

"*Curious*: Does it hold your iPod *and* your laptop?

"*Dramatic*: When it runs with the common cold—Niagara Falls!

"*Enterprising*: The perfect logo for the Snoops 'R' Us Detective Agency!

"*Poetic*: I thought that I would never see

A beak as large as Tennessee.

Yet I was wrong

For here it grows—

Our fifty-first state: Stephen's nose!"

I halted. Struck a pose offering an unobstructed view of my chaffed proboscis, a proud rocket thrusting toward the sky.

Cullen Fu Hanson laughed, his straight teeth agleam against his dark skin. He tucked his club beneath one arm and slapped his hands together. The wide palms made a popping sound as he began to applaud. Everyone (even Ace, who is too cool) joined in. Scarecrow's face darkened from cherry punch to roasted eggplant.

"S-snot-nosed p-punk!" he sputtered. "Geek! Nerd!"

"Pleased to meet you," I answered, bowing. "Stephen J. Wyatt, at your service."

Chapter Four

"Why you little—" Scarecrow lunged, putter swept high. "That nose of yours is history. A goner. A whoosher!"

I didn't know what a "whoosher" was, but I caught his drift.

I stepped backward—

tripped—

and tumbled into the Swamp.

Two inches of tepid green slime seeped over my body. My head lay cradled in the grin of Crikey the Crocodile. His gaping maw smelled of rotting algae and Trix cereal that's been soaking in rotting algae.

Clubs raised, Scarecrow and his cronies loomed, blotting out the sun.

I clenched my eyes. Waited for the excruciating impact.

"*Stephen!*" Hayley cried.

Wow, I thought in a haze of fetid fumes. *She cares.*

"Nuff already," said Cullen Fu Hanson.

I peeked through one eye. Cullen had grabbed the toe of Scarecrow's club. Scarecrow clung to the handle. The two of them engaged in a brief tug-o'-war. I say brief because if Scarecrow hung on much longer, he'd lose an arm.

"Why, boddah you?" Cullen asked.

Scarecrow scowled. "You bet it bothers me. And if you don't let go, I'll tell Coach you threatened me! With your black record—"

Cullen opened his massive paw, releasing the club. Scarecrow almost keeled over, clutching his prize. The team snickered.

I tried to ooze from the swamp, but Crikey the Crocodile's lone tooth snagged my ear.

"*What is going on here?*"

The question blared like a trumpet. The cavalry, at last! I recognized the scent of Mr. Barker's coconut sunscreen.

"Hello down there, Steve. Welcome home!" he said, his voice filling with easy warmth. "What's this, first day back and already lying around on the job? And for this I pay you the big bucks?" He laughed, jingling coins in his pocket.

"Yep, you sure do," I said, forcing a smile. I moved to sit up, but Crikey's tooth bit deeper. My head whirled with pain. The faded palm trees on Mr. Barker's aloha shirt danced a hula.

"Are you all right? What happened to your nose?" Mr. Barker faced Scarecrow & Co. "Gentlemen, I'll ask once more: *What is going on here?*"

Scarecrow smoothed his scowl. "Nothing, sir," he said. "My teammates and I were just playing a few holes, when this punk—"

Mr. Barker held up a hand. "This *punk* happens to be a valued employee at Gadabout."

(I was, in fact, the *only* employee.)

"I meant no disrespect, sir. This *youngster* charged at me with—"

"If you've hurt him . . ." Mr. Barker's words trailed a threat.

"We didn't do anything to him," Scarecrow insisted.

"Yet," Ace murmured.

"Zey meant to tenderize Sneeze like zee tough steak!" Pierre said. "To mince 'im like zee onion! To crack 'im like zee egg! To—"

"Is this true, Peach?" Mr. Barker asked.

Hayley blinked. Her lips parted, but no sound came out.

"In addition," announced a voice behind me, "they were whacking balls hither and yon, a most dangerous form of amusement."

I'd never heard Hiccup speak with such strength and confidence. And why wasn't he gasping? His usual idea of a workout is taking his own blood pressure. Scurrying to fetch Mr. Barker should've exhausted him.

"A golf ball, on impact, could inflict ocular trauma," Hiccup said. "Or a life-threatening injury called *diffuse axonal*."

"Is that a lumberjack's disease?" Goldie asked, still scribbling notes.

"I've heard enough." Mr. Barker jerked a thumb toward the exit. "You five: Out. *Now.* Don't come back."

"We demand a refund!" Scarecrow said.

"Break the rules, forfeit the cash."

"You can't treat me this way! I'm the captain of the Patrick Henry High School Varsity Golf Team!"

"I don't give a golf ball's dimple. But your coach might if he has to bail you boys out of jail. And that's exactly where you'll be if I catch any of you on my property again."

"Fat chance we'd want to come back to this pit," Scarecrow said with a sneer. "We're gone."

His triplets stepped over me one by one, their cleats barely skimming past my schnoz.

Scarecrow stepped last. Then he shoved his face so close to mine his peppermint breath stung my eyes. "This isn't over, Snot Boy," he said. "I'll teach you to keep your *nose* out of my business!"

Just once couldn't a bully say: *Whatever was I thinking? Sorry for the inconvenience. I shan't bother you again.*

"Leave the clubs," Mr. Barker called.

The clubs dropped. Cullen the Bear twirled his putter between two fingers before handing it to Hayley.

"Sorry." He jerked his head at Scarecrow. "He one *haole moke.*"

"Uh-huh," she said, the syllables as glazed as her eyes.

He ambled after the team and through Gadabout's gates.

"That's that!" Mr. Barker brushed imaginary dust from his hands. "How'd I do, Peach? Aren't you proud of your old man?"

Hayley's dad is well known for going too easy on players who ignore Gadabout's rules. That's why, three years ago, after her mom died in a car accident, Hayley acquired the SOS—and her reputation for giving *zilch.*

"Mm," she said, seemingly transfixed by the club in her hands. "Oh, yes, Daddy." She hugged him. "You did great standing up to those goons."

What about me? Hadn't I stood up to them too?

"A little help here!" I said. "Hayley? Hic? *Somebody?*"

Mr. Barker unhooked my ear, then pulled me from the swamp. I swayed, clutching his arm, dripping sludge. I sneezed. Three shades of green—pea soup, pippin apple, and Japanese jade—shot out both nostrils.

Pierre grimaced. "You look like zee coleslaw."

"With rancid mayo," observed Ace.

"I've got the *perfect* headline!" Goldie said. *"Hawaiian God Meets Grotesque Geek from Green Lagoon."*

"If he met the *naegleria fowleri* amoeba in that alleged lagoon," Hiccup warned, "he could expire within three to seven days."

"Hit the showers, Sneeze," Mr. Barker said. "I'll loan you a pair of shorts and shirt to change into."

Hayley and her dad live in a loft above an old surf wax factory, next to Gadabout.

"Thanks, no thanks!" I was embarrassingly aware that I might have to use Hayley's bathroom, Hayley's shower, Hayley's soap. "I've gotta get home."

"Need a lift?"

"I have my bike."

"I insist on accompanying you, Sneeze," Hic said, "in the event you develop seizures, confusion, headache . . ."

Ha. Couldn't fool me. He just longed to see Mom.

"Tomorrow's Labor Day," Mr. Barker said. "Any chance of getting a little labor out of you, Steve? We're three months behind on maintenance."

"Sure! I already started a mental fix-it list."

"Have you, now?"

"And while I was gone, I took the liberty of sketching a hydraulic system for Pisa. It should jack up the tower to its original slant."

"Thoughtful of you, but I'm afraid that kind of repair work will have to wait a bit longer," Mr. Barker said. "Money's tighter than usual. See you tomorrow." Whistling, he waved and walked toward the loft, coins jangling in his pocket.

"Eye regret zat eye too must depart," Pierre said. "Keep zee leftover cake, 'ayley. And pleeze—burn zee plate." He clicked his heels, kissed her hand, and skedaddled.

Hayley wiped her hand on her shorts. "Guess the party's over."

"Where's Pierre sprinting off to again in such a hurry?" Goldie mused, tapping her teeth with her pen. "He's been MIA all summer."

"Pastry camp?" Hiccup guessed.

"Nope! I checked. Here's the scoop: His family is practically *bankrupt.* Mr. Noel's fast-food joint, Lickety-Split Chick, is a *ginormous* money pit. And Mrs. Noel lost *bazillions* on her health food bakery. No surprise there. Spinach brownies and tofu donuts? Oh, *gag.*" She snapped shut her notepad. "See you all at school on Tuesday. Sneeze, you still owe me that *exclusiv*e. I'll be in touch." With a flip of her golden hair, she turned on her heel and flounced off.

I tossed my bike lock key to Hic. "Saddle us up, will ya, pardner? I want to talk to Hayley a sec."

"Time is of the essence where *naegleria fowleri* is concerned."

I gave him a *Look*.

"Going now," he said, and went.

"You too," I said to Ace, who was pinching leaves from a Tarzan vine. He lifted an eyebrow, lingered a moment like he was going to say something to Hayley, then sauntered away.

Hayley and I stood there, alone.

Too alone.

Quiet.

Too quiet.

"What did you want to talk to me about?" she asked finally.

I tried not to think about the fact that I was smelly and green, and said, "I just wanted to thank you again for the party. And—"

I gulped. I felt like I had one of Dancer and Dasher's rubber chew toys stuck in my throat.

Hayley crossed her arms. "And?"

"And, I wanted to say, I missed"—I gestured at Gadabout, but a different word flew from my mouth—"you."

She snorted. "You couldn't have missed me that much. You were gone three months and never sent a letter. Never wrote an e-mail. Not even a stupid postcard! And I *know* you had things to say."

Her SOS honed in on my face. No doubt she meant the convention. I prepared to surrender, to reveal all. But the SOS vanished. Hayley's eyes glazed again. *Where* had I seen that look before?

She turned and methodically filled her arms with the discarded clubs, placing Cullen's gently on top.

Then she whirled on me and blurted, "And for goodness golf tees! What were you thinking, sword fighting with the clubs like that?"

"What?"

"You know better than anyone those shenanigans are unacceptable at Gadabout!"

"Hayley, I was trying to *protect* Gadabout. Protect *you*!"

"We don't need protection." She strode to the office.

What was going on? Earlier, she seemed happy to see me. Now she acted like she never wanted to see me again.

I trotted to keep pace, my sneakers squelching swamp juice. "Are you mad because I didn't write? You know I hate writing."

"That's never stopped you before."

True. A year ago, in summer school, I'd written a funny instruction manual called *101 Ways to Bug Your Parents*. Last spring I'd written the sequel, *101 Ways to Bug Your Teacher*, for another school "project."

"If you mean my books," I said, "they don't count. I wrote those for personal reasons. Important reasons."

Hayley glared.

Geez, what had I said wrong now?

"Good-bye," she said, wrenching open the office door.

"Fine. *Good-bye!*" No, that wasn't what I wanted to say. "Thanks again for the party. It was great."

Another snort.

"No, really."

"No problem."

"Hayley. *Wait.*"

We faced each other. She, beautiful and angry. Me, smelly and green.

Should I hug her?

No, Sneeze. You're smelly and green.

Should I kiss her on the cheek?

NO, Sneeze. You're smelly and green.

"See you tomorrow," I said.

"Don't be late."

"I won't." I thrust out my hand. For a brief second, I felt the lovely snag of her calloused finger. Then her hand jerked from mine, trailing a stringy, slimy strand of moss. She wiped it on her shorts the same way she'd wiped off Pierre's kiss.

I wanted to shrink to the size of a golf ball. Roll myself into the Bottomless Pit.

Instead, cheeks blazing, I turned and slunk through the rusty gates of Gadabout Golf.

Chapter Five

"Let's go," I said to Hiccup through cringed teeth.

"See you Tuesday, Hayley!" he called with a vigorous wave. He buckled his helmet. "And it would behoove you to check the pH levels of the Swamp—"

"Hiccup, I said *let's go*."

"—acid/alkaline imbalances may create teeming cesspools of—"

"*NOW*."

He gaped at me. "But the Health Department warns—"

I pushed off on my bike with a fierceness that made the tires spit gravel.

He hurried to follow. "Your face is red. Perhaps you've been exposed to scarlet fever. Or the 'slapped face' virus."

"I'm not sick, Hic."

"Lupus also manifests—"

"Give it a rest, okay?"

"You're flushed! I'm endeavoring to diagnose the problem!"

"*You* are the problem!" I banged a fist on my handlebars. "Man, you bug me bonkers sometimes. Can't you ever talk about anything besides death, disease, and destruction? And what part of '*let's go*' didn't you understand?"

I spurted onto the road, not caring that I left Hic in my dust. I careened corners. Wove between cars. Pumped like crazy till my legs cramped, my lungs burned, and my cheeks radiated a heat that didn't come from embarrassment.

Exhausted, I slowed to a coast. The breeze cooled my sweaty face and stiffened my jeans. An aroma of baked bog tickled my nose and I sneezed. Four times.

I heard a rattling. Hic and his hand-me-down bike pulled alongside. He stared straight ahead, lips pursed over his braces in a classic "silent treatment." That's another thing that bugs me about him. When he's angry, why doesn't he just admit it? Rant and rave and wave his arms like normal people?

Huh. Probably because if he tried that at home, his five older brothers would pound him.

We rode block after block, the silence thickening.

"Sorry, Hic," I said when I couldn't stand it anymore. "I didn't mean it."

He let slip a smile. "Irritability is not one of your traits. Nor is it a symptom of the *naegleria*. May I assume something irritating happened at Gadabout?"

"Yeah. *Hayley* happened."

"Care to elaborate?"

"What's to elaborate? Hayley and I had a weird conversation, is all."

"Define *weird*."

"I don't know, Hic! *You* know. Just . . . *weird* weird."

"Hmmmmm," he said.

"I see," said he.

Then: "Ah-*ha*!" He halted, brakes squealing, tires skidding.

"What's wrong?" I yanked a U-turn. "Flat tire? Chain fall off?"

"You like her!" he shouted.

"What?" I almost toppled off my bike. "Who?"

"Hayley, who!"

"Shhhhhhh! Not so loud!" I waited till three cars whizzed past, then muttered, "Hayley's my boss. My friend. Of course I like her."

"No, you *like* like her!" Hiccup grinned like a madman. "When will you confess to her your affections?"

He *was* a madman. Any second, he'd start frothing at the mouth. Drooling into his pocket.

"I'm not telling Hayley anything! What if she laughed at me? Or threw up on my shoes?"

"Don't be ridiculous. Hayley is not the type to regard re-gurgitation as an effective means of communication."

He had a point.

"Besides, she likes you too."

"Yeah, right."

"I witnessed it. When you were fencing words with that goon. Her face radiated fear—and pride."

"Yeah, right." But a scrap of hope fluttered in my chest. "Really?"

"MM never lies." Hiccup flashed Medicine Man's sign for *Truth, Justice, and Vitamin C for all.*

I gazed west toward Gadabout. The sun slipped between the tips of the eucalyptus trees, striping the street with burnt-pumpkin shadows.

Stephen!

Hayley had shouted my name the instant Scarecrow tried to tee-off my nose. Yeah, there'd been worry in her voice. Yet, minutes later, she'd practically fired me. And then—

"You will tell her?" Hiccup asked.

I jerked my head at the memory of Hayley wiping off my mossy handshake.

"No way, Hic. Nope. No. Never. I mean, what would a beautiful, brilliant girl like Hayley see in a chapped-nose geek like me?"

Hic bristled. "Do not accept that golf goon's estimation! You are a talented wordsmith, a faithful friend, a brilliant inventor—"

"HA!" I shoved my bike onto the sidewalk, tore off my helmet, and threw it onto a gopher hole.

Hiccup followed, clattering over the curb. "Sneeze, what exactly transpired at the Invention Convention®?"

"I don't want to talk about it."

"This does not solely concern Hayley, does it? MM's X-ray vision reveals difficulties with the Nice Alarm. Also, that you are in desperate need of"—he made a mechanical noise while examining my butt—"new underpants."

I couldn't help it. I laughed. "Medicine Man has X-ray vision?"

"In actuality, no. Today's sophisticated superheroes are endowed with CAT scan capabilities. Incidentally, your right sock has sustained a hole in the vicinity of the littlest piggy."

I dropped my bike, grabbed him in a headlock, ripped off his helmet, and knuckled his carrot hair with noogies. He yelped. Then, in a maneuver worthy of Houdini, he escaped, twisting my arm behind my back.

"My clavicles!" I groaned.

He froze. "Your *what*?"

"Gotcha!" I aimed to elbow him in the stomach.

With a sharp cry that sounded like *kee-yap,* his ankle hooked mine—and jerked. I toppled, dragging him with me. We thudded onto the grass, laughing like loonies in a painful jumble of punches and spokes, legs, and gears.

"Impressive," I admitted when we untangled ourselves. "Where did you learn that stuff, a ninja correspondence course? Or from your brothers?"

He folded his arms beneath his head and grinned at the leaf awning above us. "I acquired my self-defense techniques in a hapkido class to protect myself *from* my brothers."

I jolted upright. "*You*? Mr. Don't-Breathe-on-Me-Because-I-Might-Bruise, taking martial arts?"

"Six days a week, three hours a day, the entire duration of your absence."

"No wonder you're in such great shape! Can you break a board with your bare hands?"

"And my bare feet."

"Without getting a splinter?"

"I carry tweezers, just in case."

"Hiccup, this is huge! Why didn't you tell me? We're best friends!"

"Why haven't you told me about the Invention Convention®? We're best friends!"

Ouch. Or should I say: *Touché.*

Hiccup knew all too well about the endless hours I'd spent toiling on the Nice Alarm. He was the alarm's first test subject, an experiment that nearly resulted in a nose amputation—his.

He knew too about the endless hours I'd toiled at Gadabout, scrimping and saving every dollar to pay for the convention. He actually overcame his fear of rust long enough to sand the corroded sluice at Hole #10, the Abandoned Gold Mine—presenting me with his meager wages.

Then there was *101 Ways to Bug Your Parents*, the book I wrote in summer school last year and hawked from the boys' bathroom at Jefferson Elementary. Hiccup's last-minute wacky cartoons were what made the cover eye-catching, each page hilarious. I could've sold thousands of copies and used the proceeds to attend the convention a whole year earlier—if the book hadn't been confiscated by the school board and practically gotten our sixth-grade teacher fired. (But that's another story.)

Hiccup deserved to know. He'd *earned* the right to know.

So I told him. About marching through the great glass doors of the convention center in San Francisco, the Nice

Alarm tick-ticking as proudly, eagerly as my shoes on the polished linoleum floor . . .

About shaking hands with Mr. Sterling Patterson, president of Patterson Novelty Enterprises: the man who answered my query letter requesting a demonstration, who'd considered mass-producing my invention . . .

Last but not least, I told Hic about that long-awaited, dream-come-true meeting . . .

. . . and how it had ended quickly, nightmarishly, with four curt words:

"Sorry, kid. Not interested."

Chapter Six

"But! What?! Not!" Hic sputtered like popcorn in hot oil. "Didn't Mr. Patterson give you a chance to properly demonstrate the alarm?" He clapped a hand to his mouth, eyes wide with dismay. "Oh, doh! You dibn't ambudade his dose, dib you?"

I laughed. "No, I didn't amputate his nose. The Nice Alarm worked *nicely*."

"Then what was the reason for his negative response?"

A rusty nail scratched a painful memory in my head: Mr. Patterson's polite smile erasing even before the alarm's second tap on his shoulder.

"He thought the alarm was *too* nice," I explained. "He told me"—I imitated his booming voice—"*Mr. Wyatt! In this tech-savvy world, our customers want novelty items that offer more whiz-bang for their buck!*"

"*Whiz-bang?*" Hic frowned. "I don't understand. Would he prefer an alarm clock that launches fireworks?"

"Maybe."

"But an incendiary device wouldn't awaken sleepers gently. It would jolt them to consciousness, forcing them to flee their beds to extinguish a fire!"

"Which defeats the whole purpose of the alarm."

"Exactly!"

"*Exactly!*" I nodded, relieved we agreed, relieved that I'd told him—and that he understood.

"To whom will you demonstrate the alarm now?" Hiccup asked.

"What do you mean?"

"Surely Patterson Enterprises is not the only company producing novelty items."

I kicked at my bike tire. Hic didn't understand after all. "Didn't you hear what I said? The Nice Alarm is a flop! A failure! It fizzled—end of story."

"Don't be ridiculous!" Hiccup leaped to his feet like MM come to life: fists on hips, jaw set. "You cannot surrender now, Sneeze! Mr. Patterson is just one person, one opinion. You must demonstrate the Nice Alarm to others. If it is rejected again, then you must demonstrate it to someone else, and to someone else after that, until you succeed!"

Sorry, kid. Not interested.

My stomach twisted. "No. I'm done, Hic. I can't face being rejected again."

"The *alarm* was rejected," Hic said, "not *you*." He righted his bike, hooked his helmet into place. "If you choose not to contact other manufacturers, then the only person responsible for the Nice Alarm's demise is . . . *yourself*!"

42

Ouch. He had a point.

"How'd you get so smart, Hector?"

"It is the company I keep," he said, flashing an embarrassed smile. "Although, I am not totally without flaws. There exist two major snags in this scenario. First, due to prohibitive travel costs, you cannot demonstrate the Alarm in person to additional potential buyers. Second, due to extreme risk factors, you cannot ship your sole prototype to said buyers for examination."

After I'd translated his "snags" into English, the proverbial lightbulb switched on inside my head. "Ah, but that's where CAD comes in handy!"

"CAD?" Hiccup frowned. "Coronary artery disease?"

I laughed. "*Computer-aided design*. It's one of the classes I signed up for this semester at Patrick Henry High."

I'm considered a "gifted" student. So, in addition to attending Jefferson Middle this year, my parents pulled strings to allow me to take three advanced high school courses as well. I was especially excited about CAD because that class would teach me how to design, build, and test 3-D invention prototypes on the computer. CAD is a cheaper, easier way to invent because you don't have to fork out big bucks to erect a working model until you know for sure it works.

"My original plan," I explained to Hiccup, "was to use CAD for inventing stuff to ease Mom and Dad's lives after Sis is born. Stuff like the Loaded Diaper Pager and Butt-Oh-So-Fresh and the Rubber Baby Body Burper. But since Sis isn't due till December, I can use part of the semester to create CAD plans for the Nice Alarm—the kind I can submit via e-mail to other manufacturers."

"Brilliant!" Hiccup said. "And I assume you will need assistance researching names and addresses of additional novelty companies? I humbly offer my services."

"I humbly accept." I glimpsed my wristwatch. "Yikes, I gotta get home, Hic. I haven't even had a chance to say hi to the Guys!"

The Guys (Edison, Bell, Ben, and the Wright Brothers) were my tropical fish. I'm allergic to all things feathered and furred, so the Guys were the only pets I'd ever owned. Hiccup fed them at his house while I was away. I wouldn't entrust my scaly confidants to anyone else. I mean, Hic was the kind of guy who'd take a bullet for them.

"I hope they behaved themselves," I said, straddling my bike. "That ornery Ben—always first in the chow line. And Bell! Does he still play hide-'n'-seek in the sunken treasure chest?" I chuckled. "Never mind. Fill me in tomorrow, okay?"

"I, ahem, would prefer to accompany you now. It's imperative we discuss a matter of great sensitivity. After you disinfect yourself, of course."

"Of course."

"And perhaps I might stay for dinner? That is, if *She* doesn't mind."

Hiccup's eyes glazed like dreamy donuts. They tend to take on that look whenever one of us mentions Mom.

"We're having pizza," I warned. "What about your allergy

to wheat gluten? And what's this matter of 'great sensitivity' you need to—?"

Before I could finish, Hiccup vaulted his bike and blasted off.

I thunked my helmet into place and scrambled to catch up, coasting behind him into the garage and edging with care past Dad's vintage 1976 Caddy convertible. The trunk yawned. Inside it, hunched like a boxy toad next to the jumper cables, sat the Nice Alarm.

I leaned in. Lifted it out. The clock tick-ticked in perky, perfect time. Its arm with padded glove fell forward and patted me twice on the shoulder as if to say: *You did your best, Sneeze. Thanks for trying.*

I returned the reassurance: *I won't give up. Someday, you'll be built for thousands to enjoy . . .*

"Steve?" I heard Mom call. "That you?"

"It's me, Mrs. Wyatt!" Hic yipped, charging through the back door. "Hector! Hector Denar—*gaaack!*"

Ah, he'd spotted the Belly.

I placed the Nice Alarm on the kitchen counter and hurried to the living room. Hic stood staring, stammering, "You're—you're—"

"Behemothic?" Mom guessed with a weary smile. She lay on the sofa, her swollen feet propped on pillows. The Belly served as a mounded desk with letters, bills, and catalogs cascading into a mail moat below.

"No, no!" Hiccup insisted. "You're *small*, Mrs. Wyatt! Infinitesimal!"

"Dear, sweet Hector. You lie like your dogs. But you've grown faster than E. coli this summer, hasn't he, Steve?"

I hadn't noticed (how had I *not* noticed?) that Hiccup stretched at least three inches above me now. His face was a battlefield, freckles engaged in a great civil war against a battalion of red, angry zits.

"I'm starved," Mom said, arising with a grunt. "Stay for dinner, Hector? We're having pizza, curdled milk, wilted lettuce, and a bag of Halloween candy I found in the freezer. That's all we've got till I buy groceries tomorrow."

"Mm-*mm*!" Hiccup exclaimed. No surprise. He would cheerfully snack on broken glass if it meant dining with Mom.

"*Stephen.*" She grimaced. "You're *green*. Did one of your inventions decompose again?"

"No, Mom."

"Then what—?"

"It's a long story, Mom."

"Do I want to hear it?"

"No." I grinned. "I'll go shower now."

"Yes, you will. And Hector: Call your mother and let her know you're staying for dinner. I don't want her to worry."

"I shall do that," Hic lied, and Mom pretended to believe him. She knew he wouldn't bother to call because his mother wouldn't bother to worry. Not with five other boys, seven dogs, seven cats, and a husband or two to worry about.

After only minutes in the shower, I was lassoed by the succulent scent of re-heating pizza. (*Mental note: Design a "Mama Mia! Alarm" that tantalizes you to consciousness with pizza aromas.*) I didn't even bother going to my room to dress. I just snagged Dad's ratty robe from where it hung behind the bathroom door and leaped the stairs, three at time, to the kitchen. There I found Dad tossing a limp salad, Mom fussing with the silverware, and Hiccup fussing over Mom. He pulled out her chair and, with a flourish, draped a napkin across the Belly.

"Hector, I'm pregnant, not an invalid," Mom said with a hint of exasperation, although I could tell she enjoyed the attention.

Dad studied the kitchen clock. "Hector, my boy, you've set a personal record. Two months, three weeks, four days, five minutes, six seconds since you last dined with us. But I'm sure you'll make up for lost time in no time."

It needles Dad that Hiccup spends so many "family meals" with us. Probably because Hiccup spends so many of our family meals needling Dad about his questionable food choices.

Hiccup eyed the bowl of wilted lettuce with his own version of Hayley's SOS.

"Don't you have any tomatoes, Mr. Barker?" he asked. "They're an excellent source of vitamin C that will boost the baby's immune system."

Dad yodeled into the cavernous fridge, "Hel-loo! Any tomatoes in there? Nope, sorry. Will ketchup or moldy salsa do?"

Hic sniffed. "I think not."

"I'm impressed with your nutritional knowledge, Hector," Mom said. "Perhaps we'll hire you as the baby's dietician."

Hic looked hopeful, but Dad sniffed. "I think not."

We tore into the pizza. Not Hic. He selected one slice, peeled off the cheese, discarded the crust, and lectured us on the dangers of sodium nitrates in pepperoni. Mom made him lick at the tomato sauce, though, because tomatoes are an excellent source of vitamin C.

For dessert we gnawed on the frozen Milky Way bars (except Hic, who fretted about cracking a tooth). That's when Dad ruffled his already ruffled hair, cleared his throat, and announced, "Stephen, I'm afraid we have bad news."

I felt a queasiness that had nothing to do with sodium nitrates. "Plain, ordinary bad news?" I asked. "Or 'We bought you a new tropical fish' bad news?"

My parents have a nasty habit of springing bad news at the dinner table and bribing me with a new fish to ease the springing of bad news at the dinner table.

"*Our* news isn't fish-worthy," Dad said, shooting a glance at Hiccup. "But—*ow!*" He gawped at Mom. "Did you just *kick* me?"

"Sorry," she said, nibbling her candy bar. "Crossed my bloated ankles."

Hic snatched our plates and began scrubbing them in the soapy sink.

I gripped my chair. "I'm ready, unless I need a cigarette and a blindfold."

"Your schedules for both schools came in the mail while we were gone," Mom said, slipping an envelope from beneath her placemat. "You got all the classes you registered for—except PE."

"That's *good* news!" (I'd made a point of *not* registering for PE.)

"You're required to take phys ed," said Dad. "And in order to get yourself from Patrick Henry to Jefferson Middle in time for PE, I'm afraid you'll have to drop your third period class."

I swallowed. *"Which. Class. Is. That?"* I asked, knowing the answer before Mom took a printed form from the envelope and read aloud:

"Computer-aided design."

Chapter Seven

"Oh, no," I said. "I can't drop that class. I won't!"

"I understand your disappointment," Mom said, "especially coming on the heels of Mr. Patterson—"

"You don't understand at all, Mom. CAD is crucial for the Nice Alarm—and all the other inventions bursting to get out of my brain!"

Dad said, "Maybe next semester you could—"

"I can't wait four months to work on my inventions!"

"No one's asking you—"

I shoved backward, chair shrieking against the floor. "CAD is the main reason I agreed to take morning classes at Patrick Henry. And now you're making me drop it? *Why?* So I can trot around a grass-infested field, sneezing my nose off?"

"Sweetheart, it's out of our hands," Mom said.

"The state requires that every student your age take PE," Dad explained.

"This is unacceptable!" I kicked my chair. It crashed onto its side.

Hiccup jumped, soapsuds flying.

"Stephen Wyatt." Mom's tone was scarily calm. "Right now it's your behavior that is unacceptable."

Dad pointed his candy bar at me. "Enough with the melodrama. Go to your room. We're all punchy from traveling. We'll discuss this in the morning."

"But—"

"Now."

"But—"

"What part of *now* don't you understand?"

"Fine, okay, whatever," I grumbled. "C'mon, Hic."

"Hector goes nowhere but home," Dad said.

"I cannot depart just yet, Mr. Wyatt." Hic stood twisting a dish towel. "There is still the sensitive matter I must discuss with him."

"Do you mean to say you haven't told him yet?"

Hiccup's freckles blotched.

"Told me what?" I asked.

"Pretend it's a bandage, Hector," Mom advised. "Best just to rip 'er off fast and get it over with."

Hic nodded, mouth grim.

"You're scaring me, people," I said. "What's going on?"

Hic sighed. "I shall explain everything, Sneeze. Will you please accompany me upstairs?"

"Gladly," I answered, although what I felt more was dread.

Hic knotted the dish towel into an origami flower. Ears pinking, he presented it to Mom. "A blossom for a blossom . . . to remember me by."

"How thoughtful, Hector," she murmured. "It's very . . . cottony."

"Maybe we should offer *him* a blindfold and cigarette," Dad muttered.

"Hush," Mom said.

As we left the kitchen, you could've heard a cat whisker drop.

Hic led the way through the living room, up the stairs, and down the hall to my bedroom. He paused outside the door, straightening his shoulders before nudging it open.

I craned around his tall, skinny form and glimpsed my aquarium. It sat, as usual, on the desk next to my bed. I felt a thrum of excitement.

The Guys!

I burst into the room. Snatched a small yellow container from my bookshelf, ready to sprinkle the food flakes, eager to watch my buddies zip to the surface, tails wriggling, mouths gulping, blowing kiss-bubbles of thanks . . .

But—

The Guys were gone.

So was the water . . . and the turquoise gravel . . . and the plastic kelp . . . and the little plastic treasure chest with diver.

"Hiccup," I said, facing him. "Where are the Guys?"

He stared at the carpet, rubbing a stain with the toe of one sneaker.

"Where. Are. The. Guys."

He rubbed harder.

"WHERE?" I demanded.

In the olden days (meaning every day of Hector's life until last May), this was the moment he would've started hiccupping. Hic used to hic whenever he felt flustered, flummoxed, frightened, fretful, or fraudulent (hence, the nickname Ace bestowed upon him). The hiccups lasted hours, often a week or more.

But those days were gone. Hiccup had been cured. There were no hics forthcoming this time to help him stall for time.

"The Guys . . ." he admitted at last," . . . expired."

"No." I felt numb. Dumb. "I don't understand."

"Expire: to die. Cease to exist. Perish. Succumb. In other words, the Guys are"—he gulped a nervous giggle—*"ex-fish."*

"I know what 'expire' means. What I don't understand is *how.* Sure, Edison was old, possibly senile. But the others—"

"It was an accident," Hic said. "A terrible, terrible accident." He slumped into my desk chair, head in his hands. "The aquarium needed cleaning. I followed your instructions exactly. Yet, afterward, there remained the most disgusting, decaying organic matter stuck to the glass." He shuddered. "So I used cleanser—"

"You used *cleanser?"*

"—and bleach—"

"You used *bleach?"*

"—to scrub every nook and cranny—"

"You used cleanser and bleach!?"

He lifted his head, eyes shining at the memory. "Sneeze, you should've seen it! The aquarium sparkled like new. The

53

Guys were dazzled! Grateful! They waved their little fins at me from where they watched in the auxiliary bowl. But within moments of being reintroduced to the tank, Edison began swimming perpendicularly. Ben darted to his aid, but halfway there he lost all volition. Then they were floating, belly-up—"

"You didn't really follow my instructions, did you?" My voice sounded scarily calm like Mom's had minutes before. "And the Guys, they didn't just expire, did they? They were murdered. By *you*."

"It was an accident! You must believe—"

With a strength and fury I didn't know I had, I wrenched Hector to his feet. Shoved him out the door. Slammed it in his shocked and zitty face.

I flung myself onto my bed, trying not to cry.

A minute—or a million—passed.

Then—a tentative knock.

The door creaked. Hic tiptoed into the room again. "Please, please, *please* forgive me, Steve," he said, his voice ragged.

I hunched toward the wall.

"It was a grievous mistake. I swear on MM's cape that I'll buy you as many fish as you want to replace—"

"Replace? Ha!" I said, my words bitter yet muffled against the pillow. "*Nothing* can replace good friends, Hic. The Guys and I, we've been through everything together: building the Nice Alarm, writing the 'bug' books. My inventor's block, your hicking marathons. They deserved better than"—

I rolled to face their executioner—"*death by disinfectant!*"

He flinched, eyes red.

"So where are they now?" I demanded. "What did you do with their bodies? Tell me you didn't"—my voice broke—"*flush* them?"

"Don't be ridiculous!" He was aghast. "I planned a proper burial. Composed a requiem: 'Ode to the Inventor's Fish.' But before I could begin the ceremony, another catastrophe occurred. Dasher, or maybe Dancer—"

My heart squirmed. "Oh, no."

Hic released a long, shuddering breath. "After I scooped the Guys from the aquarium—deceased fish decay rapidly, you know—I relocated them to a sterile dish while I searched for a suitable coffin. But the bleach fumes triggered a fainting spell. I put my head between my legs for a second, two at the most, and while distracted, Dasher or Dancer"—he choked—"*slurped the Guys up.*"

I felt sick. Tears welled in my eyes. I faced the wall again. I couldn't bear the sight of him. "Go home, Hector."

"May I get you a glass of water? A cup of soothing chamomile tea?"

"Good-bye, Hector."

"Yes, perhaps that would be best for now." He covered me with a blanket. Switched off the light. "May I call tomorrow to check on you?"

I didn't answer. Just clenched my eyes and wished him away.

"Sneeze?"

"Don't. Bother."

He made an odd sound like a cough-choke. "I said I was sorry! I loved the Guys too! And I took expert care of them every single day for almost three months until—well, at least you could say thank you for that!"

"Thanks," I hissed into my pillow, "for nothing."

Chapter Eight

I jolted awake.

What time is it? Where are we? Still on the road . . . ?

A frayed edge of satin tickled my cheek like my blanket at home. The familiar scent of WD-40, oozing from well-oiled inventions, lingered in my pillow.

But I didn't hear the soothing burble of my aquarium. And I couldn't see the Guys, their iridescent scales disco-dancing under the tank light.

A faint warning bell rang deep inside my head.

My heart revved. I groped for the bedside lamp. Squinted in the glare.

Whew.

I was home after all, surrounded, comforted by the gadgets I'd invented over the last ten years. Contraptions spilled from my closet, filled my shelves: the Keep Kool Baseball Kap with attached mini-sprinkler . . . See to Pee, the glow-in-the-dark toilet seat . . . Lazy Lick, an electronic ice-cream-cone holder . . . Cut 'n' Putt, the golf club that trims your lawn as you play.

And the Nice Alarm.

Mom or Dad must've brought it from the kitchen after Hic left and I fell asleep. It hunched on my dresser, merrily informing me of the time: 5:30 a.m.

I yawned, flopping on my side toward the aquarium. "Guys, you won't believe the nightmare I had last night . . ."

Then I remembered.

With a moan, I sagged back against my pillow, my mind churning everything that happened to me yesterday. I mean, I hadn't even been home twenty-four hours, and already I'd:

1. Fallen into a swamp
2. Fallen in love
3. Been attacked and threatened by golf goons
4. Been ordered to dump the class I needed most for my inventions
5. Lost my beloved fish to a deranged hypochondriac and his seafood-loving dogs
6. Possibly been exposed to *naegleria fowleri*, the amoeba notorious for nibbling brains into Swiss cheese.

Would Hayley sit at my deathbed? Wipe my feverish brow with a golf towel, wet with her tears . . . ?

Yeah, right.

Stomach knotting again, I flung aside the fantasy along with my blanket. I was looking forward to working at Gadabout after such a long break. But I also felt apprehensive about seeing Hayley. Who would greet me today? The no-

nonsense girl I knew and (eep!) loved? Or the one-second-I'm-happy-to-see-you-the-next-I'm-peeved-for-no-reason girl?

Even more worrisome, could she tell from my face how I felt about her?

Only one way to find out . . .

I opened my suitcase and dumped the wadded contents onto my bed. Everything smelled of sea salt, damp French fries, and flowery motel soap. I plucked out the least wrinkled shorts and T-shirt I could find and got dressed.

Mom and Dad snored away across the hall. Downstairs, I scribbled a note to them, dabbed sunscreen on my tender nose, hooked on my tool belt, hopped onto my bike, and headed to Gadabout.

The cool morning air already held a hint of heat. My nose felt dry and crackly inside and out. I stifled a sneeze. Maybe tomorrow—my first day of high school!—would bring fog. Drizzly weather is much easier on my allergies.

Halfway to Hayley's, my stomach grumbled a breakfast reminder. *Rats.* I'd forgotten to grab the last two pieces of cold, congealed pizza from the fridge.

I about-faced and pedaled toward Dave's Donuts. I'd just reached the gas station next door to Dave's when I spotted a regal Roman nose and an elegant French braid.

Eep!

I slammed on my brakes.

The nose and braid belonged to the last person in the universe I wanted to see today, or *any* day: July Smith, a.k.a. Ace's older sister (though he was loath to admit it), a.k.a. The

59

Queen of the Clubs (because to give the illusion of school spirit she always belongs to at least fifty of 'em), a.k.a. the Nice Alarm thief (though she was loath to admit it—but that's another story). July and a cluster of girls wearing jean shorts and burgundy T-shirts were unrolling a huge banner that read *PEP CLUB CAR WASH TODAY! SUPPORT THE PHHS GOL—*

I didn't bother to read the rest of the banner. I about-faced again, telling my stomach it would have to be satisfied with a vending machine breakfast at Gadabout.

I reached the course just as Big Ben bonged seven times. I parked and locked my bike, peeking up at the Barkers' apartment. The kitchen lights blazed. My stomach squeezed.

How should I act when I see her? Friendly, miffed, cool? Definitely cool. Hey, it works for Ace . . .

I sniffed my armpits, smoothed my hair, and assumed an expression of nonchalance.

"Morning," I drawled, striding into the gingerbread office.

Hayley wasn't there.

I grabbed my Gadabout cap and name tag, and hurried to the greens.

She wasn't there either.

Maybe she's in her hiding place.

When Hayley was little, her mother, an engineer, built a secret hideout on the course for Hayley to play in. After her mom died, Hayley would creep inside it whenever she needed time alone to think—or cry. I was the only person she'd ever told about it, the only person she'd invited inside.

I knew Hayley's MO. She wouldn't come out till she was good and ready. If that was sooner than later, I should get busy. Hayley didn't tolerate slackers.

I spent the morning on neglected maintenance stuff: unclogging the mossy mechanism of King Arthur's moat filter, oiling ore cars from the Abandoned Gold Mine, performing the Heimlich maneuver on the golf-ball-choked Volcano.

Usually when I'm focused on mechanical things, the joy of work eclipses everything else. A gadget's workings unroll in my head like a wall map in geography class, and I'm the explorer, discovering the New World of wrenches and wheels . . . rivets and steel . . . pliers, polly-toggles, and gears.

Huh. Not that day. Every time I heard the scuff of shoes on plastic grass, the crunch of gravel, or the click of putter against ball, I'd veer off course, heart leaping, expecting Hayley. But it was only kids playing a round of mini-golf . . . or Mr. Barker with his jingly pocket-coins and more stuff to add to my fix-it list.

Finally, at noon, while helping him with lunch in the Snack Shack, I screwed up my courage to ask: "Where's Hayley today?"

"Didn't she tell you?" Mr. Barker poked a long fork at four hot dogs that hissed and spit on the grill. "She left early to go shopping."

"Grocery?"

"Clothes."

Clothes? *Hayley?*

I peeled open four buns. Tried to keep my voice Ace-cool. "Who'd she go shopping with?"

"Goldie."

"Goldie?" The buns fell to the scuffed floor.

"Five-second rule!" Mr. Barker snatched them up and laid them across the grill to toast. "Have to admit, I was surprised too," he said, chuckling. "Goldie and Hayley mix about as well as oil and water."

Ha. More like crude oil and sea lions.

"This could be a good thing," he went on. "Hayley hasn't been interested in girl stuff since her mother died. That was fine for a while. But now, well, I'm not exactly the role model a budding young woman needs." He waved at his baggy shorts and rumpled aloha shirt, then scratched his unruly curls with the fork handle. "I'm a dad. A guy. What do I know about mascara and bras?"

My cheeks blazed hot enough to char a cow at fifty paces. I opened the fridge to chill my head in the lettuce drawer.

"She needs a feminine touch," Mr. Barker continued. "So shopping with Goldie seems healthy. Normal. Know what I mean?"

I nodded, although *healthy* and *normal* weren't adjectives I (nor, ordinarily, Hayley) would've used to describe Trudy Laux. I mean, Ace hadn't assigned her the nickname Goldie (inspired by a snoopy resemblance to Goldilocks in The Three Bears) for no reason. She would gleefully rat out her own great-grandma if it meant obtaining juicy *information.*

"They'll be home after dinner," Mr. Barker was saying.

"Goldie's mother drove them to San Diego to some big sale at the outlet mall." He plopped the hot dogs on paper plates, shook a bag of Fritos over them, and handed me a napkin. "Is there a problem? I have Goldie's cell phone number if—"

"No, no! Just wondering. Thanks for lunch." I took my food and soda outside, sitting at the lone picnic table beneath its lopsided umbrella. The dogs, nestled in their buns, glistened with grease beads. Despite not having had breakfast, I pushed the plate away.

How could Hayley scamper off on my first day back at Gadabout? To go *shopping*, of all things? With *Goldie*, of all people? Didn't she know how much I'd looked forward to working here with her again? Didn't she know I wanted to talk to her about the convention and the alarm and the Guys? Didn't she remember that I was starting high school tomorrow—without her and Hic? Didn't she *care*?

"Hey."

I jumped. Ace appeared, hands in his pockets.

"Geez," I said, heart stuttering, "where'd *you* come from?"

"Nowhere."

"What's up?"

"Nothing." Over the top of his sunglasses he perused the patio, Snack Shack, and greens as if searching for someone.

"Who you looking for?" I asked.

"Nobody." He turned to leave.

"Where you going?" I called.

"Nowhere." He disappeared behind the Pirate Ship.

What was that all about?

I splotched ketchup onto the hot dogs.

"Good afternoon."

I jumped again, splotching ketchup on my shorts. "Ace, if you don't—"

Hiccup bowed, his elongated body so stiff and straight you could've ironed a shirt on it. Sweat darkened his hair to a leaf russet color. He wore a martial arts uniform—white with a red fire-breathing dragon embroidered over his heart. The flames spelled: *Hapkido Family Fitness.*

"Oh, it's *you*," I grumbled, wiping at my shorts. "What do *you* want?"

"I came to inquire after your emotional state."

"Oh."

"And?"

"And what?"

"How do you feel?"

"My fish are dead. I'm smothered in ketchup. How do you think I feel?"

"I am sorry."

"So I've heard." I chomped the first dog in half.

"May I sit down?"

"It's a free country." I ripped another savage bite.

Hiccup adjusted the umbrella to give himself a scrap of shade. Then he examined the bench splinters, chewed gum wads, and termites. Satisfied, he spread out a napkin, sat, and said: "You probably prefer that I leave—"

"You got that right."

"—however, I have something of importance to tell you."

"Yeah? Whose fish did you kill today?"

Hiccup squirmed. "I learned of it this morning in my hap-kido class. It should be of great interest to you."

I chug-a-lugged my soda and belched.

Hiccup coughed delicately into a napkin and continued: "Master Yates, my instructor, informed us that if we train at the *dojang*—the studio—for at least an hour every day after school, we can waive our physical education requirement."

"Thanks for that riveting news bulletin."

"Don't you understand the implications? This waiver applies to *all* students. If you register for martial arts classes, *you won't be required to take PE.*"

I stopped chewing. "Is this a joke?"

"The school district just needs a form, signed by your parents and Master Yates, affirming that you are getting consistent, challenging exercise every day."

My hopes leaped. "I won't have to drop CAD?" My hopes belly flopped. "But I don't know squat about martial arts. I'd make a complete fool of myself!"

"Sneeze, every student begins as a white belt—a beginner. Every student makes mistakes. That's a good thing. It's the best way to learn."

"True . . ." I said, remembering the seven prototypes I'd built of the Nice Alarm. With each model, each improvement, I'd discovered what worked and, more importantly, what didn't.

Hiccup went on: "The degree of discomfiture I experienced during my first class nearly incapacitated me. Yet, determined to improve, I returned the next day, and the next day, and every day since. Why? My choices were clear: I could risk the fear of embarrassment—or suffer the pain of my brothers forever slicing me into sushi." He threw back his shoulders, thumbs stuck into the orange belt cinching his waist. "I chose the former."

I marveled again at his new height, at the Medicine Man–like confidence. If hapkido could do this for *him* . . .

"But I'm not tall like you," I said. "I'm a wimp. A shrimp!"

He waved away an invisible fly. "Size and strength are inconsequential. Master Yates will teach you how to divert or suppress an attacker's force, how to use an attacker's power against himself. Besides, you are coordinated. Quick-thinking. In no time at all, you'll be able to do *this*."

He leaped to his feet and performed a whirlwind of kicks, punches, and jabs—accented with cries of *kee-yup*!

He finished with a solemn bow.

I breathed a solemn WOW.

"If not for yourself," he added, a smile flicking his mouth, "do it for Hayley. Women cannot resist a man in uniform. Or so MM tells me."

"Ha." I sneezed into my sleeve. "Hayley won't find me irresistible if I'm at the hapkido studio five afternoons a week instead of working here."

"At least consider the option." Hiccup removed a packet of papers folded over his belt and held them out to me. "Here is the *dojang's* brochure and registration form. Class begins

66

tomorrow at four p.m. sharp. You will need to obtain the PE waiver at Jefferson Middle's main office."

I stuffed the papers into my pocket.

His hand continued reaching toward mine. "Good luck tomorrow morning at Patrick Henry."

I kept my arms at my sides.

He sucked a breath and held it, as if willing me, begging me to shake hands. His fingers trembled. His cheeks reddened, then blotched blue.

He's gonna faint! Do you want to be held responsible for him passing out, plunging headfirst onto this filthy table, and getting splinters in his brain?

I shook his hand. Fast.

"Thanks for coming to tell me," I said. "And for the papers."

Hic squared his shoulders. Tug-tightened his belt. "I hope to see you at hapkido."

He loped toward the exit. When he reached Gadabout's gates, I hollered, "Hey, Hector!"

He stopped.

"I'm still mad at you, you know!"

"I know!" he hollered back, and waved without turning around.

11:57 p.m. My second night at home. While I was trying to fall asleep without the reassuring burble of my aquarium, the phone rang.

I groped for the receiver.

"Hic?" I grunted. "Hayley?"

"Nopey-dopey!" a smug voice sang. "Guess a-gain!

I sighed. "Goldie, it's almost midnight. Don't you ever sleep?"

"I've told you a *bazillion* times: I'm *nominal*."

"Absolutely," I said with a yawn. "But I think you mean *nocturnal*."

"What*ever*. Don't you want to know why I called?"

"No."

"Yes, you doooOOOOOoooo," she singsonged.

"If this is about that exclusive interview, could we do it another time? Like when that big ball of gas is shining bright in the sky?"

She trilled a laugh. "Lunch. Tomorrow. Behind Jefferson gym."

"Fine. Good-bye, Goldie."

"Not so fast!" Her voice returned to singsong mode. "I have a mes-sage for you-uuu. From *Haaay-leeee*!"

I bolted upright. "What's the message?"

"I need to talk to you. Meet me tomorrow. You know where. Seven a.m."

"That's it?" I asked.

"That's it."

"Nothing else?"

I could practically hear her eyes rolling. "She *might've* said please."

"Wait a sec." I shot an SOS through the phone wires. "Why are *you* delivering this message? Why didn't Hayley call me herself?"

Goldie gave a conspirator's giggle. "Here's the scoop: After your party, she called to ask if I'd take her shopping today. It's obvious she couldn't care less about how she looks, so I suspected right away she had *inferior* motives . . ."

"*Ulterior,*" I said.

"What*ever*. Do you want to hear this or not? Anyway, as soon as Mother and I picked her up, I could tell she—Hayley, not Mother—was freaking out about something but couldn't or wouldn't spill it. So I used my new Spy Camp interrogation skills on her, and they worked like a lucky charm! Get this: *Hayley is in love!* Since you're her best friend, she wants to confess *everything*, but she's afraid you'll laugh at her or be grossed out or—"

My heart skipped. Tripped.

In love? Hayley? Could this mean she . . . ? Me . . . ? We . . . ?

"Goldie, are you absolutely positive about this?" I asked. "Because if I find out you're messing with my head, I swear I'll—"

"Sneeze, I don't care if you believe me or not. I get paid either way!"

"Hayley *paid* you?"

"She will. With . . . *information*." I could almost hear Goldie's smug smile curling. "So where's this *you know where* Hayley asked you to meet her?"

"None of your business," I said. "Thanks for the message. In return, you'll get your exclusive about the convention. But that's all. Understand?"

"*Hmph!*" Goldie replied, and clicked off.

Chapter Nine

Tuesday. Seven a.m. Gadabout Golf.

Hole #13, the Great Pyramid, rose before me. Steep. Silent. Solid.

Only Hayley and I knew what secret lay within.

At the base of the giant triangle, my fingers searched the rough, rectangular blocks for what my eyes couldn't find in the fog: a smooth metal bump poking through the jagged cement.

Where . . . ?

Here!

I pressed it. The bump clicked. A nearly invisible door sprung open.

I crouched. Ducked inside. Scuffle-crawled through the dark tunnel, scraping my knees on the gritty floor. I conked my head twice, zigging where I should've zagged. Ahead, I spotted an ocher glow.

I scuffled faster.

"Sneeze? That you?"

"Yep!" I emerged in the Tomb Room, squinting against

the glare of a camping lantern. "Unless you've told someone else—"

Hayley snorted. "Never." She plunked the lantern on a rickety table. An old teddy bear, missing one eye, toppled to the floor. "I wasn't sure Goldie would give you the message. Or that you'd show up."

My heart flip-flopped. The room seemed smaller, stuffier than I remembered. "Why wouldn't I show up?"

Hayley didn't answer. Instead, she plunked onto a cushion, her back resting against the wall. She arranged her skirt to cover her legs.

Wait—Hayley was wearing *a skirt*.

And *a blouse*.

And sandals with teeny-tiny doo-dads on them.

Never, ever, had I seen her wear anything except jeans or shorts, tees, and sneakers. (And her dangling golf ball earrings, of course.)

"Whoa," I said.

"Wow," I said. "You look—"

Her SOS zeroed in on my face. "I look what?"

"Nice," I managed to gasp.

"Huh. I don't usually look nice?"

"No. Yes! I mean, today it's a—nicer nice."

She plucked at a ruffle. "Goldie helped me shop for this stuff. It's the first day of school, so I thought I should look—nice."

"That's—nice," I said.

She tossed the Cyclops bear at me. It smacked my face and I giggled.

Gaaa! I just giggled!

I found another cushion to sit on. "Why didn't you think I'd show up?"

Hayley kept plucking at her skirt. "I was rude to you the other day. For not writing to me this summer."

"I should've sent a postcard."

"Yes, you should have."

"I saw one that made me think of you, though."

"Yeah?"

"Yeah." My memory traveled to a funky roadside diner. Redwood grizzlies, carved by chain saw, guarded a cob-webby rack of faded postcards. One pictured a mini-golf course called Wacky Woods.

"With a Paul Bunyan and Babe the Blue Ox, just like yours here at Gadabout," I said. "Except their Babe has more bird poop."

Hayley laughed.

Omigosh she's beautiful when she laughs.

Omigosh she's beautiful, period.

No matter what I'd vowed to the contrary, I had to tell her. I had to tell her how I felt. IHADTOTELLHER-HOWIFELTRIGHTTHISVERYINSTANT!

Both of us blurted: "I have something to tell you!"

She laughed again. "Mine's important!"

"Mine too!"

"I wasn't sure I should tell you. But it concerns you."

"Mine too! I mean, mine concerns you."

Hayley rose to her knees, the skirt pooling around her like a blue pond. "You go first."

My heart thumped so hard my lungs felt squished. "No. You. First."

"I'm not sure how to begin," she began. She gazed at the ceiling as if it held the answer. "I've never felt like this before. Filled to the brim with—I don't know what, but I'll explode if I don't say it quick, so here goes: *Ilikesomeone!*"

"What?"

She repeated slower, louder: *"I. Like. Some. One."*

My breath caught. "Me too."

"Someone who doesn't know."

"Me too."

"But I want that someone to know."

"Me too."

"Today."

"Me too."

"I feel so much better talking to you about this!"

"Me too!"

We grinned at each other. Breathed at each other.

What should I do now? Move closer? Hold her hand? Or just sit here grinning and breathing for the next forty years?

I would do that—if I could do it while looking at Hayley.

"Tell me all about him," I said.

"You really want to know?" she asked with a shy smile.

Shy was not a word found in Hayley's smile dictionary. I felt a rush of pure, sure confidence, like the first time I tested the Nice Alarm—and it worked.

"Absolutely!" I scooted closer to better hear.

"Well . . ." Hayley peeped at me through her lashes. ". . . from what I hear, he's very smart."

"Oh?"

"And clever."

"Oh!"

"And funny."

"Ho-ho!"

"He has an inventive way with words."

"Yo-ho!"

"He just changed schools. He's never attended Patrick Henry before."

"Oh no?"

"He's actually in one of your classes."

"Oh-ho!"

"And he's so *handsome*!"

Uh-oh.

"His last name is Hanson, but Goldie says his nickname is—"

My voice came out flat. "Cullen Fu Handsome."

"You *know* him?" Hayley looked as if she didn't remember we'd all been at Gadabout the other day, as if no one had been at Gadabout except her and . . .

An icy hand plunged into my chest and ripped out my heart.

I jerked to my feet. I had the urge to fling my cushion at the wall, to fling Cullen at the wall. Seemed fitting, as that's where my heart had been flung.

SPLAT.

Funny how a heart can keep beating despite its squashedness.

In my coolest, calmest imitation of Ace, I pinched a lint speck from my shirt. "I was there too, you know. He's that Hawaiian guy on the golf team. The team that was gonna whomp me. How could I forget the guy who insulted you and Gadabout by calling mini-golf *jungle ball.*"

"I'm sure he didn't mean that the way it sounded," Hayley said. "And he stopped the team from whomping you, remember?"

"No, your dad did that."

Get out now, Steve. Quick—before you start blubbering.

I pretended to gasp at my watch. "Yikes, I've gotta go! Mr. Handsome isn't the only guy starting his first day at Patrick Henry."

Hayley caught my arm.

I froze. Afraid if I moved, she'd let go of my arm. Afraid if I moved, she wouldn't let go of my arm.

"That's the other reason I wanted to talk to you this morning," she said. "I have a couple of favors to ask."

"What kind of favors?"

"Goldie did a little investigative journalism for me—"

"You mean *snooping?*"

"—and found out Cullen's got a computer class with you.

Since you're such a computer whiz, I was hoping you might help him—if he *needs* help, that is. Goldie says he got into some nasty trouble when he lived in Hawaii, so he's on academic probation here. If he doesn't get a B in every class, the coach will kick him off the golf team."

"We wouldn't want that," I said under my breath.

"What?"

"I said, what's the other favor?"

She tucked her bangs behind one ear. The golf ball earrings quivered. "I'm embarrassed to ask. But you're my best friend. I don't trust anyone else . . ."

"Ask what?"

"Would you ask him . . . ask Cullen . . . if he *likes* me?"

SPLAT.

I didn't know I had a second heart. But there it was, oozing to the floor, joining its mate in a gory gelatinous puddle.

"I'm late," I said.

I dove into the tunnel. Scrambled gopher-like through the black. Welcomed the whimpers of my shredded knees. That was pain I understood.

"Steve, wait!"

Hayley scrambled out behind me, hair mussed, skirt dusty.

"I feel rotten," she said. "I shouldn't have made you come here this morning. I shouldn't have bugged you with favors. I'm sorry! That was inconsiderate of me. This is your first day of *high school*! You must have other stuff—important stuff—on your mind. Forget I asked. It's lame to think that he . . .

that I . . . we only saw each other once, anyway. Love at first sight! Huh. It's crazy. It doesn't exist, right?"

The fog swirled around Hayley's head like a halo. Wet diamonds clung to her cheeks, her lashes.

In a voice I didn't recognize, I said, "All right. I'll ask him."

"What? Really? Are you sure you don't mind? Oh, *thank you*." Hayley scrunched me in a hug. I smelled sun-warmed peaches. A silken thread of her hair caught on my upper lip.

Then she was skipping backward to Gadabout's gates. "Meet me for lunch! Our usual spot, under the pine tree, behind Jefferson gym. You can tell me everything then. Not just what Cullen says, but about your first morning as a high-schooler. And who it is you like! We didn't have time to talk about that. And I want to hear about the convention!"

"Sure."

Hayley halted mid-skip. Her SOS powered up. Locked on target.

Yep, she knew. She knew me well, Hayley did. Kind of . . .

"Mr. Patterson doesn't want to buy the Nice Alarm, does he," she said.

I shoved my hands into my pockets. "Nope."

"Huh. What does *he* know." Defiance blazed in her eyes. "You'll keep inventing anyway. The Nice Alarm will get built. *No. Matter. What.* Right?"

"Right."

Hayley placed a hand over her heart, eyes still ablaze. "This is gonna sound corny, Steve, but you—you're the bravest person I know. Attending that convention alone, taking the risk to show Mr. Patterson the alarm, putting yourself and your dreams out there. That. Was. So. Brave."

She turned and, tripping a little on her new skirt, raced through the gates.

"I've been braver," I whispered into the fog.

Chapter Ten

I caught the school bus around the corner from Gadabout, diving through the doors a nanosecond before they clamped shut. I thudded into the last half-empty seat. The guy snoring at the window snapped awake, hugging his skateboard like a baby blankie. "'Lo," he said groggily, emitting raspberry Pop-Tart fumes. He smacked his lips and slumped back to sleep.

I don't remember the rest of that ride. Only that my heart beat in funny jerks. My brain chanted along: *Don't. Think about. Her. Don't think. About. Her. Don't. Think . . .*

Airbrakes hissed. The bus lurched to a stop. We'd arrived.

A human tsunami roared down the aisle, spewing students into the parking lot. Pop-Tart nudged me with his skateboard. "End of the road."

"Eep." I sneezed six times, fumbled in my pack for my official Patrick Henry High School student ID card (in case anyone challenged my right to be there), and stumbled down the stairs. Pop-Tart nudged harder and a bazooka blast of adrenaline panicked me into the fog and through the main doors of my first morning at PHHS.

Surprisingly, high school wasn't that different from middle

school. Everyone still rushed around, overwrought, clanging lockers, lugging books, hunting for classes, racing to beat bells. Yeah, at first I felt like I'd crashed into the Land of the Giants. Bodies were bigger. Voices, deeper. Faces, hairier. (I'm talking guys here.) Otherwise, it was déjà vu all over again.

Especially when I heard two familiar squeals:

"Is *that* who I *think* it is?

"I think it *is*!"

Rats. The Amys.

The Amys are inseparable best friends, both named you know what, who had morphed into inseparable identities. I'd met them last spring when I joined Jefferson Middle's Inventor's Club. At the time, their idol, the aforementioned July Smith, was prez and the Amys served as her minions-turned-veeps. Their reign ended when July attempted to pass off the Nice Alarm as her own creation.

Due to that minor (her word) patent infringement, the school district banned July from all future student invention activities. She also lost her scholarship to an elite private high school. That meant that if the Amys were here, July was holding court close by. And since she blamed me for her plummet from grace, well, let's just say the last thing I needed today was her royal wrath.

"Are you *positive* it's him?" I heard the Amys say.

"*Pretty* positive!"

"We could ask him!"

"Yes! Let's ask him!"

Let's not and say you did.

I about-faced and escaped by plunging into another student tsunami. I washed up in homeroom barely in time for attendance.

My first two periods that morning featured "tree" classes: chemis*try*. trigonome*try*. I regretted not taking baske*try*. My parents had decided I should skip eighth grade because most of the courses at Jefferson didn't challenge me enough. No chance of that here. *"Master the material and be ready for an overkill,"* my chem teacher announced as she distributed our textbooks. My trig teacher began: "Trigonometry comes from the Greek words *treis,* meaning three; *gonia,* angle; and *metron,* meaning measure." The remainder of his lecture was, well, all Greek to me.

Third period, at last! *Computer-aided design.* Now that was a language I could understand.

I clutched my campus map and jostled giants to the second floor, my book pack thumping against my thigh. What a relief Mom and Dad okayed Hic's suggestion that I take hapkido instead of PE. I couldn't wait for this class to begin, couldn't wait to tackle the animation modeling software, to "draw" the virtual model of the alarm.

The CAD room greeted me with three long rows of gleaming white, state-of-the-art computer stations, each with flat-screen monitors and ergonomically correct chairs. A chemical odor emanated from the new electric-blue carpet. The computers hummed.

I grabbed a chair next to the wall, slung my pack under the desk, sank into the cushy seat, twirled twice in excitement, and gave the keyboard a flick. It glided into position.

Atlantis . . . Shangri-la . . . Utopia . . .

Cullen the Bear shambled in and overtook the seat beside me. My stomach lurched, colliding with my heart.

Hades . . . Purgatory . . .

I shrank in Cullen's shadow, practically diving to the bottom of my pack, pretending to search for a pencil.

"Howzit," he said, not unfriendly.

"Mmpf," mmpfed my pack-covered head.

Students streamed in and chose seats. The bell rang, the door closed, and class began.

I came up for air. Slumped lower in my seat. I felt sick. Dizzy.

You can do this, Steve. You will do this. You promised Hayley, remember?

Half an hour later, the teacher finished her lesson and suggested we experiment with the software. Since I hadn't heard a word of her lecture, I tippy-tapped random keys while sneaking peeks at Mr. Handsome.

He wore shorts and a faded yellow tank top with a drawing of a sno-cone on it. The tank read *Haleiwa Shave Ice.* His wide, dark brown fingers capered across the keyboard like he was playing jazz piano.

What the golf tees did Hayley see in this guy, anyway? Sure, he was tall. Muscle-y. Handsome . . .

Oh. Right.

Okay, so I wasn't tall. And my muscles were as rubbery as overcooked spaghetti. And my nose looked liked it had barely survived a nasty altercation with a garlic press. But I had something Cullen didn't have: *B-R-A-I-N-S*.

I emerged from Cullen's shadow and, before I could change my mind, blurted, "Hi! Hello! Need any help?"

"No tanks, brah," he answered. "Got it wired."

Great. Just great. The guy has computer smarts too.

Well, at least I could tell Hayley I offered to help and Cullen declined. One favor down, one to go. And I had an entire semester to get around to number two. I mean, I promised only to *ask* if he liked Hayley. I hadn't specified *when* I'd ask . . .

A carpet fluff snuffed up my nose.

"AH-*CHOO!*"

"Eh, don't I know you, brah?" Cullen's keen, blackish eyes regarded me and my wad of tissues.

I shifted closer to the wall. "Nope. Yep. We sorta met a couple of days ago at Gadabout Golf."

Cullen grinned. "You da *keiki* wen gave Marcos da metaphorical bloody nose!"

"Marcos?"

"Yellow rat bite. Wen threaten you wit one whoosha."

He must mean Scarecrow. But I didn't recall any rodent nibbles.

"You got *koa*, junior boy," Cullen continued. "But keep clear of Marcos, eh? No like talk stink, but from what I seen, dat *moke* make *pilikia*."

I stared at Cullen's shark-tooth necklace. It glistened bone-white and sharp under the fluorescent lights.

"I really, really, really don't want to offend you," I told him. "But—I don't understand a word you're saying."

Cullen's grin gleamed. "Sorry, brah. In da islands, when my bruddahs talk story, we speak Pidgin. Hawaiian dialect." He ticked his massive fingers: "*Keiki* mean kid. *Koa* is courage, da stuff of *ali'i*, Hawaiian royalty. *Talk stink—*"

"Bad-mouthing someone?" I guessed.

He nodded, pleased. "*Moke* is tough local guy. *Pilikia* spells trouble. *Rat bite*, dat's one bad haircut."

I laughed. "What about the other word? *Whoosher.* Is that a volcano?"

"Dat's one golf term," Cullen said. "It mean whack a ball so hard, air whooshes from da impact." He nudged my chair closer with his paw-foot. "So what's da scoops? What's a *menehune* like you doin' here?"

"You mean, what's a kid like me doing in a high school like this?"

"Yeah."

"I skipped eighth grade," I said. "Part-time, anyway. I take three classes here in the mornings, four at Jefferson Middle School after lunch."

"Fo' real kine? You serious? Cool . . ."

Cullen continued to ask me questions while we explored the software. He was surprisingly easy to talk to, and I surprised myself by telling him about the Nice Alarm. In return, he shared his love of drawing (he designed the logo on his T-shirt) and his desire to learn digital art. He hoped to get a golf scholarship so he could attend one of the California universities and study animation. Just in case a scholarship didn't come through, he'd moved to Southern California to live with his "Auntie."

"I like fo' establish residency here," he explained. "It make state college affordable."

"My best friend—I mean, this guy I know—plans to study art in college too," I said. "He's expanded his cartoon superhero into a graphic novel he wants to get published."

"Fo' reals? Cool. I like fo' see dat."

The end-of-class bell rang. I scribbled the homework assignment and hooked my pack over one shoulder. Cullen led the way into the hall, his flip-flops slapping against the soles of his brown feet. Guys leaped aside, offering a wide berth. Girls pointed and swooned. "Cullen *Handsome*," I heard one whisper.

Cullen didn't notice. "Hang loose," he said, strolling toward the stairs.

"Hey, wait!" I trotted after him. "I want to ask you a question. About . . . a girl."

"Wot girl?"

"The girl at Gadabout."

Cullen adjusted his shark's tooth. "There was *wahine* there? Oh, da girl with da notepad. Kept hopping like she needed da *lua*? Bathroom?" He shuddered. "Ho, she give me chicken skin. Goose bumps. Not da good kine."

"That would be Goldie," I said. "I meant the other one."

"Ada one?"

How could he not remember? How could anyone lay eyes

on Hayley and not have her image burned forever into his memory cells?

"Short hair the color of rice," I said. "Golf ball earrings. Ice-blue eyes."

"Oh, da one with da squint. She get one headache?"

"No, she have *koa*," I said, thinking about the way Hayley had challenged Scarecrow/Marcos.

"You're right, *menehune*."

"So, do you like her?"

Cullen shrugged. "How I can like her? I don't know her."

"I mean, do you think she's pretty?"

"She 'bout the same age as my niece. Both *keiki*. Both da cute. Not as cute as *ku'uipo*. My sweetheart, Annie. She live in Hawaii. What like fo' ask me 'bout Hayley?"

"Never mind!" My chest almost exploded with joy. *Cullen didn't like her! Cullen thought she was a little kid!* "I'm meeting a friend for lunch at Jefferson Middle. Aloha!"

I sprinted down the hall, squeezing between students. The loose strap of my pack caught on a drinking fountain, jerking me backward. I yanked it free—

—and smashed into a tight stomach clad in a burgundy knit shirt.

"Watch it, punk!" the shirt said. It smelled of peppermint.

"Sorry," I mumbled, and looked up, up, up into the face of Scarecrow—aka, Marcos the Moke.

Chapter Eleven

"Eep!" I said, and sneezed four wet times.

Marcos chortled in disgusted glee. "Look who it is!" He gripped my shoulders. "Right *under our nose!*"

His golf goons sniggered and contracted around me like a giant noose.

"Ha-ha" I said, struggling to break free. "Never heard *that* one before. Thought it up all by yourself, did you?"

His fingers burrowed deeper. He gave me a hard shake. "What are you doing out of your swamp, punk? And why are you at Patrick Henry? *Brown-nosing* your future teachers?"

"*Ow!* I mean, no, I'm delivering a note. To my brother. My older, *hulking* brother. He's on the football team. He *tackles*."

"You're a pathetic liar." Marcos yanked the pack from my shoulder and began rummaging.

I tried to snatch and sprint, but his three look-alikes muscled closer.

"Ugh, just clumps of wet snot rags. But what's this?" Marcos flashed my ID card, then flicked it across the hall. He tossed my chem and trig books too. "We're in the presence of a brainiac: a nerd who keeps his *nose to the grindstone*. Bet he even has his *nose in a book* while sitting on the john!"

His goons guffawed.

Ah, bathroom humor: The last refuge of kindergarteners.

"So that's why he *thumbed his nose* at us the other day!" chimed in Goon #3, beeping my sore schnoz. "That's why he had his *nose in the air*. He thinks he's smarter than us!"

"A judgment error," I insisted. "My allergy meds make me delusional."

"Maybe we should *rub your nose* in it," said Goon #4.

Talk about flogging a dead joke . . .

"Walk with us, punk," Marcos said. "I have a cramp in my arm. Nothing a few rounds with my club won't cure."

"I don't have time to play golf," I said with another futile struggle.

Marcos smirked. "Who said anything about golf?"

I gulped. Goons #2 and #3 pinned my arms to my sides, sandwiching me so tightly between them I felt like a slice of bologna. With Marcos in the lead and Goon #4 cutting off my escape route from behind, they hustled me to the double doors overlooking the quad. Below, students lunch-munched.

"Which way?" #2 asked.

"Through the industrial arts building, to the lower field," Marcos said. "Take it nice and slow. We don't want anyone getting suspicious. We're just giving our new pal the fresh-man tour . . ."

They lurched me down a flight of stairs and edged the

noisy crowd. Flocks of seagulls wheeled overhead, dive-bombing for French fries, splitting eardrums with their frenzied squawks. Even if I braved a cry for help, no one would hear me above that racket.

The fog lifted. I blinked in the bright sun. Probably the last time I'd see it—provided none of the birds left a farewell donation in my eye.

Two high-pitched shrieks rivaled the decibels of the gulls.

"You *didn't*!"

"I *did*!"

"You *couldn't*!"

"I *could*!"

I'd recognize those shrieks—and gull-like brain cells—anywhere.

The Amys!

I grasped at a straw of hope.

Would they help me? Had they forgiven me for ratting out their idol?

I scanned the quad for July Smith's Roman profile, her elegant French braid . . .

No sign of her. Probably at a club meeting. I had to take that chance. I had to flag down the Amys. There was no one else—

—and time was running out.

With every ounce of my strength, I wrested one arm from Goon #2's grasp, waved it like a rogue windshield wiper, and screamed: "Hey, Amy! Over here! *Amy! Hellooo!*"

The Amys turned. Cocked their heads like parakeets.

Their beaks—uh, lips—curled and dimpled and opened to shriek:

"It *is* him!"

"So it *is*!"

They flew across the quad, flung themselves between my captives, and smothered me in a clumped hug.

"We're *sorry* about what happened last year!" said the Amys.

"*Sorry!*" the Amys repeated.

"We feel *terrible!*"

"*Awful!*"

"It wasn't our fault. She *made* us do it!"

"*Forced* us! We couldn't help it!"

"You pretty birds know this bungled nose job?" Marcos asked.

The Amys nodded. "Uh-huh! His name is Squeeze!"

"Sneeze," I corrected.

"Uh-huh!" The Amys nodded again. "His best friend is Burp."

"Hiccup," I corrected.

"He's a brilliant inventor! He invented the Friendly Alarm!"

"Whatever," I said with a surrendering flap of my hand.

"It's going to make him rich and famous," the Amys said.

"Famous *and* rich!" agreed the Amys.

"How very interesting." Marcos popped a peppermint into his mouth. "Tell me more. What exactly is this alarm? What does it do?"

"Sneeze can explain much better than we can!"

"Better yet, he could give a demonstration!"

"Yes, a demonstration would be *much* better!"

"Sure," I said, flickering my eyelashes in what I hoped was Morse code for *SOS*. "I'm glad you've come *to my aid*. I desperately need your *assistance*."

"You've *never* wanted our assistance before," said the Amys.

"Never," the Amys said.

"Situations change." I tried to wiggle my eyebrows into arrows, pointing at Marcos. "The unexpected happens and *now I need HELP.*"

In a dim cranny of the Amys' brains, a night-light switched on.

"Help? Of course! Our pleasure!"

"We'd be delighted, of course!"

The Amys clenched Marcos around the waist and shoved him aside. "Stand here, gorgeous. Pretend you're the alarm."

Marcos squirmed and unleashed a rough laugh. *"Watch it!"*

"He's ticklish!" the Amys said. "Isn't that *cute?*"

"Adorable!" agreed the Amys.

They shoved Goon #2 in front of him. "You're the handsome prince who the alarm will awaken from a deep sleep."

"With a smooch?" His arm encircled an Amy's waist.

"Keep your flippers to yourself for a second and close your eyes. Can you snore?"

"Mmmrrrggggzzz-zzz!"

"Window-shattering," the Amys said.

"Wall-buckling," agreed the Amys.

They faced Goons #3 and #4. "You two hunks can be the

prince's brothers. You spent a wild night doing hip-hop in the pond. Close those eyes. All together now: *Snore!*"

"*ZZZZZZZzzzzZZZZZZ!*"

"*Mmmmrrrggggzzzzzz!*"

"*SNNNNerrrrrrrrrrcckk!*"

"Awesome!"

"Radical!"

The Amys whispered to me, *"Get ready."*

Whispered the Amys: *"Get set."*

"Raise your right arm," the Amys told Marcos. "Higher. Better raise your other arm too. *Perfect!* Now open your mouth and close your eyes, and you will get a big surprise!"

"Froggies, keep snoring!" the Amys instructed. "When I count to three—"

"Froggies?" said Marcos. "I thought they were princes."

"ONETWOTHREE!" the Amys yelped.

"THREETWOONE!" yelped the Amys.

The girls attacked with ferocious tickles.

Marcos and Goon #2 contorted to escape the onslaught while their team members snored with continued fervor.

I filched my pack—and ran.

I glanced back only once, hollering: "Thanks, Amys! I owe you!"

"Nope," hollered the Amys. "We're even now!"

"Even-Steven!" The Amys' fingers dove again into Marcos's armpits.

"Get—him—!" Marcos choked, cap tumbling. With an an-

gry convulsive *ha-ha-ow,* he collapsed against his cronies and I ran on . . .

After sprinting several blocks, I slowed to a trot, clutching a stitch in my side. Still two miles to Jefferson Middle and I needed to pace myself.

I arrived just before lunch period ended. I squeezed through a misshapen section of chain-link fence and hurried to the pine tree behind the gym, where I was greeted by:

Pierre, his forehead creased with anger beneath his beret;

Goldie, tapping her foot and flipping her hair with furious impatience;

Hiccup, studying my face with MM's superior vision for signs of forgiveness;

Ace, asleep, head lolled against a tree-root pillow;

And Hayley.

She'd changed out of the clothes she'd worn earlier in the dusty Pyramid. Now she wore another new skirt and blouse of blue that deepened her eyes. They gazed with expectance through me toward Patrick Henry.

"Hi," I said to her, because there was only her.

"You're *late!*" Goldie snapped. "Late for the *exclusive interview* you *swore* you'd give me! My first gossip column of the year is due *Thursday* for the first edition of *The Jeffersonian Times* on *Friday,* and *you* are my lead story! We *have* to do the interview *today. Now. Or else.*"

"St-Stephen," Hiccup interrupted, "have you been diligent about monitoring your condition after Sunday's unfortunate exposure to the *naegleria fowleri*? If you're not too angry, I would like to run through the checklist of symptoms."

"My electric *beeters*!" Pierre said, holding out a wrapped bundle. "You feexed zem last spring, oui? Once again zey are massacring zee meringue! You must fix zem before my 'ome ec class zis afternoon."

"Yo." Ace yawned. "Keep it down."

I stared at them in disbelief.

Why did I hang out with this bunch of bozos, these ingrates, these *non-friends*? If they bugged me so much, why hadn't I told them to beat it, get lost, take a hike? I mean, with "friends" like these, who needed enemies?

"Excuse me!" I said. "I have an announcement to make!" I kicked Ace's foot. "You too."

He arced an eyebrow at me over the top of his sunglasses.

"You're right, I'm late," I continued. "Do any of you care *why*? Do any of you care that I just completed my first morning as a high-schooler? That I was kidnapped by those goons from the Patrick Henry Golf Team? That if it weren't for—I can't believe I'm saying this—*the Amys*, I wouldn't be standing here now while you harass, insult, and *threaten* me?"

"Did they hurt you?" Hayley asked. "Cullen wasn't with them, was he?"

"I smell a *scoop*!" Goldie exulted, nose wrinkling with delight. *"Golf Goons Grab Gadget Guy."*

"We are reeleeved you escaped wisout injuree," Pierre said. "Eye cannot say zee same for zee beeters. You must tend to zem wis haste. Eet eez your dutee! You took an oath, no?"

94

"He's an inventor, not Hippocrates," Ace commented.

The first end-of-lunch bell rang.

"Get yourself another mechanic, Pierre," I said. "Your beaters have whipped their last cream, frothed their last meringue. I can't do anything else for them. I *won't* do anything else for them. Buy new ones. Move on."

I turned on Goldie. "Holster your microphone and stow your notepad, Goldilocks. You're not getting an exclusive. Not now. Not *ever.*"

"But you promised you'd tell—"

"There's nothing to tell," I confessed. "Mr. Patterson rejected the Nice Alarm. His company won't manufacture it. End of story."

I faced Hic. "As for you: Yeah, I'm sick. Yeah, I'm angry. Sick of your germaphobia, angry about the Guys. I'll get over both. Not today. Probably not tomorrow. But eventually. So cease and desist with the worrying. I'll see you this afternoon at the *dojang.*"

Hiccup shot a hapkido kick at the pine tree and whispered, *"YES!"*

Needles rained onto Ace's face. He rose on one elbow, brushing them off.

I booted his foot again. "What a waste," I said. "Why don't you go to class for once? That's where I'm headed."

I marched toward the logjam of students all trying to cram into the main building at the same time.

A familiar callus snagged my wrist.

Zap!

Every nerve in my body electrified to attention.

"Aren't you going to tell me off too?" Hayley said. "I deserve it."

"Maybe later." I scratched my wrist to subdue the lingerings of her touch.

"I'm sorry your morning was so rotten. I'll bet you never got to eat either." She offered a pear from her sack. "What's your next class?"

My teeth sank into the sweet pear flesh. Juice dribbled down my chin, raced along my arm. "I've got English with Mrs. Hobbs," I answered, surreptitiously using my jeans as a napkin.

"I've got English with Hobbs too. Do you mind if I walk with you?"

"First I have to get a form from the main office."

We wormed through boisterous kid-clots to the front desk. I asked a secretary wearing spiky heels for the Permission to Waive Physical Education Requirement form. "One moment," she said, clip-clipping into the next room.

Hayley stood beside me, the cloth of her blouse touching the sleeve of my tee. I'd finished the pear, tossed the core, and now didn't know what to do with my hands. They felt huge and clumsy and sticky, like I was wearing baseball mitts made of flypaper.

I waited for Hayley to ask about Cullen. I knew she was *dying* to ask about Cullen. But she didn't. She wouldn't.

I sighed and said, "Goldie's information was correct. He's in my computer class."

"Who?"

"You know." I wanted her to say it.

"Cullen?"

"Yeah."

"Did you talk to him?"

"Yeah."

"And?"

"And what?"

"Stephen J. Wyatt!" Hayley shoved her hair behind her ears and shot me an SOE (Squint of Exasperation). "*You* know. Does he . . . ?" The SOE softened into an expression of trust I didn't deserve. She whispered, *"Does he like me?"*

I opened my mouth, ready to hurt, to blurt: *No! He barely remembered you! He thought you were a kid! And you are! You're only an eighth grader! He's a senior! So just forget it. Forget him! He's already forgotten you . . .*

But I couldn't bring myself to say it. Because . . .

I knew how Hayley would feel. I knew how her breath would stop. How her heart would splat against the wall, oozing to the floor in a quivering clump, where it would jerk-jerk, jerk-jerk, each beat a painful wrench, a rip, a reminder . . .

I didn't want her to feel that. I didn't want her to suffer. I wanted to save her. Protect her.

So I swallowed against the dryness in my throat and listened as the lie crept along my tongue, squeezed through my lips, and sidled to her ears:

"Yes, Hayley. Cullen Hanson likes you."

Chapter Twelve

Hayley squealed.

I winced in pain and shock. Hayley had always firmly believed that the serrated squeals of girly girls were a moral flaw of character. Yet, here she was, morally flawing away in a pitch that could slash tires in Montana.

To save her soul (and my ears), I did the only thing I could think of: I clamped a hand over her mouth.

"Mmmpppfft!" Her eyes stretched. She scrambled to pry off my fingers.

"Young man!" The spiky-heeled secretary had returned with my form. "If you don't stop that this instant, you're going straight to the principal's office!"

"Gaaa!" I reclaimed my hand and took the form. I'd seen quite enough of Mr. Garrett's accommodations last year, thank you very much. (But that's another story.)

"PDA is seriously frowned upon at this institution," the secretary said with a serious frown.

"What's Pee Dee Ay?" Hayley asked.

"Oh, *puh*-LEEZE," Goldie said, materializing beside us. "Public Displays of Affection!"

"Pub—Affec—No!" I said. "That wasn't—I didn't—I was just—"

"Helping me hold my breath," Hayley said. "I've got— *hic!*—hiccups."

The secretary's frown grew seriouser and seriouser. "I seriously doubt a case of hiccups could be serious enough to warrant such serious—"

"Oh, hon, you must be *new*." Goldie patted her arm. "Lemme give you *the scoop* on Hiccup Denardo."

"I don't get hiccups often," Hayley said, "but when I do"— she lowered her voice to a conspirator's whisper— *"Steve was just trying to stave off the projectile vomiting."*

The secretary took two serious steps backward. "In that case, perhaps you should see the nurse." She scribbled a hall pass and held it out by the tippy-tips of her talon-like fingernails.

Goldie snatched the pass. "I'll see that she gets there safely."

Hayley snatched it from her. "I'd rather Steve went with me."

"But I've got *gobs* of experience treating your affliction." Goldie snatched the pass again.

Hayley re-snatched and held the pass aloft, forcing Goldie to leap like a poodle desperate for treats. "Since when do you have a nursing degree?"

"Since when do you have projectile vomiting?"

"Since the moment I first read one of your nauseating gossip columns."

"Well!" Goldie stamped a hoof. "You didn't think my *investigative reporting* was nauseating two days ago! For your *information*, Hayley Barker, you wouldn't know *half* of *you know what* about *you know who* if it weren't for *me*! *And* you still owe me a *scoop* as payment!"

"I'm sure the janitor has something you can scoop," Hayley said coolly.

The second warning bell rang, drowning out Goldie's retort.

"Enough with the Hall Pass Ping-Pong," I said. "We're late." I whisked Hayley into the hall, smacking into Ace, knocking his sunglasses askew.

Both dark brows arced in mild surprise. He brushed what were probably my "cooties" off his shirt. "Where's the fire," he asked with a yawn.

"That-a-way," I said, motioning into the office. "And I wouldn't go in there if I were you." I whisked Hayley to the right toward our English class, my chest full-to-bursting with admiration. "Wow, Hay, I've never seen girls spar like that before. You really nailed her!"

"Huh. You're next, buddy boy. You almost smothered me!"

"You *squealed*."

"I never."

"It's true! You sounded like Goldie."

She snorted. "There's no reason to insult me!"

"Don't you remember? Right after I said Cullen likes you, you—"

Hayley squealed again—then clamped a hand over her mouth.

"*Golf tees,*" she muttered. "It *is* true!" She gave a weak laugh. "It's just—I can't believe he likes me. It's crazy. He's a senior. I'm a middle schooler. Yet, he *likes* me! Did he say anything else? Tell me from the beginning! What was he wearing, how did you ask, does he want to meet me?"

Geez, I've created a monster . . .

"Look behind you," I instructed. "Where's Goldie? Is she following us?"

Hayley risked a peek. "She's outside the main office, talking to Ace. She's reaching for her tape recorder . . . slinking this way! I never should've asked for her help. She'll stalk me to my grave to get the scoop about me and Cullen!"

"Yep, especially now that I've ruined her exclusive," I said. "So it's time for evasive action. You've got the hall pass—and I've got a plan."

I grabbed her elbow and whirled us in the opposite direction, struggling like salmon against the powerful stream of students. I waved at Goldie, who scowled as she was swept past.

The final bell rang.

We launched into my sanctuary-away-from-sanctuary: the nurse's office.

"Boy, howdy!" The school nurse greeted me with a weathered smile, a Texas twang, and a hearty back clap. Then he pulled me into a rough hug. "Long time no see, Sneeze!"

Tony Sandoval used to ride buckin' broncs in the rodeo circuit till he traded his saddle and spurs for thermometers and doctor scrubs. Hiccup and I spent so much time in his office last year (me because of my allergies; Hic because of his hiccups), Tony considered us his *wheel-horses* (good friends).

He tipped an imaginary hat at Hayley. "Afternoon, Miz Barker. To what do I owe the pleasure?"

Goldie's face appeared in the doorway, gloating her *I've-got-you-now!* smile before jerking from sight. She'd lurk out there indefinitely, waiting for us to leave or waiting to over-hear something juicy—whichever came first. My plan was to make her believe Hayley's hiccups warranted treatment. Long, tedious treatment.

"HAYLEY HAS A NASTY CASE OF HICCUPS," I said.

"That a fact? No need to shout, son."

"It's true, Mr. Sand-*hic!*-val," Hayley said, catching on. She handed him the hall pass. "I'm *hic*ing like crazy."

"Well, ma'am, I got just the thing to fix you fine as frog's hair!" Tony opened a cabinet. He pushed aside containers of rubbing alcohol, cotton balls, and bandages before choosing a slim-necked bottle. "Heard 'bout this remedy from a lady-friend of my acquaintance. Thought our friend Hector might be needin' it first, but no matter." He tipped the opaque green bottle. Thick dark stuff oozed onto the spoon. "Down the hatch!"

Hayley eyed it with an SOS.

Outside, in the hall, I heard Goldie exclaim: "What are *you* doing here?"

"AND AFTER HAYLEY DRINKS THIS POTENT MEDICINE," I said, glancing at the exit, "SHE'LL NEED TO LIE DOWN FOR AN HOUR, RIGHT, TONY? SO YOU CAN MONITOR HER PROGRESS?"

A smile twitched his lips and he winked one sun-strained eye. "Hard t' say, son. Could be longer. Ev'ry case responds differently."

I motioned for silence. Tiptoed to the door. Poked my nose, then head, into the hall.

"Is the coast clear?" Hayley asked, *sotto voce.*

"Unless she learned at Spy Camp how to disguise herself as a drinking fountain."

"Is that nosy slanganderer gunnin' for you again?" Tony asked.

Hayley snorted. "If you mean Gossiping Goldie, the answer is yes. Are you sure she's gone, Steve?"

"Positive."

"Then so are my hiccups, Mr. Sandoval."

"Dang. I wanted to see this remedy in action. Well, no sense wastin' it." Tony slurped, coughed, and wiped his mouth with the back of his hand. "Not bad. Needs lettuce, is all."

Hayley sniffed the cap. "What *is* this stuff?"

Tony laughed. "Balsamic vinegar." He settled into his leather swivel chair, legs stretched onto his desk, boots crossed at the ankles. "Time to 'fess up, wheel-horse," he drawled. "What can I really do ya for?"

Tony could read me like a Zane Grey novel. "Hayley and I need a private place to talk."

"'Zat so? Where you two supposed t' be right now?"

"English. But we only need five minutes. Ten, tops."

Tony's chili-brown eyes regarded me. One wiry caterpillar-brow raised a notch higher than the other. But he didn't ask why. He wouldn't. He trusted me. And I, him.

"Aw right." He slapped his knees, pushed back his chair. "Mind the store while I mosey out for a new stack of hall passes." He ripped a pass from its pad and stuffed the remainder into a cluttered drawer. "This one seems t' be my last," he added with another wink.

After he'd gone, Hayley perched on the cot beneath the window. I moved to sit beside her. Then, remembering her entrancing scent of fresh peaches, I veered to Tony's leather chair. It smelled safely of saddle soap.

"Ask away," I said.

Hayley tried to smile into my eyes, but one corner of her lower lip trembled.

"What's wrong?"

"Nothing. Everything." She crumpled a fistful of skirt, then smoothed it again. "It's just—this is pointless. It doesn't matter what Cullen said about me. *'No dating till you're fourteen,'* Daddy says. That's a whole year away! By then Cullen will have graduated. Moved back to Hawaii . . ."

"But we've gone out together lots of times," I said. "To the movies and on hikes. Bike rides to the beach. Your dad's always been cool about that."

"Those weren't dates, Sneeze. Daddy trusts you. You're my *friend.*"

I spun the chair so Hayley couldn't see the arrow protruding from my chest.

"Besides, we're rarely alone," Hayley went on. "Hiccup joins us. Or Ace appears. He hung out at Gadabout practically twenty-four/seven this summer. Weird, huh? Do you think maybe he has a thing for Goldie?"

I choke-laughed.

"Ridiculous, I know. But she lurked there almost every day too, interrogating us about Pierre. I saw him only twice. At least, I *think* it was him: once slinking out of Lickety-Split Chick with a greasy bucket o' wings. The second time, buying a package of powdered donuts—at a carwash!"

"Mon Dew," I said with another choke-laugh. "Neither could've been Pierre!"

"Probably not. This guy had a mustache too." Hayley stood to pace, fists clenched. "What's happening to me? I'm acting insane. I never should've asked Goldie what classes Cullen's in. I never should've asked you to find out if he likes me. It was crazy. Stupid. And it just makes everything harder."

She sighed. The sound resonated inside my chest like a sad echo calling from the deep darkness of a dank well.

I ached for her . . . with her. . . .

And answered her sigh the only way I could.

"Maybe . . . maybe I could arrange for you and Cullen to meet at Gadabout one afternoon," I suggested, without even the faintest glimmer of how to arrange *that*. I'd just have to worry about those pesky details later. "You could pretend he'd come to play mini-golf," I went on. "Your dad wouldn't suspect a thing."

"But Daddy threatened the entire Patrick Henry Golf Team! They'll go to jail if any of them steps foot at Gadabout again."

No wonder I like Mr. Barker . . .

"Well, um . . . what about phone calls?" I asked. "That's not dating."

"Money's tight, so Daddy canceled our cell service. And if he heard Cullen's voice on our landline, I wouldn't be allowed to date till I'm forty."

Really, really like Mr. Barker . . .

Hayley thumped onto the cot, then heaved herself up again. "You're sweet, Sneeze, trying to help and all, but it's hopeless." Resignation drenched her voice. "Let's go to class. If we stay put any longer, Goldie will start a rumor that I'm dating Tony."

I swallowed. Then blurted: *"E-mail!"*

"What?"

"Cullen can write to you. By e-mail."

"No way. Daddy and I share the same computer. If I start getting e-mails from a stranger, especially a strange guy—"

The proverbial lightbulb clicked on inside my head.

I had a plan. The only question was: Would it work?

Worry about those pesky details later, Sneeze.

"What if . . ." I began, "what if Cullen sent the e-mails to me first and then I forwarded them to you? Your dad would see only *my* return e-mail address. He wouldn't care about my e-mails. After all, I'm just a . . . a *friend*."

Hayley fingered a golf ball earring. "That might work! Cullen and I could get to know each other through e-mails. Then I could talk to Daddy about changing his mind, about letting me date sooner."

"Um, yeah."

She faced me, body straight and solemn like the other day when she stood atop the North Pole. "You'd do this for me?" she asked, blue eyes unblinking. "You'd let Cullen send e-mails for me to you first? And you'd forward them?"

"Of course."

"You wouldn't read them?"

I squelched a squirm. "Of course not."

"You'd send him my answers?"

"Of course."

"You wouldn't read them?"

Another squirm-squelch. "Of course not."

"I could send them to him myself," she went on, "deleting them from my Sent Mail folder afterward so Daddy wouldn't see. But in case I forget or something, it would be so much safer if—"

"I said I'd do it, Hayley."

Her face lit with the spit and flash of a Fourth of July sparkler and she whispered: *"You are the Best. Friend. Ever."*

Chapter Thirteen

What. Had. I. Done?

What in the name of Thomas Alva Edison had possessed me to tell Hayley that Cullen would e-mail her?

Sure, my plan was simple: *I* would impersonate Cullen. *I* would write the e-mails. That way, Hayley wouldn't get her heart broken. But what, exactly, could I write that:

wouldn't make "Cullen" sound like a dork?

wouldn't make me sound like a dork dorkily impersonating Cullen?

Those were the not-so-simple, gee-I-really-should've-thought-of-those-pesky-details-before-I-promised-he'd-write-her parts of the plan.

Hunched over my notebook, I spent most of English, history, Spanish, and art scribbling down, then scratching out, fits and starts of "Cullen's" letter while simultaneously trying to ignore the attempts of my "friends" to bug me, such as:

The *tunk-tunk-tunk* of Goldie, in full pout mode, kicking the back of my chair;

Ace snoring a two-note, tone-deaf tune;

The guilt-inducing barbs Pierre muttered in murdered "French";

Hiccup peeking at me every two seconds with the same woe-is-me expression Dasher and Dancer wear whenever their food bowl has been licked clean for a whopping thirty seconds;

Hayley's glazed glow.

Even my teachers seemed bent on bugging. They expected me to parse sentences, recall long-dead emperors, direct Paco y Felipe a la biblioteca, and mix a batch of gloopy papier-mâché that reeked like curdled oatmeal.

Didn't these people realize I had more important things on my mind?

Tunk-tunk-tunk.

I whirled on Goldie. "Sssssstop it!"

"Stop what?"

"Stop kicking my chair!"

"Okay."

Tunk-tunk-tunk.

I whirled again. "You said you'd stop!"

"*You* said I'd get an exclusive! And I will. I always get my . . . *information.*"

"Not this time," I said.

"Then you force me to dig up something juicier."

I felt what Cullen called "chicken skin" prickling my neck.

I scooted my desk out of Goldie's reach and returned to more pressing issues, such as how to weasel out of my sticky situation without:

Hayley finding out and firing me and/or never speaking to me again;

Cullen finding out and adding my pearly whites to his shark-tooth necklace;

Having to immigrate to Antarctica.

Considering my dislike for writing, the South Pole seemed the best solution. Brutally cold, yes. But at least I could live a life virtually sneeze-free. I mean, what were the odds I was allergic to penguins and lichen?

After school, I rode the city bus to the hapkido studio, making a point to sit six seats *behind* Hiccup. I knew he wouldn't attempt to glance at me over his shoulder for fear of a recurrence of torticollis, a neck injury he imagined he'd sustained during the first test of the Nice Alarm. (But that's another story.)

Unfortunately, I wasn't so lucky at the studio. By the time I handed in my registration form and purchased a uniform, Hic was the only person left in the boys' locker room who could help me dress. I slipped easily into the elastic-waist pants, but the button-less shirt looked like an IQ test for Einstein. And we were due in the *dojang* in two minutes.

I swallowed a fish scale of anger—but could not, would not, gulp my pride.

Instead, I shook the shirt, bull-fighter-cape-style, hoping how-to instructions might flutter out from inside.

No such luck.

Time passed . . .

Hiccup lingered.

Finally, I let slip a faint *"Help."*

Hiccup had been waiting for just that moment.

He leaped, MM-style, over two benches to my side and showed me how the shirt crisscrossed in front, tying beneath with a hidden string. "The outer flap will stay in place once we get your belt on," he explained. "Take off your shoes. We train barefooted and—*Oh, my.*"

"What's wrong?"

"Your pants!"

I took a gander—and groaned. Hiccup and I wear the same waist size. But where his pants barely brushed the top of his bony feet, mine dragged behind me like the train of wedding gown.

"Maybe if I do this"—I hiked the pants under my pits—"and keep my arms pinned to my sides . . ."

"Not a good look for you." He jerked my uniform waist-level again. "And without the use of your arms, you will be incapable of defending yourself properly. This will solve the problem"—he rolled each hem into a thick wad at my ankles—"until *She* can alter them."

Ha. Dad did all the hemming, patching, and button sewing at our house. Mom proclaimed herself Non-Seamstress for Life the Halloween I turned seven. That's when she stitched me a Frankenstein costume that featured two left legs.

Hic completed my ensemble with a stiff white cotton belt, tied in what I assumed was his own complicated version of Goldie's knot.

"Make haste and follow me." He padded briskly into the *dojang*, a gigantic workout area with glaring fluorescent lights and whirling ceiling fans. Spongy blue mats, edged in red, covered the wide expanse of floor. Mirrors lined one wall. Above it were the words:

Courtesy, Integrity, Perseverance, Self-control, Indomitable spirit.

"Those are the five tenets of hapkido," Hiccup explained. "We recite them at the end of every lesson."

He bowed before stepping onto the blue mat. I did the same, feeling dizzy.

We joined a cluster of about twenty uniformed girls and guys. They sat stretching their hamstrings and other assorted muscles I didn't know the names of and had probably never used before.

A tall, taut man with a salt-and-cinnamon beard strode into the room. A black belt encircled the waist of his uniform. Joining him was a girl with almond-shaped eyes and shell-pink toenails. She was the size of a fourth grader, but she carried herself as someone older—despite the inky ponytail sprouting from her head like a sea anemone.

An older student in a red belt leaped to his feet and barked, "Attention!"

Everyone lined up, bowed, and chanted, "Good afternoon, Master Yates."

I copied them, almost toppling as the blood rushed to my brain.

"Good afternoon, students," Master Yates replied with a solemn bow. "I'd like to introduce Joonbi Park."

112

An excited murmur rippled across the room. Students nudged each other. One whispered: *the Bee!*

"Since Ms. Park's reputation precedes her," Master Yates continued, "you know what an honor it is to have her with us."

"Hic."

My head snapped toward Hiccup.

Was that you? I mouthed.

Don't be ridiculous!

"Ms. Park has just entered the eighth grade," the master continued, "but, as you may know, she has already earned her black belt in taekwondo. She chooses now, however, to walk a new path. She will train at our studio for several months, learning the hapkido principles of Hwa, Won, and Yu."

"Hic!"

Hector, It was *you!*

It wasn't . . . was it? He peered inside the front of his shirt as if his navel held an explanation.

Master Yates said, "Ms. Park, will you give us a demonstration?"

"Sir, yes, sir!" she replied in a lyrical but firm voice. "May I have a volunteer to act as my sparring partner?"

"Hic-hic!"

Hic clamped his hands over his mouth.

"Excellent," Joonbi said. She motioned for Hic to join her at the mirrors.

He twitched a *no,* staring at her with zombie eyes.

The student behind gave him a not-so-gentle push. Hiccup stumbled forward into an awkward bow.

"Fighting stance!" Master Yates said.

"Hic!"

Then—

"Ki-hap!"

It happened in half a blink.

One minute, Hiccup stood there.

The next minute, he didn't.

Joonbi hid a smile. With a jaunty shake of her ponytail, she held out a petite hand and hoisted Hic to his feet.

He gave a grin of thanks, straightened his shirt, and—

"Fighting stance!"

"Hic!"

"Ki-hap!"

Now you see him . . .

. . . now you don't.

Hiccup lay sprawled on his stomach, arm in an awkward twist, Joonbi's knee wedged between his shoulder blades.

He was up. Down. Thrown all around. *Three. More. Times.*

The room exploded with applause.

Despite the lingering anger I felt toward Hic and his role in the Guys' demise, I couldn't bring myself to clap. Instead, I felt a flush of deep embarrassment for him.

Yet Hic didn't seem ashamed at all. In fact, the more Joonbi jabbed, twisted, and threw him, the wider he grinned.

And hicked.

"Your turn," Joonbi said, her ponytail a-swish. "Show me your stuff."

"Thank you—*hic!* Perhaps another *hic!* time." Hiccup

bowed, faced Master Yates, and said, "Sir, I believe I am suffering an attack of *hic!* adhesive capsulitis. May I rest for a—*hic!*—moment?"

"Certainly, Mr. Denardo. Mr. Wyatt, please fetch your friend a cup of water."

Your friend. Ha. If only he knew. But I said, "Sir, yes, sir!" and hurried after Hiccup, remembering at the last second to bow, as he did, before leaving the mat.

He plunked onto a bench near the emergency exit and fanned himself with someone's discarded flip-flop.

"She is," he breathed, "mag*hic*ficent."

I filled a paper cup at the drinking fountain and shoved it into his hands. "Are you hurt?"

He sip-hic-gulped. "No."

"What's with the capsulitis thingy? Have you had that condition before?"

"Don't be ridiculous. It only affects men between the ages of forty and sixty."

"Then why—?"

"I did not wish to admit I am truly unwell."

I snorted like Hayley. "Hic, you are always 'unwell.' It's your state of wellness!"

"My stars, man! I just imbibed *drinking fountain water!* I must be feverish, delirious—a strong indication that I am suffering from malar*hic*ia."

"You're kidding me, right?"

He gazed toward Joonbi as she led the other students in sets of kicks, jabs, and punches. "I wish *hic!* I were. But I am

115

ex*hic!*ibiting acute ague, the most common symptom of the disease."

I plunked next to him. "In English, please."

"Chills. Nausea. Sweating."

"What else."

"Hic!"

"Other than that."

His eyes continued to gaze and glaze. "My hands and toes are numb. My heart is palp*hic*tating. I am experiencing vertigo . . ."

"Go on."

"I cannot—inhale—or—exhale."

"Hmmmmm," I said.

"I see," said me.

Then: "Ah-*ha*!"

He clenched my arm. "Malaria?"

"No, you idiot. You like her!"

"What?" He dropped his cup. *"Who?"*

"Joonbi Park!"

"Shhhhhhh! Not so—*hic!*—loud!" He hooked my elbow and dragged me back into the boys' locker room.

"It's true, isn't it?" I asked.

"It cannot be!"

"It be. *Joonbi.*" I twirled him to face the mirror. "Check out your eyes. They get this same glazed look whenever you're around Mom."

"Mom who?"

Whoa. This is more serious than I thought!

"So when will you tell her?" I asked. "Joonbi, I mean."

"Tell her what?"

"That you *like* her!"

Hiccup ogled me as if I'd morphed into a madman. "I am not telling her anything."

"But you expected me to tell Hayley!"

"That is completely different."

"How's it different?"

"This is about *me*."

Ha. He had a point—even if it was a double standard.

He slumped against the sink. "It's useless anyway. How could I profess my admiration for her when my diaphragm is afflicted with these infernal spasms? She would only point and laugh at me."

"She wouldn't laugh."

"She would point?"

"Yes. No! *Neither*."

"She *would*!" He pounded an angry fist against his chest. "Stephen, I do not comprehend this predicament. I've experienced nary a half a hic these last four months. *So why today?*"

"You're not hicking now," I said. "That episode in the *dojang*, it must've been a fluke. An isolated incident."

"Even if it was, I cannot risk telling Joonbi of my affections. What if she already"—he gulped—"*likes someone else?*"

My heart clenched. My stomach twisted. "It happens."

"You told Hayley?" He searched my face. "You told her! And she said?"

"She—she likes Cullen Hanson."

Hiccup's voice scaled up an octave. *"The golf goon?"*

"Huh. He's not as goonish as we thought. He's in my CAD class. We talked. He's actually"—I winced the word—*"nice."*

"He could never be as nice as you."

"Um, thanks," I mumbled. Man, this guy made it hard to stay mad at him. Although with all the hicking and ki-yupping, I'd sorta forgotten to be mad.

Hiccup cleared his throat.

I cleared mine too. "We should go back to the *dojang.*"

"You go." Hiccup wrenched on the faucet, splashing water on his malarial-flushed face.

"You might feel better if you, you know, *talk* to her."

He swooned. Dripped. Gripped the sink. *"Talk? To? Her?"*

"Not about your feelings, Hic. Just stuff."

"Define *stuff.*"

"School. The weather. Childhood diseases. Or what you learned from sparring with her."

"I don't know . . ."

I yanked his belt. "Mr. Denardo, are you a man or a mouse? Where's your perseverance? Your indomitable spirit? MM has them . . . *do you?*"

He raised his head. Threw back his shoulders. Puffed out his chest. "I shall agree to a casual discourse under one condition."

"What's that?"

"You will accompany me."

"Sure."

He released a long breath. "Does this mean . . . we are friends again?"

I flashed on the Guys. I really missed them, but . . . I had to admit, I missed Hic even more.

"Friends can get mad at each other, sometimes bug each other, right?" I asked.

"Right."

"Then I never *wasn't* your friend, Hiccup."

He blinked. Nodded. Grinned. "Man hug!" he cried, and pounced, crushing me, slapping my back so hard I almost coughed up a lung.

"Ow! Get off me!" I half laughed, half gasped.

He eyed himself in the mirror, adjusted his belt, combed a hand through his hair. "How do I look?"

"Courteous," I said. "Self-controlled."

"That will suffice." With a slight swagger, he strode from the locker room.

Chapter Fourteen

"Students dismissed!" Master Yates announced.

I shuffled off the mat, muscles sore and squeaky. Hiccup's bangs were plastered with sweat, his eyelids drooped with tiredness. But I could tell from the way his eyes glittered that it was a good kind of tired. The kind I often feel while wrestling with one of my inventions—meshing gears, adjusting torques, tightening screws—when *SNAP!* everything fits, clicks, runs Just Right.

A straggle of students followed us to the sidelines, heading for the locker rooms. Most, though, clustered around Joonbi Park like she was a movie star or something. Voices trampled voices to ask advice, offer compliments, beg for a handshake. A camera appeared. Joonbi's polite smile seemed to levitate in flash after flash after flash.

"You're not the only one who thinks she's magnificent," I said to Hic.

"Mm-*hic!*-hm," he replied, mesmerized.

We hung back until the adult class started and Master Yates shooed Joonbi's throng of fans off the mat. She made a beeline for a bulky equipment bag.

"Excuse us, Joonbi," I said. "My friend and I, we—"

"No more pictures," she said, dabbing her face with a towel. Her voice still had its firm lilt, but it flowed younger, softer than it had on the mat.

"We just wanted to introduce ourselves. I'm Steve, and this is—"

Where did he go?

I found Hic crouched behind me, attempting to take his pulse. I yanked him up. "This is Hector."

"We've met," she said, tossing the towel aside. "Thank you for sparring with me, Hector. You have excellent falling skills."

My hackles stiffened. "That's harsh!"

"That's a compliment," Joonbi said. "You probably didn't know, being a white belt. When you take a fall, it's crucial to avoid hesitating or tensing up. You need to relax, to flow through the fall. Otherwise, you can get hurt. Remember: Keep it smooth."

Hic bobbed in agreement. "Smooth. *Hic!* Good."

Joonbi hefted her bag over one petite shoulder and waited.

Hiccup and I exchanged looks.

"I expect you want something else?" she said.

Hiccup and I exchanged looks again. His mouth and eyes formed three panicked *O*'s.

"Like what?" I asked.

She released a light sigh. "The usual? My autograph, my father's autograph? Then I suppose you want my sisters and me to perform at your next birthday party. Sorry, I'm temporarily retired."

"We just wanted to say hello," I said.

"Truth?" Joonbi released her ponytail. Black hair rippled to her shoulders in liquid waves. Her voice rippled with enthusiasm. "Hey, you guys really don't know who I am!" She swung around, almost knocking Hic to the floor with her bag. "Will you join me for a snack? There's a fast-food place on the next block. The chicken is greasy, so I'm forbidden to eat it, but they serve awesome smoothies!"

"Sure," I said. "We'll grab our gear from the locker room, then meet you outside. Okay with you, Hector?"

"Smoothies. *Hic!* Good."

Joonbi winged out the door. Hiccup stood gaze-hicking after her, so rooted to the spot I'd either have to drag him— or spray weed killer on him. It seemed easier to fetch his gear myself.

"Why are you talking like a caveman?" I asked, thrusting his bag into his arms, urging him toward the exit.

"I don't know!" he wailed. "Each glimpse of her transforms my brain into cerebellum slush. Perhaps I had best head home to feed D and D."

"Oh, no you don't. Dasher and Dancer can snack on a rug till you get there. For now, just focus on being less monosyllabic and you'll be fine."

We emerged from the studio. When she spotted us, Joonbi zipped away like a bumblebee, whiz-zigging and buzz-zagging pedestrians, hum-hovering at a stoplight, then darting across the street and to the entrance of Pierre's dad's fast-food joint, Lickety-Split Chick.

A cowbell clanged as Joonbi pushed open the door. The fowl odor of batter-fried drumsticks assaulted my nose and I sneezed. "Hector and I know the owner of this place, don't we, Hector?"

"Hic!" he answered.

"That isn't something to brag about," Joonbi said with a twitchy smile.

"Their son feels exactly the same way," I continued. "He's a wannabe French chef. Puts béarnaise sauce on PB-and-Js. His mom is a total health freak. Serves tofu molded into the shape of turkey at Thanksgiving, with minced rice cakes as 'stuffing.' Hector can fill you in, right, Hector? You two grab an empty booth and I'll get the smoothies."

"HIC-HIC!"

I translated that to mean *Please don't leave me alone with her!* Or *Please don't order me a strawberry smoothie because I'm allergic to strawberries and my face will blotch like pepperoni pizza!* Or both.

"I'll. Be. Right. Back," I promised his pleading expression.

"A fruit smoothie for me," Joonbi said. "Milk products disagree with my stomach."

I winked at Hiccup. He and Joonbi had something in common already!

I followed a trail of chicken footprints painted in mustard yellow on the floor leading to the front counter. A kid wearing an egg-yolk-colored uniform and a beak-red paper hat posed behind the cash register. A badge pinned over his heart read: *Your order is free if it's not ready lickety-split!*

"Welcome to Lee-kee-tee-Spleet Cheek, sir," he said. "May eye pleeze take zee order?"

"Pierre?" I couldn't believe it. "I thought you despised your dad's place! You once swore on a stack of quiches that you'd never work here!"

"Eye am afraid, sir," he replied haughtily, "zat you 'ave mistooken me for anothzaire person. Eye am not zis Pee-yaire of whom you speek. My name eez Monsewer Fee-leep de Bergerac, and you will not forget eet!"

"Uh-huh. Whatever you say, Fee-leep. But during your next break, you might want to wash your face. You've got chocolate syrup smeared under your nose and just below your ears. Or is that tar?"

He bristled. "Zat, sir, eez my moosetache and sideburnz!"

I choked on a laugh. "Did you draw them with Magic Marker?"

"Bah! For your eenformation, eet eez wis eyebrow penceel zat eye—" Realizing his mistake, Pierre clutched for his beret, which was not on his head, and instead crushed the red paper hat. "Sacré bleu, zat eez zee third 'at today! She will be fureeous wis me!"

"She who?" I asked.

"Never zee mind. Now pleeze—be gone!"

"I haven't ordered yet. I'd like three smoothies, please. Nothing with strawberries or milk products. What flavor do you recommend?"

"Zey are all good," Pierre insisted with an anxious glance over his shoulder.

Hiccup appeared at my elbow. "You have been gone an interminable interval! I cannot stop hicking when I'm around *Her*, yet here you stand, frivolously conversing with—*Pierre*!"

Pierre threw up his hands. "Oh, *carotte*!" he spat, using his favorite blasphemy, which, unbeknownst to him, is actually French for carrot.

"PIERRE!" Hiccup repeated, louder. "Is this where you've been all summer? You abhor this establishment! Whatever induced you to—"

"Philip!" a female voice called from the kitchen. "What's the trouble, are you swearing at the customers again, don't make me come out there!"

Cold worms slithered down my neck.

That voice. It sounded uncomfortably familiar . . .

"Do not trouble yourself, my leetle cheeken wing!" Pierre called, panic strangling his words. "All eez under control!"

"Did you squash another hat, you're only issued four a month, they don't grow on trees, I don't want to dock your pay, but as assistant manager—"

Pierre frantically ironed his hat with his hands. He wrenched it onto his head. "My 'at eez fine, Juliette! Every-zing eez fine."

"Don't call me Juliette," ordered the voice, distaste saturating her tone. "And I am not your little chicken wing! When you've finished with that customer, get back here on the double, I've got two club meetings I'm late for and this grease trap isn't going to clean itself!"

"Oui, my leetle sweet beak!" Pierre crooned. He glared

125

at us and skittered from view. I heard slicing and scooping and pouring, then the roar of ice-grinding blenders. He reappeared and thrust three overflowing "peech smoozies" across the counter. "Zay are, 'ow you say, on zee house. Take zem and go! Queek-lee. And pleeze—" Pierre glanced over his shoulder again and whispered, eyes desperate: "Do not breethe a word of zis to Goldee."

I zipped my lips. "Your secret is safe wis us."

"Zank you for dining at Lee-kee-tee Spleet Cheek, sir! Do come visit us again"—he lowered his voice to a growl—"over your dead bodeez!"

I handed two smoothies to Hiccup, grabbed mine, and headed to the booth where Joonbi waited. I elbowed Hic to sit beside her, but his face paled as if stung. He scooted next to me instead.

"Is one of those mine?" Joonbi asked.

I elbowed Hic again. He inched Joonbi's cup across the table, never taking his eyes off her.

"Thank you!" She plunged in a straw.

"Hic!" said Hic.

My brain floundered for something to say besides *Nice weather we're having* and *Pardon the drool, but my friend is in love with you.*

"So tell us," I began, "why were those hapkido students taking your picture and asking for autographs?"

"Truth?" Joonbi sucked a long slurp and dabbed her mouth with a napkin. "You two really don't know?"

I shook my head.

"That's so refreshing, I'm not sure I want to tell you!" she said, but she smiled.

"We could talk about something else. Like . . . Hector! Hector is an amazing artist. Tell Joonbi about the graphic novel you're drawing, Hector."

Hiccup hic-choked on his smoothie.

Joonbi removed the straw from her drink and licked it. "Okay, you twisted my arm. Here's the thing. Father and my *harabuj y*, grandfather, are taekwondo grandmasters in Korea. They're world famous. Best of the best. If you're serious about taekwondo, you want to train with them."

"Are you famous too?" I asked.

"My sisters and I are. Were. As a team. There are six of us. I'm the youngest."

"That's just like Hector," I said. "Except he has five older brothers, right, Hector?"

Hic hick-nodded.

"My sisters and I, we've studied with Father and Harabujy practically since we somersaulted out of our cribs," Joonbi went on. "My entire life, I've done nothing but train, travel, compete; train, travel, compete! Until now." She slurped more of the frosty drink.

"Why did you stop? Were you injured?"

Joonbi twisted the straw. "In a way. My stomach is giving me trouble. The doctors say stress, the pressure of competing, blah, blah, blah. They're running all kinds of tests on me." She made a face. "Last week, I had to drink the most awful, chalky stuff!"

Hiccup straightened. "Barium," he said. "A metallic powder. When mixed with *hic!* water and imbibed, it coats the inside of the upper and lower GI tract, making the intestines visible via *hic!* X-ray."

"That's the stuff! How did you know?"

"As a youngster," Hiccup went on, "whenever my older brothers *hic!* found me to be interminably annoying, they would lock me out of the house. My mother finally proffered me my own key. She instructed I should keep it somewhere safe. So I *hic!* did."

Joonbi laugh-dribbled smoothie juice, then grimaced as if something jaggedly metal was inching down her throat. *"Truth?"*

I nodded. I'd never forget the key incident because immediately afterward, Mom started letting Hiccup hang out at our house whenever he liked.

"I can top that story!" Joonbi said. "Once, during a training stunt, my *harabuji* swallowed a chopstick. It was stuck inside of him for twenty years!"

"Did he get splinters?" Hiccup asked.

"Worse," Joonbi said with an impish smile. "Termites."

Hic grinned. "Did the doctors perform surgery? Or . . . *hic!* fumigation?"

Joonbi cracked up.

Gee, these two were made for each other! Maybe I should take this opportunity to disappear . . .

"Anyway," Joonbi continued, "medical tests take time, so the doctors advised I slow down, enjoy some R and R for several months. I didn't want to quit studying martial arts completely, though. It's like breathing to me! So I switched to hapkido. It's not easier. But it is a less competitive discipline. Already my stomach's a teensy bit better. But until the doctors know for sure what's wrong, we're staying put. No traveling, no competing."

"Here *hic!* good," Hic said.

"Yes, but now I've got a different kind of stress." Joonbi ripped open another straw, twisting that one too. "My sisters are furious with me! Like I'm doing this stomach thing on purpose just to break up the act. Umma, my mom, she understands. Father is . . . disappointed. But he keeps it mostly to himself. Not my sisters! They love the limelight and the paparazzi and the fans and the traveling and the boys. So they remind me, every single day, that I've ruined their lives. It makes me feel so guilty . . ."

"Hector's brothers use him like a personal punching bag," I said. "That's why he signed up for hapkido, isn't it, Hector?"

"In*hic!*deed," he answered. "But a physical defense is not always enough. Verbal attacks can be more painful, as Joonbi is aware."

"But I found something to help ease that pain!" Joonbi unzipped her bag and dug deep. "Don't worry, it's not barium." Then, with a yip of delight, she held aloft a tattered, handmade booklet. "I found this in the house we're renting. It was rammed into a corner closet. Whenever my stomach hurts, and especially when my sisters are torturing me, I lock myself in my room and read this from cover to cover. It's hilarious! I laugh so hard I can't help feeling better—for a while, anyway. Too bad it wasn't written about sisters. Take a look!"

Hiccup didn't have to. I didn't either. We both recognized the thin, stapled pages, the red construction paper cover . . .

"He *hic!* author," Hic said, pointing at me.

"What?" Joonbi asked.

"He said I'm the author," I confessed.

"What do you mean?"

"I wrote it."

"You wrote what?"

"The book."

"What book?"

"That book."

"*This* book?"

I nodded.

"*You* wrote this book? *You wrote 101 Ways to Bug Your Parents? You* are Stephen J. Wyatt? *TRUTH?*"

I nodded again.

"Oh!" Joonbi gasped, her eyes aglaze. "I think I love you!"

Chapter Fifteen

Five minutes later, Hiccup stomped like a tantrum-throwing toddler down the street toward the bus stop.

I waved good-bye to Joonbi and hurried after him.

"Wait up!" I yelled. "What's wrong?"

He hurled the accusation in my face: "You're secretly writing another book!"

"What are you talking about?"

"As if you did not know!"

"I don't!"

"You do!"

I didn't.

Back at Lickety-Split Chick, we'd just finished our smoothies when Joonbi spotted her mom's car zipping past the window toward Hapkido Family Fitness. "Early, as usual!" she groused, scooting from the booth. "That's number fifty-two on her list of *101 Ways to Bug Your Youngest Daughter*."

"We should trade mothers," I said. "Even if Mom swears she'll pick me up in exactly one hour, I always have to multiply that number by a factor of four. Don't I, Hector?"

He pursed his lips, but a gruff *hic*! escaped.

"Truth?" Joonbi twisted her hair back into its spiky pony-tail. "How buggable!"

"She doesn't do it on purpose," I explained. "Mom's a scientist who also has ADHD, so she gets distracted easily. Dad too. That's one reason I wrote *101 Ways to Bug Your Parents*—to get their attention."

Joonbi hoisted her gear bag. "I have a million questions about your book! How you researched it, how you wrote it, did you test every suggestion? My favorite is number nine: *Laugh with a mouthful of milk until some squirts out your nose.* I accidentally tried that last Sunday morning while eating a bowl of Rice Krispies. Snap, crackle, *yuck!* Umma didn't notice, but my sisters were so grossed out they steered clear of me for half an hour. Best thirty minutes of my life—till now!"

Another gruff *hic!* from Hic.

"After hapkido tomorrow," Joonbi said, "want to get together again for smoothies? My treat. I can't believe it! Usually *I'm* the person people are in awe of. But I've met Stephen J. Wyatt: author, inventor . . . my hero!"

Then she'd buzzed off to meet her mom—but not before *blowing me a kiss.*

Eep.

"Your feigned innocence is futile," Hic continued now, "and an insult to my intelligence. It is clear you are writing a new book entitled *101 Ways to Bug Your Friends*. And number one on that list is: *Steal your best friend's girl!*"

I would've laughed if he didn't look so murderous. "I didn't steal your girl. How could I? She's not even yours! And it's not like I *tried* to make her like me."

"I witnessed, firsthand, your brazen, blatant flirtations!"

I touched my cheek where the invisible smooch had landed. "Trust me, Hic. I wasn't the one flirting."

"Then please explain your flushed expression."

"Joonbi's gushiness is embarrassing!"

"Then why encourage her with all that smiling?"

"That's called acting *friendly*."

"And all those questions?"

"Somebody had to ask her questions, Hic! Why didn't *you* jump in? Didn't you notice how I kept steering the conversation your way?"

"Yes, of course. Did you not notice Joonbi's and my humorous interchange? Things were going swimmingly, until—"

"Ha. Did you bother to utter more than a couple of sentences? More than a couple of syllables? NoooOOOOooo."

"I had the hiccups," he defended. "I was awaiting their termination before engaging in a lengthy discourse."

"Yeah," I muttered, "like that was going to happen in this century."

Without even checking for graffiti or gum wads, Hiccup flung himself onto the bus stop bench. He held himself tight as if wrapped in MM's cape against a chill.

"Maybe we should trade mothers," he mimicked. "How dare you do this to me, your best friend! Joonbi and I, we are

a perfect match! She likes hapkido. I like hapkido. She has five annoying sisters. I have five annoying brothers. She has medical issues and I have—"

"Hiccup, read my lips." I thunked beside him and focused on his zit-freckled face. "*I'm. Not. Interested. In. Joon. Bi.*"

"Why not? What's wrong with her?"

"Nothing's wrong with her!"

"Is she not beautiful? Brilliant?"

"Sure!"

"Brawny?"

"She could toss you across the street farther than I could spit, but that doesn't mean I *like* her."

The bus arrived. The doors flumped open.

Hic toddler-stomped up the steps.

I started after him.

He whirled on me and said through gritted teeth, "*Take the next bus.*"

"*What?*"

He dropped his bag and snapped into a fighting stance. His eyes blazed a ferocity I'd only seen in his drawings. "These hands are not officially registered, but make no mistake: They are lethal weapons. *Take the next bus.* I no longer wish to be best friends. I no longer wish to be friends, period."

"Fine!" I shot back. "Who needs friends like you? Not when you're working on a 'bug your best friend' list of your own! Not when number one on that list is: *Offer to take care of his pets while he's on vacation—then murder them!*"

The blaze in Hic's eyes sputtered, shrank—and died.

"Door's closin', boys," the bus driver said.

"Endeavor to keep your trousers on, sir!" Hiccup snapped.

Then, voice thin, he said, "Stephen. I already apologized. What more can I do? What happened to the Guys was an accident. I offered recompense, a sincere gesture of atonement. How did you respond to my overtures? *With revenge!*" Embers smoldered again in his eyes. "So I swear—no, I *vow*—on the sacred cape of MM: Joonbi is the only love of mine you will ever steal from me!"

That night, alone in my room, I tried to do my first-day-of-high-school homework. This was difficult because:

1. I hadn't retrieved my chem and trig books from where Marcos the Moke tossed them into the hall at Patrick Henry

2. The phone kept interrupting me. I didn't want to talk to anyone unless it was Hiccup calling to apologize (which it never was), so I asked Mom and Dad to tell people who called me that I'd been forbidden to chat until my homework was finished (which it never was—see numbers 1, 2, and 3)

3. I was too busy worrying about:

    a. How to prevent Marcos and his goons from finding me again at PHHS and using my sore nose as their personal golf bag

b. Hiccup hating my guts and every other organ in my body (as if I cared!) because of his mistaken assumption that I'd stolen Joonbi

c. The heart-wrenching hurt and disappointment Hayley would feel if "Cullen" didn't send her an e-mail

I stared at the empty aquarium and sighed. In the olden days (three months ago!), whenever I had a problem and Hiccup wasn't around, I consulted the Guys. They'd been perfect confidants, expert listeners who never argued with me, never accused me of stealing their little fishy friends . . .

But now—

I hoisted the tank and shoved it into a moldy corner of my closet (where my failed invention Flapjacks in a Can had oozed through its aerosol nozzle). Into it I flung everything I could find of Hiccup's: a hypoallergenic sweatshirt; two early editions of Medicine Man comics; rough drafts of the cover drawing for *101 Ways to Bug Your Parents*; stubs of stray colored pencils; and a half-empty box of surgical masks.

Last, I tossed in the container of fish flakes, and slammed the door so hard my window rattled.

The Nice Alarm *tsked-tsked*.

"It's just the two of us now, kiddo," I said, "so no scolding."

I sank into my desk chair and pulled from my pack the

notebook in which I'd scribbled and scratched ideas for Cullen's e-mail to Hayley.

Ugh. Even worse than I remembered.

"Why is this so hard?" I asked the alarm. "Maybe I'm not as good at writing as I am at inventing. Or sneezing. But I'm a clever wordsmith. Everyone says so. Mom. Dad. My teachers. Hayley. Even the great Mr. Sterling Patterson!"

I traced the outline of the Nice Alarm's toad-like body with a finger.

"That's how I got the interview with him at the convention. I wrote a humdinger of a letter as president of a phony invention company. Remember how surprised and impressed he looked when I waltzed in with you?"

The alarm *tsked-tsked* again.

"Yeah, too bad he wasn't as impressed with what you can *do*. But when I told him I'd written and sold *101 Ways to Bug Your Parents* to earn extra money for my trip, he asked for a souvenir copy! He asked for my 'Bug Your Teachers' list too. So if I can write well enough to impress—and fool!—a man of Mr. Patterson's intelligence, stature, and experience . . ."

Do-it, do-it, do-it, ticked the Nice Alarm.

"Okay, okay. Don't rush me!"

I switched on my computer, clicked into my e-mail program, cracked my knuckles, and typed:

TO: Hayley@gadaboutgolf.com
FROM: Sneeze@stephenjwyatt.com

SUBJECT: Homework assignment ;-)

Dear Hayley,

How are you? I am fine.

Ugh. That was the kind of letter Cullen would've written in second grade—to his *grandmother.*

You can do better, Steve. Think "Cullen." Think "Hawaiian."

Howzit, Hayley!
The first time I saw you, I got chicken skin.
My brain turned into a whoosher. That's what
a cute wah-hee-nay like you does to a Hawaiian
lug like me. I wish you could be my kwee-poe.
But I don't have enough koa to stand up to your dad.
I don't want to talk stink about him, but he thinks I'm
a moke (rhymes with Coke) and you're a kaykee.
So to stay out of peeleekeeya, we'll just have to be
satisfied being pen pals.
Aloha, Cullen H.

Double ugh. Hayley's SOS would spot this fake faster than you could say *forgery.* And if Cullen ever read it (perish the thought!), he'd sic the goddess Pele on me with a volcanic vengeance.

I nibbled a fingernail.

How in the name of Thomas Alva Edison did people compose love letters?

My brain rewound to the creation of the Nice Alarm and my bugging books. All three required two crucial elements: *research and experimentation.*

I'd already tried experimentation—and failed. So maybe research . . .

I went online to my favorite search engine and typed: *How to write a love letter to a girl.*

Page after page of websites appeared. I scrolled through dozens until my vision blurred and my mousing finger cramped.

At last—*Bingo!*—I spotted a site that looked promising because it claimed to be written *for* teen boys *by* a teen girl.

WWW
Wooing with Words
Six Secrets to Writing WOOn-derful Love Letters to Your Girl

1. The Presentation:

Always compose your love letter on a sheet of elegant stationery. No lunch bags or lined binder paper, please! Use a fountain pen with blue or black ink. Writing missives using pencil, crayon, grape-scented markers, or your computer are taboo. Remember: Your beloved may desire to keep your letter as a treasured memento, so compose it using your very best handwriting.

Huh. Surely there were exceptions? I mean, what did folks do if their fountain pen had been stolen or they were fresh out of Egyptian papyrus? Wasn't a computer-composed letter better than nothing?

2. The Atmosphere:

Create a romantic mood in which to write. Draw the drapes, dim the lights, turn off your cell phone, play soft music, light a candle. Choose a quiet, secluded room free of nosy parents, nose-picking siblings, and other interruptions and distractions.

Double huh. Before the demise of the Guys, their aquarium used to bathe my room in a ripply, romantic glow. But now, well, at least it was quiet. The only sound I could hear was the muffled bang-bang of Dad's favorite TV cop show and the slam-slam of cupboards as Mom searched for her stash of dark chocolate (which Dad had hidden because her pregnancy doc said she was gaining too much weight).

3. The Salutation:

Begin your love letter with a greeting that is heartfelt, such as "Dearest" or "My Darling." At all costs, avoid: "Yo, mama!" "Howdy," and "What's Up, Doc?"

As Goldie would say: Well, duh.

4. The Body:

Tell your beloved why you are writing. You may wish to recall the moment you first met (unless you barfed on her blouse). Explain how you've changed for the better since that magical moment. Describe her unique qualities, what makes her different from other girls. (Avoid commenting on tics, split ends, or BO.) Enumerate what you two have in common.

Now we're getting somewhere!

5. The Valediction:

Close your love letter with a fare-thee-well that is tender and meaningful. Avoid terminology such as "Smell ya later" or "Ta-ta, toots!"

6. K.I.S.S.:

Keep It Simple, Stupid! Tell her how and why she's important to you. Say what you feel.

Of course! I'd learned all about that last year in the summer school creative writing class my parents had forced me to take. The teacher, Mr. Powell, had constantly sledge-hammered into our heads the very same thing:

Write what's important to you, important to your life.

I'd been going about this the wrong way. I'd been trying

to write a love letter *to* Hayley *from* Cullen. But *Cullen* didn't love her. *I did!*

I logged off, reopened my e-mail program, retyped Gadabout's address, cracked my knuckles, and began to write.

And write.

Hiding behind Cullen's shadow, I found it so easy to tell Hayley how I felt that I didn't stop at just one letter. Or two.

Or even three.

By the time I tapped the SEND button for the final time and collapsed on my bed, the number of e-mails rocketing through cyberspace to Hayley Barker's waiting in-box numbered a grand total of seven.

Chapter Sixteen

"Howzit!" Cullen shambled into CAD the next morning and overtook his chair. His fingers tap-danced across the computer keyboard until he spotted my textbooks. "*Menehune*, wat doing?"

"I didn't do anything," I grumbled, and sneezed a nose-full of pink eraser dust. "But I'll give you three hints who did: Marcos. The. Moke."

High School Trigonometry disappeared within one of Cullen's paws. He flipped page after scribbled page, shaking his head at the spew of intricate threats and crude graffiti. "He need some lickens."

I mulled a moment. "He needs . . . a spanking?"

He cuffed my shoulder. "You catch on quick. Bo-da-dem like dis?"

"Huh?"

"Your books—both of dem stay scribbled?"

"Yeah. Look what Marcos did in my chem book."

"Ho!" Cullen fingered his shark tooth. "How he wen cock-aroach—steal 'em—da first place?"

I explained about my "reunion" with the goons the day

before. "I found these—complete with, uh, marginalia—in the lost and found. I've been erasing nonstop, but the pencil lead has become one with the paper molecules."

Cullen wrinkled his nose. "Dey smell like my armpits after one jog."

"They were buried under a pile of old gym socks."

"Bummahs."

"Yeah." I flicked the eraser nub into the open mouth of my pack. "My chem teacher was mad enough to spit sulfuric acid. She says I owe the school sixty-seven bucks." I slammed shut the book. "I don't understand. I'm a peon! A nobody with a runny nose! Why is Marcos out to get me?"

"You wen challenge him, brah," Cullen said. "And you wen shame him—twice—in front of his braddahs."

"But the second time, it was the Amys who—"

"No matter. Dey your sistahs, eh?"

"The Amys? Ack! No!"

Cullen chuckled. "Dey *friends*, like you my braddah, my brah, eh? So in Marcos's mind, stay your fault. Moke like Marcos, dey no like fo' be challenged, tricked, humiliated. Especially not by two wacky *wahine* and one *keiki* with hanabaddah." He tapped my runny nose.

I winced and blew into a tissue. "What should I do? Apologize?"

Cullen laughed.

"Then how do I make him stop wanting to—let me paraphrase one scrawl—'Sever Sneeze's spleen and feed it to the girls.' Wait, that's *gulls*. His handwriting is pathetic."

"No can make dis moke stop anything," Cullen said. "No try. Mo bettah you lay low till he forget you exist. Or till he find a new victim."

I slumped. "I have to spend the next nine months skulking around in case of an ambush?"

"Maybe not stay. It golf season, so we supa busy. Da team got practice or one match every afternoon till da final championship. Dat's in two weeks."

"Golf season is only two weeks long?"

He shook his head. "In dis district, we start in July. So Marcos got ada tings on his mind right now. Just in case, tho', I watch your back, eh?"

"Really?" Then, feeling guilty about the e-mails I'd ghost-written to Hayley, I said: "No, thanks, I can't let you do that."

Cullen chuckled, flexing his paws. "How you going stop me?"

"Let me get this straight: You'll act as my personal bodyguard? Beat up the goons if they threaten me?"

"If I hear dem comin' your way, I warn you. More den dat? Sorry, ah? No can."

I hated the whiney fear eking into my voice: *"Why not?"*

The teacher bustled into the room. "Take your seats, people!" she said. "We've got a lot of territory to cover today."

Students stowed packs and positioned keyboards. Beneath the noise, Cullen continued: "Back in small kid time—sorry, when I younger—I make much *pilikia* at my school on Oahu. To me, brah, is history. *Pau.* I finish with dat life. But I still need fo' prove myself to Auntie and Coach and da principal at dis school."

The students settled, focusing on the lecture. Cullen signaled me to wait. He jotted notes, absorbed by the teacher's every word.

A girl made a joke. The class cracked up.

Cullen's bear-bulk reclined as if to share the laugh with me. Then, in a low voice, he said, "Marcos know about my past. Don't know how, but he does. No can buss him up—hurt him. No can geevum stink eye, even. He going tell Coach for sure, and if dat happen"—he thumb-slashed his throat—"I'm off da team. Tossed out of school. No can risk dat. I no like."

"It's okay, I understand," I said, dying to ask what kind of *pilikia* he meant but afraid to ask in case it involved the dismemberment of overcurious *keiki*. "So other than laying low, any advice for me regarding Marcos?"

"Yeah. No humiliate dat moke one third time. Could be your last."

"My 'last' what? Last time I shame him?"

Cullen regarded me with keen grizzly eyes. "No, *menehune*. Da last time you stay living, brah."

I spent the rest of third period thirstily gulping info about templates and symbols and digital files till my brain swelled like a sodden sponge: thick, heavy, and dripping with data. Next week, I'd wring it dry of the basics and start transferring my hand-drawn plans of the Nice Alarm into something I could e-mail to other novelty companies.

I wondered, had Hiccup researched the names and addresses of any of those companies yet—?

Oh. Right.

Like I'd told the Nice Alarm: We were on our own.

When class ended, Cullen escorted me to the edge of campus. I felt safe with him beside me, my body a chink of meteorite eclipsed by his supernova.

"Hang loose," he said, and lumbered off in search of "grinds"—food, I think.

With him gone, I felt more exposed than if I were stark naked. I darted behind a molting eucalyptus tree and scanned the perimeter. There were a bunch of popular fast-food joints at the end of the street. Groups of students approached, hustling in that direction to buy lunch, including—

—eep!—

The Amys.

And

—yikes!—

July.

I dove into a bush.

Yeah, the Amys had saved my hide yesterday. But for all I knew, they'd only done it so that at some future time— now!—July could happily skin it.

"How about hamburgers today?" I heard the Amys say as they neared.

"Hamburgers sound fab!" said the Amys.

"Hot dogs sound fab too!" the Amys said.

"Then how about hot dogs today?" said the Amys.

Heart th-thumping, I peered through prickly twigs and thick leaves and crossed my fingers that this wasn't one of the 174 types of foliage I'm allergic to.

"Nix on both hamburgers and hot dogs," July said, floating past, one wing of the chocolate-colored cape she wore swirling against my hiding place. "I get enough of that junk every afternoon at work. I've put on five pounds just breathing all that grease, and I'm not eating lunch today anyway. I've got a dinner date with my guy."

"Pish! You're soooo slender!" the Amys said.

"Pshaw! You're soooo willowy!" said the Amys.

And then they were gone.

I breathed a stream of relief, but waited five minutes to make sure the coast was clearly July- and moke-free.

Satisfied, I scarpered down the street.

Half a block from Jefferson, my heart th-thumped again.

Hayley!

She stood waiting inside the school's fence, fingers threaded through the wobbly metal, her face a crisscross of chain links and impatience.

My cheeks engulfed in flames till I remembered that "Cullen" had written last night's e-mails, not me.

"Hhhhhhi," I breathed. She looked fresh, cool, and beautiful in another new skirt, this one of deep lake-green.

"Where have you been?" She gave the fence a shake.

"It takes time to walk two miles, Hayley."

"I don't mean now. Where were you yesterday? You never

showed up for work at Gadabout! I left a message with your mom last night, but you never called back."

Great golf tees! I forgot to tell her about hapkido class!

"Oh, Hayley, I'm sorry!" I explained about substituting martial arts for PE. "That's why I got that waiver form from the office yesterday."

"You mean you won't be working for us during the week?" She crossed her arms. "Stephen, Daddy is depending on you! We're already behind because of your vacation."

"I know, I know. I'm sorry."

"Can he at least count on you for the weekends?"

"I'd never give that up!"

"Huh. Well, I guess it's okay—if you promise to get your work done."

Was work all she cared about? Was "Daddy" the only one who'd miss me?

"Why are you waiting for me here?" I asked, hiding my disappointment with grumpiness.

Hayley stretched the buckled fence-hole so I could squeeze through more easily. "Can't I wait for a friend if I want to?"

"No. Yes. It's just—we always meet under the pine tree."

"Goldie and Pierre are there and I don't want to sit with them. Did you know you have twigs in your hair?"

Without waiting for my response, she led the way to a shady, deserted patch of grass behind the library, where we sat to eat.

I opened my water bottle and took a tepid sip. "Was Hiccup at the tree?"

"I haven't seen him at all today. He's not sick, is he?"

"Naw. He's . . . avoiding me."

"How come?"

"We had a misunderstanding." I unwrapped my sandwich. "So, did you receive any e-mails from He-Who-Must-Not-Be-Named?"

Hayley bit a squeal in two.

I flashed an innocent smile. "Is that a yes?"

"You know it is. You forwarded his e-mails from your address!" She beamed at me from under coy lashes.

Omigosh, she's wearing mascara.

Omigosh, she's acting coy!

This wasn't Hayley. Not even close. Who was this simpering Southern belle and what had she done with the girl I loved?

The coyness vanished as Ace appeared, one hand shoved into a jeans pocket, the other holding . . . a *book*.

A *textbook*.

He gave me half a nod. "Hey," he said to Hayley.

"Hay is for horses," Hayley replied.

One dark brow twitched, which for Ace is the equivalent of laughing in hysterics.

"What's up?" I asked.

He pinched a hair from his shirt. "Nothing."

"What's the book for?"

He glanced at me over the top of his sunglasses like I was a moron or something. "Algebra."

Algebra? Ace?

"Was there something you wanted, Ace?" Hayley asked

politely. "We're in the middle of a private conversation."

Ace plucked another hair. "I didn't write down our homework assignment."

ACE? DOING HOMEWORK?

"Sure." Hayley flipped through several pages in her binder. "We're supposed to do the exercises on pages twenty-four through twenty-eight."

Ace took a pencil from behind one ear and scribbled inside the front cover of his book. "Thanks."

"Anytime."

He slid the pencil back into its "holder."

"Was there something else?" Hayley asked.

He half hesitated. "Nope."

With a nod at me, he disappeared.

Bewildered, Hayley and I stared at each other.

"*What* was *that?*" we blurted at the same time. Then we both laughed and I had an overwhelming urge to hug her. Hayley was still Hayley after all, somewhere deep inside . . .

"About those e-mails?" I prodded.

"Oh! Yes! They were—" She stopped to SOS. "Hey! How did you get Cullen to write to me last night? You didn't see him until this morning in class!"

Yike. Glitch alert!

"I, uh, he gave me his e-mail address yesterday," I fibbed. "So I can, you know, help him with stuff. Like you asked me to."

The SOS eased, then flashed again. "You kept your promise? You didn't read his e-mails to me?"

"*Yep* to your first question, *nope* to the second."

"You *swear?*"

I raised my right hand. "I solemnly swear on this bologna-and-Frito sandwich that I did not read Cullen's e-mails to you." (Technically true, because Cullen hadn't actually e-mailed her.) I took a crunchy bite. "How come you didn't write him back? I *know* you had things to say."

Hayley blushed. "I wanted to, but Cullen asked me not to. Not yet, anyway. He thought it would be safer, less of a chance of my dad finding out. Also, he said"—she closed her eyes—"*My words are my gift to you. For now I want nothing in return other than the delight of knowing you are reading my deepest emotions.* Isn't that beautiful?"

"Are all his e-mails as *handsome* as his face?"

Her eyes flew open and she snorted. "Handsomer!"

I imitated her snort.

"Huh." She pointed her apple at me. "Just because a guy is gorgeous doesn't mean he's got the brains of lava rock!"

"Cullen's smart, is that what you're saying?"

"Smarter than you!"

I smiled. "Can't argue with that. But is he a good writer?"

"Better than good. He's brilliant!"

It was my turn to blush.

"It's like he's known me for years," she continued. "We're that linked, that in tune with each other. Listen!" She removed several computer printouts from her notebook, smoothed them against her skirt, and read:

"*Dear Hayley: I'll never forget the moment we met. You didn't like me. You were angry with me. Yet, it was your anger I found appealing. Because when I searched beyond the clenched fists, the suspicious squint, and the sharp edge of your voice, I saw pride and confidence and the reason behind your anger. You were protecting what you love, what you believe in: Gadabout Golf.*"

"Is *golf* all he can think about?" I asked.

"He's romantic too! Listen to this: *I didn't believe in love at first sight—until you walked by again.*"

"I think I read that once on a Valentine card."

"And this! *You've taken my heart, Hayley. I'd beg you to return it—except the more you take, the more I seem to have.*"

"Oh, golf tees! First he doesn't have a heart, then he has too many. Can't he make up his mind?"

Hayley gaped. "You're—*jealous!*"

"I'm *what?*" My nose tickled. I scrubbed at it—ow!—to subdue the sneeze.

"You heard me! *Jealous.* Because he writes better than you do. Even his subject matter is better than yours. Cullen doesn't make lists of how to annoy parents or teachers. He writes about important, enchanting things. *If a kiss could be sent through cyberspace, you would read this e-mail with your lips.* There! Isn't he a master of eloquence?"

I rolled my eyes. "A master of mush, maybe."

"Think what you like. *I* think he's a genius."

"Let's not exaggerate."

"*G-E-N!*" Her chin tilted. "*I-U-S!*"

"If you insist," I said with a bow.

A golden tornado whirled between us. "Gotcha!" Goldie exclaimed, sending my sandwich and Cullen's letters flying.

Chapter Seventeen

My stomach gurgled as I looked forlornly at my sandwich.
"Thanks heaps, Goldie," I said.

"Is *this* the *you know where* you two met yesterday morning?" she asked with a smirk of disappointment. "Not much of a hiding place. I found you like *that*!" She snapped two ring-encrusted fingers. "*Ooo*, what are *those*?" The fingers itched toward Cullen's e-mails.

"Fritos," I said.

"Not those. *Those*."

"None of your business." Hayley zipped the printouts into her pack with a *rrrrip* of ultimatum: *Don't touch—Or. Else.* "What do you want? Sneeze and I are having a private conversation."

Goldie flicked at her hair. "I'm here to offer my congrats on your *miraculous* recovery from the hiccups! And speaking of hiccups, I just got *the scoop* that Sneeze is *persona au gratin* with Hector!"

"Unless he's a potato," Hayley said, "you mean *persona non grata*."

"What*ever*. Sneeze, *dish* the *dirt!* What's with you and Hic?"

"They had a misunderstanding," Hayley said. "Now scoop somewhere else, please. We'd like to be left alone, if you don't mind—"

"Oh, but I *do*!" Goldie wriggled with smugness. "And it was *way* more than a misunderstanding." She flipped through several pages of her notepad. "Here's the *buzz*: Sneeze stole the Bee directly from Hiccup's hive!"

"That's a lie!" I said.

Hayley frowned. "Who, or what, is the Bee?"

"Hiccup's one-and-only true love!"

"Hic has a girlfriend?" Hayley gave a *whoop*. "That's great! Good for him! Good for *her*! It's about time someone realized what a sweetie he is. When did this happen? Who is she? What's her name?"

"Joonbi Park," Goldie went on, consulting her notes again. "She's a *major* celeb in the world of marital arts, known competitively as the Bee because she swarms to quick victory, her opponents defeated before they know what's stung 'em."

"Martial arts, Goldie," I said.

"Huh?"

"Joonbi is trained in *martial* arts, not *marital* arts."

"What*ever*." She clicked her pen. "Hiccup's told me *his* version of this sordid story of friendship, betrayal, and karate chops. How about *you*?"

"Steve!" Hayley shot me another SOS. "You stole your best friend's girl?"

"He's not my best friend," I said.

Hayley snorted. "Since when?"

"Since he stole Hiccup's Bee!" Goldie said.

"Joonbi is *not* Hic's girlfriend!" I said.

"But you admit you stole her," Goldie said.

"Did you?" Hayley asked.

"No! You should know by now that ninety-nine point nine percent of anything emanating from Goldie's mouth is highly suspect."

"Hmph!" Goldie hmphed. "Is that *so*? Then *why* is the Bee buzzing around telling *everyone* that she *loves* you?"

"What?"

"And *why*," Goldie continued with a head flounce, "is she asking *what* classes you have, *who* your friends are, and *where* you hang out? *Hmmmmm?*"

"I don't know. But if she's my girlfriend, she wouldn't have to ask, would she?"

"Sounds like a flimsy argument to me," Goldie said. "Maybe it's time I interviewed Joonbi myself. Her side of this love triangle should make an *excellent* lead story for my gossip column on Friday!"

I leaped to my feet. "That's it!" I said. "I'm done. I'm gone!"

"Just *where* do you think *you're* going?" Goldie demanded.

"We haven't finished our talk!" Hayley said. "You haven't eaten lunch!"

I didn't intend to do either. Not there. Not now. There comes a point when a guy can take only so much soap opera before he starts needing an acid bath.

Without a backward glance, I hotfooted straight to my school sanctuary: the nurse's office.

"Com bin, Steeb, com bin!" Tony said, chewing the words through a meaty sandwich. He downed the mouthful with a swig of soda, then brushed crumbs from his scrubs. "Is Miz Barker with you again too? No? More's the pity. I like her salt. But I s'pose a man's gotta sit with his own, now and again, away from the buckle bunnies."

I didn't know what buckle bunnies were, but if furry, diminutive rabbits were involved, most likely so were girls.

"What's your pleasure today, Steve? Allergy shot or grub?"

"Grub."

"Take a seat and strap on the feed bag!" Tony leaned forward in his leather chair, grabbed another soda from the mini-fridge, and lobbed it (the soda, not the fridge) across his desk.

The cold, wet can smacked into my hand. I spritzed it open and copied his swig. Sharp, sweet bubbles fizzed my nose. I sneezed.

"I'm right honored to see ya twice in two days," he said. "Specially since you must be busier than a one-toothed man in a corn-on-the-cob-eatin' contest. How's things at Patrick Henry? Keepin' above snakes?"

"I think so." Conversations with Tony were sometimes as difficult to translate as Cullen's. "My classes are tough, but a good kind of tough, if you know what I mean."

"I do." More crumbs snowed onto his shirt. "Makin' any friends?"

"One or two."

"Makin' any enemies?"

"One or two."

He laughed. "Then you're doin' sumthin' right. Say, what's happenin' with that ingenious alarm clock o' yours?"

I'd forgotten he didn't know what happened at the convention. Quickly, I filled him in. But as he started to offer condolences, I added: "I'm okay with Mr. Patterson's decision, Tony. He isn't the only fish in the sea. I'll use what I learn in my CAD class to design a virtual mockup I can submit to other companies."

"That's what I like to hear. No hangin' up the fiddle for you!" Tony wedged the last of his sandwich into his mouth and extended a hand. We shook, his encouragement sealed with mayo.

"Sweet on any gals yet?" he asked next.

"No." I twisted the stem off my apple.

"Not even the salty Miz Barker?"

"No!" I studied the apple for wormholes.

"Now that's a yarn if ever I heard one. C'mon, Stephen, acknowledge the corn and let's talk about it. Might as well, seein's how you obviously didn't come here to eat."

I plopped the untried apple back into my sack. "There's nothing to talk about. I like Hayley. She likes someone else. End of story."

"Oh, that'll happen a lot."

I choked on a gulp of soda. "You mean . . . I'm gonna feel like this . . . more than once?"

Tony winked. "How ya think I got hitched four times?"

"*Four . . . ?*" The room reeled. "Man, how'd you do it? How'd you let yourself fall for girl after girl *after girl* if you knew things wouldn't last?"

He grew a Cheshire cat grin. "Ya don't never got a say 'bout where that heart of yours is goin' or who it's goin' with! A heart has its own mind, and that's a fact. Besides, when you start courtin' a gal, your brain's not thinkin' one twitch o' a cat's tail about The End. No sir. It's too busy bein' roped and tied and led around by your heart to allow much thinkin' 'bout anythin' 'cept . . ." Tony paused, his chili-brown eyes trance-like, his voice tumbled low. ". . . 'cept the fresh-cream scent o' her skin that makes ya dizzier than any fancy perfume. The way her hair flows black as a river on a moonless night. Or how when she looks at ya, your insides shiver like a lake when a breeze breathes over it."

I swallowed. "Is that a poem?"

"Naw. But *she* was."

"Which one?"

"All of 'em."

I crumpled my sack. Hurled it into the trash. "I don't want to feel like this again," I said. "Never. Ever. It—*hurts.*"

"I didn't say it don't," Tony replied. "That kind o' pain compares only to a good tramplin' by a fifteen-hundred-pound rodeo bull. 'Course, ya don't think about that happenin' neither. The moment you touch his back, there's nuthin' on your mind 'cept *hang on.*" He tapped a picture frame with a calloused finger. "Remember this?"

I'd seen the photo last year. But to be polite, I peered again at the faded picture of a much younger Tony—clad in jeans, boots, and plaid shirt—hovering over a Hummer-like beast with sharp horns the size of bazookas.

"This here's the famous Red Rock," Tony explained. "World Champion Buckin' Bull. He's tossin' me like he tossed the other three hundred an' eight cowboys who tried to sit him."

"Wow. You *rode* that sucker?"

"Ain't you listenin'? Red Rock *was unrideable.* He retired undefeated. But I gave him a go. Three times."

"*Three . . . !* Tony, you could've gotten maimed. *Killed.* Why'd you do it?"

With his thumb he wiped dust from the frame's wooden edge. "'Cause Red was the greatest challenge. And each time I gave him a go, I knew I'd learn somethin' important about him, somethin' important 'bout myself that I could use one day. So the risk of not ridin' him was greater than the fear, greater than the risk it took to give him a whirl. Get what I'm sayin'?"

"I think so." I peered a final time at Red Rock's massive body, his sharp horns, roiled dust beneath jackknifing hooves. "You're saying that compared to love, bull-riding is a piece of cake."

The end-of-lunch bell rang.

Tony shook his head. "Why do I even try with you, boy? Might just as well be a guard dog barkin' at a knot." He swept off his hat and swatted me. "Get outta here. Go on, move your tail to English before I buck you there myself!"

Laughing, he planted a boot on my butt as I escaped out the door.

Chapter Eighteen

Time oozed the rest of that hot school day till I felt as melted as the clocks Salvador Dalí painted in the picture my art teacher discussed. Of course, it didn't help that my classes were made further surreal by:

1. Hiccup, radiating at me the vengeful fury of a thousand suns
2. Goldie, emanating gloat rays I took to mean *I-found-Joonbi-and-guess-what-she-told-me*!
3. Pierre, peeking fearfully at me from beneath his beret in case Goldie's gloat rays meant I'd told her where he'd been MIA all summer
4. Ace, holding another *textbook*. (And he wasn't even using it as a pillow!)
5. Hayley, engrossed in writing, over and over in her binder: *Cullen Hanson, Mrs. Cullen Hanson, Hayley Hanson, Hayley Barker Hanson, Ms. Hayley B. Hanson,* ad nauseam

I couldn't wait to get to hapkido. Today, with any luck, I'd learn how to kick something. *Hard.*

Have you ever been walking along, deep in thought, when a bee zips out of the wild blue yonder and bounces off your face?

That's what happened to me at Hapkido Family Fitness as I left the boys' locker room.

Except this Bee zipped faster than your average insect.

And weighed eighty pounds more.

"Steve! *There* you are!"

Bounce.

"Aaaaaa!" I stumbled backward into the door. It swung outward, smacking me into Joonbi's slender arms.

"Aaaaaa!" I bounced off her again, landing on my butt.

A petite but strong hand with dainty shell-pink nails hauled me to my feet.

"I finally found you!" Joonbi said in her lilting laugh. "Did you get my messages? I called you four times last night."

HIC!

I turned toward the angry sound. Steps away, Hiccup stood, arms crossed, at the entrance to the *dojang*. His eyes bored into mine in an SOAA (Squint of Attempted Assassination).

"I couldn't wait to talk more *101 Ways to Bug Your Parents*," Joonbi continued without my answer. "I tried to find you at school this morning, but no one knew what classes you're taking."

I started to explain about Patrick Henry, but thought better of it.

"At lunch, I met this girl who claimed to be one of your 'bestest best friends.' But she wouldn't tell me anything about you unless I agreed to an interview for the school paper. When I said no, you should've seen her reaction! She actually stamped a foot! Reminded me of Jek ki, my oldest sister. Truth!"

"That would be Goldie," I said, relieved that Ms. Snoop hadn't succeeded in getting or giving any . . . *information.*

"I hope she's not your sister or something."

I choked. "Great golf tees, NO!"

"Are you still free to get a smoothie after class? *Aigoo*, don't let Master Yates see your belt dragging on the floor like that! Allow me."

Joonbi's arms encircled my waist, lassoing me with the belt. She stood so close that the inky tuft of her ponytail itched my nose.

I sneezed.

"Steve, I can't tie this when you're arching away like that. I don't bite. Truth!"

HIC-HIC!

Two more angry eruptions from Hiccup. His SOAA practically bored straight into my skull, through the wall, and into the skateboard shop down the block.

"Tuck one end of your belt under like this, bend the short end over . . ." Joonbi hum-buzzed while she worked. ". . . pull both ends to tighten and the finished knot resembles a fortune cookie! See?"

"Cool," I said, free at last to sidle away and scrub my tickled nose. "Thanks."

"Now for your fortune!" Joonbi pretended to read from a scrap of paper: *"You will share secrets with a new friend while imbibing a liquid refreshment."*

"Secrets? But I don't have any—"

"HIC-HUMPH!" Hic stomped into the *dojang*.

"Business before pleasure, though," Joonbi said. "Today you'll be learning how to defend yourself with an unlikely weapon."

"What kind of weapon?" My mind swirled with exciting possibilities: nunchuks, bokkens, maybe even the *'alngegh*, a Klingon battle ax.

"A cane!" Joonbi announced.

"A *cane* cane? You mean like what little old men use?"

"I told you it was an unlikely weapon!" Joonbi zipped into the *dojang,* where the rest of the students had assembled.

I hurried after her and tripped—sprawling onto the padded mat.

"Excellent falling skills!" For the second time in five minutes, she hauled me up.

I glanced back to see what I'd tripped over.

"My apol*hic!*gies," Hiccup said with a bow. "My left foot inadvertently strayed into your path."

Inadvertently, my foot!

"Apology accepted," I said coolly.

"Attention!" a red belt ordered.

Students bowed to Joonbi and raced to form lines on the mat.

I turned to take my place with the other white belts—

—and sprawled in another face-plant.

"My apol*hic!*gies," Hiccup said. "Restless Leg Syndrome."

"I'll Restless Leg Syndrome you," I muttered.

I didn't get the chance.

Master Yates strode into the *dojang*. Class began immediately with warm-up exercises and forms. Then, after dividing us into groups of separate belt levels, Master Yates ran through a series of basic blocks, strikes, and kicks. I punched and *ki-yupped* till my muscles shrieked, but I managed not to embarrass myself.

The "best" was saved for last. Fifteen minutes before class ended, Master Yates clapped his hands for silence and gestured at the equipment shelves. "Choose a cane for today's weapons lesson."

Several younger students gamboled across the mat to snatch canes. They hobbled in circles, clutching their backs, cracking geezer jokes, and cackling like wizened crones in a fairy tale.

Master Yates clapped his hands again and murmured a reprimand. Red-faced, the students slunk back into line.

"Your perception of the cane and its owner is a common one," Master Yates said with a wry smile, "and may be used to your advantage. There is hidden strength in appearing weak, frail, or injured. An assailant may make the mistake of assuming you are easy prey, discovering all too late that you are not.

"The greatest strength of the cane is this: It is a potent defensive weapon! Unlike most weapons, it is already drawn. Therefore, if an attack is imminent, you can strike with instantaneous, dramatic speed and power to disable your assailant. Like so."

Master Yates motioned for Joonbi to join him at the mirrors. "Fighting stance!"

Joonbi pretended to rush him with a knife.

Cane in hand, he pantomimed several fast, hard strikes and hooking techniques to disarm and take her down. Each movement was focused and controlled; never once did he actually touch or hurt her with the cane, although she pantomimed that he had. The entire demonstration took seconds. Joonbi faked a grimace from where she lay on the mat. Then she sprang to her feet and bowed.

Everyone applauded.

"Choose your sparring partners!" Master Yates said.

Hiccup headed straight for me.

Joonbi zigzagged between us. "If we're quiet," she whispered, "we can talk while we train."

She proceeded to show me the correct way to hold the cane, block an attack, and take down an attacker.

"I was wondering," she murmured, "if you've ever thought of writing another bugging book? *101 Ways to Bug Your Sisters*, perhaps?"

"I don't have a sister—yet," I answered. "But my mom's pregnant. Baby Sis is due in December."

"But if you had a sister now, how would you bug her?"

"Why would I want to bug her?"

"Just wait. You will!"

"I was sorta freaked out when I first heard about the baby," I said while practicing a hook move. "I mean, my life will be so different with her around. But now I'm looking forward to having a little sister."

"A little sister, maybe. Five big ones? They're an absolute pain in the . . . belt. Truth!" She moved my fingers to the correct position along the staff. "You must have at least one or two bugging 'secrets' I could use. Maybe something left over from the bug-your-parents research that didn't work on them, but might work on kids?"

"You could rip the heads off their Barbies." I concentrated on pantomiming a block.

"Excellent. Try a first strike," Joonbi said. "But your suggestion won't work. My sisters haven't played with dolls in years. What else?"

"Read their diaries?"

"Yes! Baekjool keeps a journal under her mattress. What else?"

"Would you show me how to do that first strike again?"

Joonbi huffed a sigh, but her small hand grasped mine firmly.

"This strike can travel in two directions," she explained. "Straight up, to hit the hand, wrist, or funny bone of the weapon-bearing arm. Or, if your attacker is right-handed, strike cross-body like *this*. To be effective, you have to use a great deal of speed and power. Try it."

I clutched the cane hook. Took a deep breath. And—

Whoosh.

The cane flew over my head, narrowly missing Hiccup before clattering against the mirror.

I cringed. "Oops!"

Hic glowered and clenched his cane, knuckles whitening. "Eep!"

Hiccup advanced, lips pursed, eyes blazing, cane held high.

"Yipe!"

Joonbi's face paled. "Hector! That's not—!"

"Enough." Master Yates stepped in front of me. The room fell silent. "Lower your weapon, Mr. Denardo."

Hic stared at his arm, his hand, the cane rising high. He stared as if they belonged to someone else. Then he turned and stared at our classmates. Like Joonbi's, their faces were pale with shock.

Hiccup's cheeks blotched. "Sir, yes, sir." He hung his head. The cane dropped to the mat. "I apologize, Master Yates. I apologize, Mr. *hic!* Wyatt." He bowed. "I—don't know what *hic!* came over me."

Master Yates did not return the bow. He moved, unhurried, to the front of the room. "Line up!" he instructed.

We snapped to attention.

"Hapkido is not street fighting," the master said, hands

169

clasped behind his back. "There will be no conflict of ego on the mat. There will be no competition on the mat. The purpose of hapkido is not to fight and defeat an enemy. The purpose is to train your aggressive instincts and reactions. We spar not to win, but to learn. Is that understood?"

"Sir, yes, sir!"

"It is your moral responsibility," he continued, "never to use your martial arts skills on anyone except in an emergency—and only to defend yourself and your family. Is that understood?"

"Sir, yes, sir!"

Master Yates focused on Hiccup—then me. "The *dojang* membership is one of family," he said, his voice kind, compassionate. "The secret of hapkido is harmony. Remember that."

"Sir, yes, sir!"

"Recite the tenets!"

"Courtesy. Integrity. Perseverance. Self-control. Indomitable spirit."

"You would do well, all of you," Master Yates finished, "to think hard about number four. Now bow to the flags, bow to the black belts. Thank you. Class dismissed."

Chapter Nineteen

"Smoothies, here we come!" Joonbi burst from the *dojang*, tugging me out to the sidewalk.

Hiccup shuffle-hicked from a way-too-close distance behind us. I shot him a wary glance. Why was he following? Was he biding his time, waiting for the right moment when he could push me into the path of an oncoming cement mixer?

"I shouldn't, Joonbi," I said, fidgeting to flee. "I can't miss the bus. I have a lot of homework tonight."

"Just half an hour! Afterward, Umma will drive you home. She was so excited when I told her I had smoothies with you yesterday. She's always pressuring me to *socialize* more. That's number four on her *101 Ways to Bug Your Youngest Daughter* list. Anyway, remember what the 'fortune cookie' predicted!"

"*You will share secrets with a new* hic! *friend,*" Hiccup quoted, "*while imbibing a liq*hic! *refreshment.*"

"That's right, Hector!" Joonbi said, impressed. "You'll join us, yes?"

"*Love* to! Where are we going?" Goldie said, whirling

between us from behind a tree. "To the place where true *looo-oove* blossomed?"

"*HIC!-HIC!*" said Hiccup with a squirm of humiliation.

"Who *are* you?" Joonbi asked. "I already said no to an interview."

Goldie *tsked*. "I *told* you at lunch: I'm *Goldie Laux*, the *Snoop with the Scoop!* I always get my . . . *information*. 'No' is simply *not* in my dictionary."

"Vocabulary," I said.

"What*ever*. It's not in either one."

Ace appeared in his magical fashion. "Then how about: *Go away?*"

Goldie stamped a hoof and started to shove him.

Ace stared at her over his sunglasses as if he'd detected a curious species of beetle squashed beneath his shoe. Goldie sidled away.

"Who are *you?*" Joonbi asked Ace.

He shrugged. "Is Hayley here?"

"Who's Hayley?" Joonbi asked.

"*Hic!*" said Hiccup.

"She, he, they're all sorta friends of mine," I sorta explained.

"Hayley's at Gadabout. She's *always* at Gadabout," Goldie said, tapping her teeth with her gnawed pen. "You know that, Ace."

Ace shrugged.

"Steve, you have so many pals!" Joonbi said. "I've never lived anywhere long enough to make real friends. Smoothies for everyone—my treat! Would all of you like to come to my birthday party? It's next weekend. I'm turning thirteen. Umma said I could have a pool party and invite whomever I want. Bring—what's her name?—Hayley too! The party will be at the Lemon County Country Club."

"*Ooo*, I wouldn't miss it!" Goldie gushed. "Mother lunched there last week and said the watercress-and-cream-cheese sandwiches are to *die* for! *Ooo*, and she spotted *Chandler Scirocco*, the snooty soap star, sashaying out of the ladies' room with *toilet paper* stuck to her shoe! Can you *imagine?*"

Joonbi slipped an arm through mine and buzzed me down the street. "I think you should write a sequel to your book. I could help you! With five older sisters, I've had plenty of experience as the buggee. Truth!"

"Sneeze already wrote a sequel," Goldie said. "*101 Ways to Bug Your Teachers.*"

"It was more a list than an actual book," I said, "and it was for my personal use only, because—"

"I was thinking of *101 Ways to Bug Your Siblings,*" Joonbi said.

Goldie gushed, "That's a *fab* idea!"

"I'm not interested in writing another book," I said.

Hiccup hic-snorted.

"I'm *not,*" I insisted, walking faster.

Goldie trotted to keep pace. "But I can see the headline now! *Brainy Bugging Boy Busily Brushes Up on Ways to Badger, Bother, and Bedevil Brothers!*"

"And sisters!" Joonbi added.

"I got into enough trouble writing the first two books," I said. "So the answer is *No. Nope. Never!*"

We'd arrived at Lickety-Split Chick. I reached for the door.

Ace stopped, his warning calm. "You don't want to do that."

"Do what—say no?" I asked. "I've got the right to not do anything I don't want to do!" I yanked. The cowbell clanged. Joonbi, Goldie, and Hiccup filed past me.

"Stephen." Ace sauntered backward. *"You don't want to go in there."*

"I'm *thirsty.*" I turned my back on him and speed-walked to the polished counter where a kid in an egg-yolk-colored uniform and a beak-red paper hat posed behind the cash register, ready to take our order and—

Great golf tees. I completely forgot!

"Pierre!" Goldie shriek-gloated.

Pierre, aka Fee-leep, paled and clutched at the Lickety-Split badge over his heart. "Oh, *CAROTTE!"* he spat.

"So *this* is where you've been hiding the last three months! No *wonder* I couldn't find you! *Never* in a bazillion years would I have looked"—Goldie's nose wrinkled—"*here!* W*hy,* Pierre? *Why* are you working at Lickety-Split, *hmm?"*

"Eet eez none of your beez wax!" Pierre said stiffly. Then his shoulders sagged. "Ah, eet eez of no use! Eye know you will chase me to zee endz of zee earth to learn zee truth." He swept off his hat, crushing it between his hands. "Eye do eet for Papa. Zis bistro, she eez loozing money and we are, 'ow you say, short'anded."

Goldie rolled her eyes. "There's *got* to be a better reason. You *despise* this place with every fiber of your croissants!" She scrutinized the restaurant as if a juicier explanation lurked in the saltshakers or was encoded in the chicken-feet hiero-glyphics.

"Philip!" a girl shouted from the kitchen.

Alarm bells tolled, sirens wailed in my head.

It was the same voice I'd heard yesterday . . .

. . . and this afternoon in front of Patrick Henry High.

"You didn't greet those customers with a *'Welcome to Lickety-Split Chick,'*" the voice said, "and I've already told you three times today that if you insist on straying from the script I'll be forced to write you up, not that I have time to keep repri-manding you, my boyfriend will be here any minute for our dinner date—"

"Do not ruffle zee featherz!" Pierre half yelled, half crooned, his face now the color of his hat. "All eez well, eye assure—wait! You 'ave a *date*? Wis a *man*?"

"No, with a chicken! What are you hiding, your tone sounds weird, what's going on, don't make me come out there—"

"No, pleeze, my leetle sweet beak!" Panic overwhelmed Pierre's words. "Eye beg of you, Juliette, do not bothaire yourself wis—"

"Ooo!" Goldie yipped. *"I know that voice!"*

"Unfortunately, I—*hic!*—as well," Hiccup said.

"It's *July!*" Goldie exclaimed.

"Who's July?" Joonbi asked. *"Another* pal of yours?"

"Zey wish!" Pierre said. "My Juliette, she eez too fine to assoceeate wis zee likes of zem!"

Goldie yipped again. "The Queen of the Clubs, working

here! *Ooo*, what a comedown. *Ooo*, what a scoop!"

"I'm not your little sweet beak and don't call me Juliette!"

July Smith stormed from the kitchen, her slender hands dusted with flour, apron splotched with grease and gravy. Her face had a flushed sheen to it from working in the hot kitchen; wisps of dark hair escaped her French braid, curling against her cheeks.

No wonder Ace had warned me! After all, July Smith was his sister. A little-known fact he took great pains to keep a little-known fact. (Why, you ask? That's another story.)

"It's obvious you can't handle these customers, Philip," July said, "so take your break now, then I can escape this hen hole as soon as my boyfriend—"

She froze. Arced a dark, elegant brow. Glared at me.

"YOU," she said.

I gulped and managed a thin smile. "In the flesh."

"I DESPISE you, LOATHE you, it's ALL YOUR FAULT I'm stuck at Patrick Henry, it's ALL YOUR FAULT I'm working in THIS . . . THIS . . . THIS—"

"Don't blame him for your *hic!* mistakes," Hiccup countered. "If you hadn't tried to steal the *hic!* alarm—"

July jabbed a floury finger into Pierre's chest. "Is Sneeze Wyatt a friend of yours? IS HE?"

Pierre choked. "Eye—eye no speeka zee Eengleesh, mademoiselle."

July glared at Goldie, then Hiccup, then jabbed at Pierre again. "I know you, all three of you, you're all with Sneeze, I remember you from the district Invention Convention® last spring when you had me disqualified!"

Pierre shredded his hat into confetti. "Eye told you yesterday not to return, Sneeze. But deed you listen? No! And now you 'ave blown my deesguise! My true identity would 'ave continued to elude Juliette eef eet were not for you!"

July gave a tinkly laugh. "THAT'S supposed to be a DISGUISE? What a laugh! I knew immediately you had to be the owner's pathetic son. Why else would he give a job to a kid with a weird speech impediment and a Magic Marker fetish?"

"I smell a *scoop!*" Goldie shoved her microphone beneath Pierre's moosetache. "Tell us, *Fee-leep*, what's the *real* reason you're working here?"

Pierre flung out his arms, showering confetti. "Eye confess! At first, eye work 'ere only to 'elp Papa. But zen—zen eet eez becuz eye fall in love!"

Goldie's eyes glittered. "With *who?*"

"Wis Juliette!"

"With *hic!* July?" Hiccup said.

"With *me?*" July asked.

"I can see the headline!" Goldie said. "*King of the Kitchen Falls for Queen of the Clubs!*"

"Are you *hic!* daft, man?" Hiccup demanded. "How can you feel affection for *her?*! I am the first to admit that Sneeze's faults are plentiful—and annoying!—but that was no reason for this woman to wrong him. She lacks *hic!* morals! She lacks *hic!* scruples! She is guilty of trademark infringe*hic!*ment"

"Eet eez true, eye *am* cray-zee! Cray-zee wis love!" Pierre bent down on one knee and clasped July's flour-y hands. "Juliette, now zat eye 'ave reveeled my feeleengs for you, pleeze tell me: Do eye 'ave your 'eart? Just say zee word and eye shall bee yours for eeterneetee!"

We all looked at July.

We all held our breaths.

"Yuck," July said.

"I quit," July said.

She yanked off her greasy apron. Dropped it onto Pierre's head. "And don't call me Juli—"

The cowbell clanged as a customer entered. A waft of pungent aftershave, mingled with peppermint, itch-tickled my nose.

My neck prickled with chicken skin.

"Ready for dinner, babe?" asked Marcos the Moke.

Chapter Twenty

My heart jackhammered in my chest.

"Well, well, well," Marcos said with a little smile. He strode toward us, his cleated golf shoes crunch-clacking across the chicken tracks. "Look who it is: my favorite post-nasal drip."

I managed a weak laugh. "Ha-ha, that's pretty good." I edged behind the counter. "You've been boning up on your puns!"

"*Zis* eez zee boyfriend, Juliette?" Pierre asked. He gave Marcos the once-over, taking in the PHHSVGT uniform with distaste. "You prefer zee *jock* to zee *Jacques?*"

"And the Drip has his little adenoids with him again," Marcos added, popping a peppermint. "How cute."

July grabbed a purse and her cape. "I'm ready to get out of here anytime you are, Marcos. *And I'm not coming back*," she shot at Pierre.

"Eez zat zee threat . . . or zee promise?" Pierre shot back.

"Be with you in five, babe," Marcos said. "First I need to have a little 'chat' with Banana Nose here. You know, the punk with the monkey food on his face." In one swift movement, he hopped the counter.

I inched backward into the kitchen. Bumped into a sink. Banged into hanging pots and pans. A lid clattered to the floor.

I looked wildly around for something, anything I could use to defend myself.

Stainless steel tables. Bowls of fresh fruit. Deep fryers. Refrigerator. Overflowing garbage can.

"*Pssst!*"

I glanced behind me.

Ace lounged in the doorjamb of the emergency exit. He beckoned with one nonchalant finger.

I faced Marcos again. He'd moved closer—too close!—with the calculated stealth of a mountain lion. Then he smiled, turned his hat backward—and pounced.

I scooted beneath one of the tables. Marcos caught the loose tail of my hapkido belt and yanked. I belly flopped, my nose connecting with—*ow!*—a metal drain. Marcos yanked again, dragging me toward him. I kicked blindly. Marcos grunted and let go. I scrabbled to my feet and shoved the garbage onto the floor.

The contents spewed.

Marcos and his cleats slipped—

tripped—

and sprawled in a slough of gizzards, gravy, and rotting banana peels.

He roared. Struggled to rise. But Joonbi was on him, wrenching his arm behind his back.

July rushed in, cape billowing, hand to her mouth.

Marcos lifted his head, spitting, sputtering, face splattered, dripping. An orange rind replaced his hat; a banana peel dangled from one ear.

I shouldn't have said it. I really shouldn't have. But I couldn't resist: "Ho! Look who's got monkey food on his face now!"

She shouldn't have done it. She really shouldn't have.

July *laughed*.

Marcos's face purpled.

No humiliate dat moke a third time. It could be your last . . .

Marcos roared again and slip-struggled to his feet, bucking Joonbi.

"Bye!" I yelled, blasting out the back door.

"Thanks!" I yelled as I blasted past Ace.

"Wait!" I yelled to the bus idling on the corner. I raced up the steps and down the aisle, diving to the crusty floor of the rear seat.

"Wouldn't you be more comfy up here?" quavered a pair of thick panty-hosed cankles wedged into turquoise sneakers. They were attached to an elderly lady who batted her crepey eyes and patted the seat beside her.

I peeked out the window. Marcos, still trailing garbage, his face purple with rage and plum juice, pounded toward the bus.

I ducked, my heart drilling a hole out my chest.

Great, just great. First I humiliate him in front of his friends, then in front of the Amys, and now his girlfriend. What's left? How can this possibly get worse?

The lady patted her seat again.

The bus lurched forward.

"No—thanks—" I gasped. "I'm—good. For now."

It was another twenty minutes before my heart beat normally again.

When I finally made it home, the kitchen phone was ringing.

"Steve?" Mom's muffled voice called from the downstairs bathroom. "Quick, get the phone! It's for you!"

How does she know that?

My hand hovered, trembling, above the receiver.

Don't answer it. There isn't anyone you want to talk to right now.

Truth, as Joonbi would say. The only people who could be calling me were: Goldie, to gossip about Hiccup, Pierre, July, Joonbi, Marcos—or all five; Pierre, to cuss me out with multiple, vehement *carotte*s! for leading Goldie the Fox straight to his chicken coop of love; Joonbi, wanting to wheedle more bugging ways out of me to seek sisterly revenge; or Hayley, to gush even more over "Cullen's" eloquent letters.

"Sweetheart, *answer the phone*! I told him you'd be home by now!"

Him? Had the King of the Goons discovered where I lived?

I approached the receiver as if it were a rattlesnake. Lifted it slowly to my ear. Uttered a wary, wavery "H-hello?"

"Is that you, Stephen!" a voice boomed, nearly puncturing my eardrum. "Sterling Patterson here! You might not remember me, but we met a couple of weeks ago at the Invention Convention®! Ring a bell?"

"Sure, yeah, yes!" Geez, how could he think I'd forget?

"I have a proposition for you, Stephen!"

My ear winced, but my heart and hopes leaped. "You've changed your mind? You want to buy the Nice Alarm?"

"Not at all! Clever item. Ingenious! But not right for Patterson Enterprises. No, it's your books I'm calling about!"

"My . . . books?"

"I passed them along to a New York friend of mine! Fess Garrison, editor in chief at Ridiculous Reads! They specialize in goofy gift books. He thinks yours could be the start of a terrific series! He wants to offer a contract!"

The bathroom door flew open with a slam. Mom burst-waddled into the kitchen, flapping her wet hands. "Who is it, is it Mr. Patterson?" she asked. "Did he tell you the great news?"

"I don't understand," I said into the phone. "A contract for what?"

Mr. Sterling boomed even louder, if that was possible. "To publish *101 Ways to Bug Your Parents* and *101 Ways to Bug Your Teachers!*"

My mouth went dry. My tongue went wooden. I looked at Mom and croaked: "C-c-con-twact!"

She bobbled her head. Grabbed my arms. Then whispered, *"How much? Ask him how much!"*

I licked my lips. "How much would I have to pay?"

He laughed. "They pay *you*, Stephen! I can't speak for

183

Garrison, of course, he'll be the one to negotiate terms with you and your parents! But you'll receive an advance against royalties somewhere in the vicinity of—"

He named a monetary figure that made my knees buckle.

I repeated it to Mom. She clutched her belly and did an awkward jig. "College!" she whispered. "That'll pay for college!"

And my inventions.

My mind reeled.

No more buying nicked nuts and bent bolts from the bargain bin at the hardware store! No more struggling to save every penny I earned at Gadabout! Sure, I'd still work there for fun. I'd never leave Gadabout—except on occasion to promote the Nice Alarm—because now I didn't have to search for a novelty company to produce it. *I could afford to produce it myself!*

"Are you there, Stephen!" Mr. Patterson boomed. "May I give Garrison your phone number so he can discuss contract details with your parents?"

Yesyesyesyesyesyesyesyesyesyes!

I cleared my throat. Tried to sound calm, professional, as a good inventor should. "Yes, that will be fine, Mr. Patterson. What about Hiccup?"

"Hiccup?" A pause. "Say again! I think we have a bad connection!"

"Oh, sorry. Hector Denardo. He's my—he's the guy who did the illustrations for *101 Ways to bug Your Parents*. Would they like his phone number too?"

"That won't be necessary! Ridiculous Reads won't be of-fering a contract for Denardo's cartoons."

"They—won't? Why not?"

Mom stopped jigging. Her gaze fixed on mine, brows crimping with the same confusion and apprehension I felt in my stomach.

"Ridiculous Reads prefers to hire from their own stable of illustrators," Mr. Patterson explained. "Their artists are professionally trained! They have years of experience in the world of publishing!"

"But Hiccup's drawings are half the book," I said. "No one at my school was interested in buying *101 Ways to Bug Your Parents* until we added Hector's drawings. They're what made my lists so funny and real!"

"Garrison is firm, Stephen!" Mr. Patterson said. "He doesn't like Mr. Denardo's drawings. He wants only you for this series!"

I closed my eyes.

I couldn't believe what I was about to do. Mom wouldn't believe what I was about to do.

"Then all I have to say is—" I swallowed. *"Sorry. Not interested."*

Chapter Twenty-one

On Friday afternoon, I found a copy of *The Jeffersonian Times*, Jefferson Middle's newspaper, wedged into my locker. A pink sticky note, embellished with *From the Desk of Goldie Laux*, was attached to it. The note said:

> See what happens when I don't get the Exclusives I'm promised?
> When you're ready to spill your guts, give me a call! –G.

My stomach clenched as I opened the newspaper and saw what splashed across the front page:

BIGWIG BUYS BRAINY BOY'S BUGGING BOOKS!

by Goldie Laux, *The Snoop with the Scoop*

Ridiculous Reads, a publishing company that specializes in goofy gift books, has offered Stephen "Sneeze" Wyatt a six-figure contract for *101 Ways to Bug Your Parents* and three sequels. The hilarious but handy self-help booklet, written by Wyatt and illustrated by former sidekick

Hector "Hiccup" Denardo during summer school last year, would've been the first of a four-book series, including: *101 Ways to Bug Your Teachers*, *101 Ways to Bug Your Brothers and Sisters*, and *101 Ways to Bug Your Friends and Enemies*. *"Would've been?"* you ask. Yep! For reasons known only to him, Wyatt has reportedly turned down the deal. This reporter's comment to Sneeze: *ARE YOU CRAZY?!?!?!?!?!?!?!?!?!?!?!?!?*

Mom had uttered a similar comment after I ended my call with Mr. Patterson.

"Stephen, are you *insane*?!?!?!?!?!"

Then she slumped onto the kitchen stool, patting her belly with one hand, fanning herself with Hiccup's dish-towel blossom with the other. "I'm sorry, honey. That was my hormones screaming. This is your decision. But such an important one! Don't you think we should've discussed it before you said no? Think of your future! It's money for college—and beyond! Help me to understand . . ."

Ha. I barely understood it myself. I mean, Hiccup and I weren't even friends anymore! Why hadn't I just taken the money and run?

Because . . .

Because as I stood there—shocked and silent with the phone in my hand, Mr. Patterson waiting for my answer—the words Hiccup threw at me the other day at the bus stop kept whirlpooling inside my head:

Joonbi is the only love of mine you will ever steal from me!

I knew what Hic's drawings meant to him. What getting them published meant to him. He loved his art way more than he loved Joonbi (though he might not know it). His work was a huge part of what made him Hector, just as the Nice Alarm and my inventions (and yeah, even my writing) were a huge part of what made me *me*. So I couldn't sell *101 Ways to Bug Your Parents* without his illustrations. It wasn't wholly mine to sell. We'd done that book *together*. It was *us*. What *used* to be us.

After a long discussion at dinner, Mom came to understand my reasoning. Dad too. They patted my back and told me how proud they were, how I'd made the right decision and what a true-blue friend of Hiccup's I was. Double ha. If only they knew that friendship had turned black-and-blue . . .

"Goldee's words are as sharp as zee guillotine, *oui*?" Pierre said from behind me now, interrupting my thoughts. He flung open his locker, flung in four books, grabbed three others, and flung shut the metal door with a fierce *bang*. "Zey can make you sick like zee poisoning of ptomaine."

"Pierre, you're actually *talking* to me?" I asked. "I figured after I blew your cover with July, you'd never speak to me again."

"Eye must admeet, at first eye wuz fureeous wis you," he said, fingering the faded moosetache beneath his nose. "But now eet eez Goldee 'oo raises my 'ackles! Now eet eez Goldee eye refuse to speek to!"

188

"Goldie? Why?"

"Zat *carotte*! Zat feemale Robespierre! She 'as told zee entire school of my fooleeshness!" He flicked a finger at the newspaper, his face reddening. "Read *Goldee's Gosseep* and weep—eef you daire!" He clicked his heels together, bowed, pulled his beret down over one side of his face—and fled.

With a gulp, I opened the paper again.

Goldie's Gossip

continued from Page One

by Goldie Laux, *The Snoop with the Scoop*

KITCHEN KING FALLS FOR QUEEN OF THE CLUBS!

Oo-la-la! Finicky food snob Pierre Noel recently traded his chef's hat for a cashier's badge when he took a counter job at Lickety-Split Chick. *Pourquoi?* you may well ask. Because he stumbled upon something there even hotter than the jalapeño wings: July Smith (former member of 50 extracurricular clubs at Jefferson Middle), to be egg-zact! Alas, Pierre's attempts to cook up a love potion filled with sugar and spice and smoothies-with-ice failed to ruffle even one of Mademoiselle Smith's feathers. Her hard-boiled response to Pierre's confession of amour? "Le yuck!" Now that July has flown the coop, Pierre is a mere shell of himself, left with nothing but scrambled dreams. This reporter's advice to Pierre: *If you can't stand the heat, get out of the love kitchen!*

Oh, man. No wonder Pierre wasn't speaking to her!

HYPOCHONDRIAC STUNG!

According to the latest buzz, Hector "Hiccup" Denardo was stung by the love bug while taking martial arts lessons from "the Bee," aka Joonbi Park, new student at JMS and a world-famous black belt in Hop-key-doe. But Hector got the anaphylactic shock of his life when long-time best bud Stephen "Sneeze" Wyatt turned waspish and stole the Bee right out of Hiccup's hive! Sneeze continues to drone on, denying any intentional involvement; but when pressed, he blurted: "None of your beeswax!" Sources close to the love triangle hint that Hiccup tried to eliminate his rival with the Vulcan Neck Pinch, but Sneeze is obviously built of sterner snot. This reporter's advice to Hector: *Try to develop your sweet side. You'll catch more bees with honey than with a punch in the nose.*

Poor Hic. All the hapkido-instilled confidence in the world might not squash this kind of humiliation.

GOOFY GEEK GOADS GOLF TEAM

I didn't bother to read *that* article. Ha. I was still reliving it all too clearly in my nightmares (and every moment Cullen wasn't by my side at Patrick Henry).

TEE FOR TWO?

During the first week of school, if you whispered to Hayley Barker the name of the Hawaiian god from the PHHSVG team, you'd count more dimples on her face than on a golf ball! But now Miss Barker, manager at Gadabout Golf, seems to have pushed her affections for Cullen Fu Handsome to the back nine . . . or is she merely sending false reads to throw inquiring minds off the scent? This reporter's advice to Hayley: *Forget Cullen and let him play through, honey! You simply can't hope for someone this handsome to swoon over you if you aren't up to par!*

Ouch.

I hoped Hayley's crush hadn't changed her so much that she'd lost her nerves of titanium.

She hadn't.

"Do you honestly think I care what that weasel-ette writes about me?" she demanded the next day at Gadabout when I asked her about Goldie's column. "Besides, we obviously succeeded in throwing her off the scent of Cullen and me. That's all that matters."

"Uh-huh," I said, thinking it a fine coincidence that we were talking about Goldie at the same moment I was peering into the odiferous bilge of the Pirate Ship. "*Pee-yew!* Hayley, hold the flashlight a little higher, will you? And hand me that wrench. I need to tighten these bolts."

"I feel kinda sorry for Pierre, though," Hayley went on. "He's an insufferable snob, but still! Goldie didn't need to strew pieces of his broken heart for the whole school to see. And poor Hiccup! He's taken to his bed, did you know?"

I shook my head. Despite his moment of thawing at Lickety-Split on Wednesday, and a few curt greetings since then, we still hadn't reconciled.

Hayley snorted. "You two are acting ridiculous. You should call him. I did. Last night. But Mrs. Denardo wouldn't let me talk to him. She said he won't be at school next week. He's got a bad case of shingles. Huh. If you ask me, it's actually a bad case of *chagrin*. He must be mortified everyone knows about his crush on Joonbi."

I sidled the subject of Hiccup by asking: "Are you sure you're not bothered by what Goldie wrote? You know, about you not being up to Cullen's par?"

Hayley snorted again. "Shows how much Goldie knows! If she read even *one* of my letters from Cullen—"

I dropped the wrench. It landed on my big toe, but the pain was nothing compared to the white-hot panic that seared my stomach. "Hayley! You're not actually going to let Goldie read—"

She snorted a third time. "Never ever. You're the only person I've shared his letters with." Eyes dreamy, she sank onto the turf, her back against the ship's hull. "His letters . . . they just keep getting better and better and better . . ."

Yeah, yeah, yeah. On one hand, I reveled in Hayley's compliments. But on the other, it was kinda weird being my own rival and all.

". . . he's been writing me for four days now. Don't you think it's time I wrote him back?"

"What?" I said. *"What? NO!"*

Hayley's dreaminess evaporated, narrowed into an SOS. *"Why. Not?* His letters are so beautiful. They deserve a response! Besides, I want to do more than just *read*. I want to write to Cullen, *talk* to Cullen, let him know what I think and how I feel."

"But he asked you *not* to write him, Hayley!"

"I know, but—"

"You haven't even known him a week!"

"I know, but—"

I kneeled in front of her. Stared directly into the depths of her ice-cream-cold blue eyes. "Promise. Promise me you won't do anything stupid."

"Stupid?" Her chin tilted. "Is it *stupid* to want a two-way conversation with someone you like? How else are people supposed to get to know each other!"

"I'm sure Cullen knows what he's doing," I said. "Wait a bit longer. Play it safe. You don't want your dad finding out."

"You're really worried about that, aren't you? That's . . . nice." She gave me a quick hug. Her peach scent penetrated even the noxious fumes of the bilge.

My head swooned.

I picked up the wrench again, polishing it furiously with a rag so she couldn't see my face. "I just don't want you getting hurt," I said.

And that was the tricky part. I couldn't, *shouldn't* keep up the charade much longer. Hayley had fallen harder than ever for Cullen—and all because of me! But how could "he" end things with Hayley without causing her to suffer? It seemed my clever little plan had totally imploded . . .

"Ho! What's da haps, Steve?" Cullen said the following Thursday as he lumbered into CAD. He stowed his pack and settled into his chair. "You been working round the clock on da drawings for da Nice Alarm?"

"Yep. How did you know?" I said with a wide yawn. I closed my eyes, laid my head on the desk. The hum of the computers created muffled, lulling ocean sounds, like when you hold a seashell to your ear.

"Mebbe 'cuz you look buss up, ready to crash."

Ha. Mebbe 'cuz along with working on the alarm the last five days, I'd been:

1. Fretting about Hayley
2. Plotting unique and furtive ways to get around Patrick Henry without Marcos the Moke and his Goon Brigade ambushing me (so far, so good)
3. Spraining and straining every muscle every afternoon in hapkido to (ironically) avoid

the discomfort and inconvenience of PE

4. Avoiding the evil clutches of a gossip-crazed girl who lurked behind every bus, bush, and baby carriage to get her ears on the "real" reason I turned down a four-book contract

And let's not forget impersonating you, Cullen Fu Hanson, by spending an hour or two every night writing WOOn-derful love letters to Hayley.

"What was the question again?" I asked with another yawn. Cullen chuckled.

"Actually, the Nice Alarm drawings are easy as pie," I said. "It's my trig and and chem classes that are killing me."

"Need any help, brah? Neva wen take trig. But t'ree years ago, I got one A in chem. I could tutor you dis weekend. Come for dinner, eh? Auntie make ono—delicious—*huli huli* chicken."

Man this guy is nice, I thought with a guilty wince. I really shouldn't accept his offer. But I really, really, really needed help.

"That'd be great," I said. "Does Saturday work for you? I'm going to a birthday party in the afternoon, but it should be over by five. My mom could drop me at your place after that."

Cullen shook his head. "No can. Big golf tournament dat day. If we win, we move on to da state championship. Coach going like fo' take us out fo' grinds afta da game to celebrate. How 'bout Sunday?"

"Sure." We exchanged addresses and phone numbers.

"*Mahalo*, Cull."

He formed a fist with his thumb and pinkie finger sticking out. "Shaka, brah," he answered.

Late that night, after I finally finished 1.) working on the Nice Alarm's cyber-drawings; 2.) oiling the Nice Alarm; 3.) writing three Cullen-letters to Hayley; and 4.) brushing my teeth, I had just hopped into bed and turned out the light when my computer beeped.

Incoming e-mail! Who would be writing to me at this hour?

Maybe it was just one of those automatic messages reminding me about Joonbi's birthday party on Saturday afternoon. The e-mail certainly couldn't be from Hiccup. I'd heard he still had shingles. Besides, he hadn't bothered to forward me so much as an influenza vaccine schedule since he ceased being my bud.

So who . . . ?

I clicked on the light. Clicked open the mail program . . .

. . . and felt a jumper-cable shock to my heart.

To: Sneeze@stephenjwyatt.com
From: Hayley@gadaboutgolf.com
Subject: Math Homework: Please forward to CFH—ASAP!

Why was Hayley writing to Cullen? Especially since she promised (she had promised, hadn't she?) that she wouldn't?

Curious fingers crept to the keyboard.

What do you think you're doing, Stephen? You promised you wouldn't read any of "their" letters!

Huh. Hayley just broke her promise, so she owes me one, right? Besides, I have to read it. She'll expect an answer from Cullen about the "math homework," won't she? How will I know how to have him respond if I don't read this letter?

I had a point.

I gulped. Opened the message. Shut one eye and read with the other:

> Dear Cullen: You made me promise not to write
> to you. I'm sorry, but I can't keep that promise
> any longer. Your letters mean so much to me!
> You deserve an answer—in person. Meet me
> tomorrow, Friday, 11:30 p.m. at Gadabout Golf.
> I'll leave the gates unlocked. Directions on how
> to find me are below. I hope you'll meet me!
> We have so much to talk about.
> —Aloha, Hayley

My heart went into cardiac arrest.

The directions at the bottom of Hayley's e-mail led Cullen directly inside the Great Pyramid.

Chapter Twenty-two

I wrenched out of my chair and began to pace, eyes burning, fists and teeth clenched.

How could she do it? How could Hayley tell Cullen—*Cullen!*—about her secret hiding place? *Our* secret hiding place?

A strange, hot anger engulfed me. My hands grabbed the first thing they could find and, grunting like a troll, I hurled it across the room.

Lazy Lick, the electronic ice-cream-cone holder I'd invented, smashed into a jillion pieces against the wall.

That felt good.

I grabbed Cut 'n' Putt and flung it at the wall too.

Grunt. *CRASH.*

Really good.

I grabbed another invention. (Grunt. *CRASH.*) And another. *(Grunt. SMASH.)*

I was just reaching to hurl See to Pee, the glow-in-the-dark toilet seat, when Dad stumbled into the room.

"What in blazes is going on in here?"

He stared at me, wild-eyed, befuddled.

I stared at the toilet seat in my hand, then whisked it behind me, dropping it on the floor. "Nothing, Dad."

"Nothing?" He surveyed the damage and scratched his Einstein-like hair. "Do you consider an earthquake 'nothing'?"

"What was that crash?" Mom called sleepily from the master bedroom. *"David, is Steve all right?"*

"Steve's fine, Barbara," Dad answered. "I think."

I snorted and flumped onto my bed.

"Are you boys fixing a snack? If so, I'll have whatever you're having!"

A ridiculous laugh bubbled inside me.

"We're not snacking, Barbara!"

"But I smell ice cream!"

Another bubble laugh. I was getting hysterical. "How do you *smell* ice cream?" I asked Dad.

"She's six months pregnant," he replied. "She can smell a double-dip of chocolate on the moon." To Mom, he yelled: "A couple of Steve's inventions broke. I'll help him sweep up. Go back to sleep, honey."

"Are you sure he's okay?"

"Sure I'm sure!" He shot me a wary glance, then shuffled out of the room. Minutes later he shuffled back carrying a broom and dustpan.

With a sigh, I moved to help.

Dad waved me away. *"Are* you okay, Steve?" he asked,

sweeping. "With your crazy schedule, we haven't had a chance to talk the last couple of weeks. Are you managing to juggle school and hapkido and Gadabout—?"

"Yeah." I stared at the ceiling. The dimpled pattern reminded me of golf balls. I turned to stare at the Nice Alarm.

"You'd let me know if you weren't okay, though, right?"

"Right."

"Don't lie to me, Stephen. I'm holding a broom and I know how to use it." He waved it with false menace, dust bunnies and metal motes snowing onto his wild hair. He looked so silly, I laughed. A normal, non-crazed laugh.

"I'm not lying, Dad," I said. "I just don't feel like talking now."

"Fair enough." He lowered the broom and swept the remains of my inventions into the dustpan. Then he dumped the lot into the trash. "But you'll let me know when you *are* ready?"

I nodded.

"G'night, then."

"G'night."

He flipped off the light.

When my door was almost closed, I called softly, almost hoping he wouldn't hear: "Hey, Dad?"

"Hm?"

"I have a—question."

"If it's about electronic ice-cream cones—"

"It's not."

"Then shoot." He came back into the room.

"I was thinking about . . . lies. Have you ever told one?"

He cleared his throat. "What kind of lie are we talking here? I want to give you an honest answer, son. But as a Concerned and Responsible Dad, I have a duty to be a proper role model."

"I don't mean the 'Officer-I-swear-I-didn't-rob-that-bank-despite-the-one-hundred-thousand-dollars-poking-out-of-my-pocket' kind."

"I see," he said, chuckling. "More like when your mother asks: '*David, do these pregnancy pants make my butt look big?*' and I answer '*No*'?"

Mom hollered: "I can hear you!"

"The second kind," I said, lowering my voice.

"Then the answer is yes," Dad admitted.

"Did any of the lies . . . ever get out of hand? I mean, let's say, for example, you lied to someone for a really, really good reason."

"Define 'good.'"

"To protect this someone, keep her from getting hurt."

"Gotcha. Go on."

I pulled my blanket around me. The frayed edge of satin tickled my chin. "And the lie I—you told," I went on, "it not only kept her from getting hurt, but made her really, really happy. So happy that you told another lie and another and another. You didn't mean for things to go that far, but they did. And now you're not sure how to stop. Because if she finds out you lied, she just might hate me, I mean, you, I mean, whoever, for the rest of your life. Has that ever happened to you, Dad? And if it did, what should I—you do?"

Dad didn't answer right away. Instead, he made his way across the darkened room and perched on my bed. The springs squeaked.

"That's a prickly predicament, Stephen," he said finally. "But if it were me, I would take the risk and tell her the truth. Because if you don't, you run the risk of hurting her even more. I wouldn't want that to happen. Would you?"

I thought of Hayley: the scratchy snag of her callus . . . the defiant tilt of her chin . . . her funny jig after shooting a hole in one . . . the blue of her eyes and the way they smiled directly into mine . . .

I swallowed at thick guilt in my throat. "No."

"Let's go downstairs," Dad said. "I'll make us some hot chocolate and we can talk more about this. What do you say?"

"Not tonight, Dad. I just want to lie here and think about—stuff. But thanks."

"*Any*time, my son," Dad answered, heading for the door. "Anytime . . ."

Friday night. 11:30 p.m. Gadabout Golf.

The Great Pyramid loomed before me in the dark. Steep, solid, mocking:

Hayley shared my secret with you, it seemed to say. *Now she's whispered my secret to someone else. It doesn't matter he doesn't actually know. What matters is this:* You won't always be the

202

only one. *Did you really believe you would be? Did you really believe you were special?*

"*Shut. Up.*" I kicked a cement block. My toes yelped. I crunched a swear word and tasted blood.

I deserve this pain. It's my fault Hayley shared our secret. If I hadn't sent her those e-mails, hadn't pretended to be Cullen . . .

I hobble-hunched along the wall, my fingers feeling for the small, smooth bump—

There.

Click.

The door sprung open.

From within the tunnel, Hayley's voice floated out into the night: eager, echoy, tentative. *"Cullen?"*

My anger and determination drained away. I deepened my voice, trying to sound like Cull, trying to sound Hawaiian and handsome and muscley. "Yeah, it's . . . me."

"Come on in!"

"No can."

A snort. "Of course you can! Crawl. The Tomb Room isn't far."

"No."

"What's wrong? You sound . . . weird."

I forced myself to speak from deeper within my chest. But the words lurched, scratching my throat. I coughed. "I too big for da tunnel."

"I'll come out!" I heard scuffling. Saw the faint glow of her lantern bobbing toward me.

"No!" I jerked away from the entrance.

The scuffling stopped. "Don't you want to see me?"

My heart flip-flopped. I croaked: "More den I want to breathe."

"Do you have a cold? Why can't I come out?"

I crouched and spoke into the tunnel again. "If your dad see us, you get into much *pilikia*—trouble."

"I just want to *talk*."

"Hayley, dis not right. I too old for you. I not . . . who, or what, you think I am."

"What does *that* mean?"

I sucked in a breath. Forced it out. Steam rose, mingling with the evening chill. "I was wrong to write you da e-mails, Hayley."

"What?"

"I'm pau—done with dem now. I'm sorry I sent dem."

I could almost hear arms crossing, her chin tilting. "Well, I'm not! They're the most beautiful things I've ever read. Nobody writes like that anymore. Nobody!"

Oh carotte, she's going to cry. I've made Hayley cry . . .

"But I'm seventeen, almost eighteen. You're only thirteen. If your dad read doz letters, he could make *pilikia* for you *and* me. Dat's why no can e-mail you anymore. Why no can be friends. If we seen together, I might get kicked off da golf team. Or out of school."

Hayley's voice stretched thin and tight. "I wouldn't want that . . ."

"Mahalo. Thanks for understanding." I leaned closer toward the tunnel, and whispered, "I'm sorry, Hayley. I gotta go now. Aloha."

"Cullen, don't go yet! Cullen, are you still out there?"

I crouched again at the tunnel opening. "I'm . . . here." *I'll always be here . . .*

"Couldn't we just keep talking like this—me inside, you outside—for a little longer?" she asked, voice desperate. "My dad's asleep. No one can hear us. I won't come out. I promise."

I glanced around. The course was quiet and empty and the air smelled of all the things I loved: King Arthur's murky moat . . . the lemony tang of golf-ball-washing solution . . . the oily metal of machinery . . . and the faint sweetness of late-summer peaches.

"Just a little longer?" Hayley asked.

I closed my eyes. Slid to the ground, my back resting against the pyramid's slanted wall. The concrete blocks still held the day's heat, *her* heat. It seeped deep into my shirt, into my skin, my heart . . .

Against my better judgment, I said in a hoarse whisper, "Okay, Hayley. Just a little longer."

Chapter Twenty-three

"Talk to me," Hayley said. "Talk to me the way you did in your e-mails."

I didn't answer. I lifted my head to take in the enormous star-studded sky. No words could describe . . .

"Cullen? You still there?"

"Yeah."

"You don't sound very sure."

"It's the tunnel. My words have to grope their way through the twists and turns to find your ears."

"Huh. My words don't have that trouble!"

"That's because they already know the way by heart—to my heart."

"Your words could see better if I brought the lantern closer!"

I heard her scuffling, creeping toward the entrance.

"That's far enough!" I said. "This is better. Me, a shadow. You—a glow."

"Why is it better?"

"Because this way," I whisper-rasped, "I can actually tell you how I feel. Not by writing the words, but by speaking them in my Very. Own. Voice." Or a hoarse facsimile thereof.

"You sound so different now! Nothing like the day Marcos hit the golf ball through my window."

"Because I'm not speaking Pidgin English?"

"I don't know . . ."

"I think I do. It's because tonight . . . for the first time . . . I'm not scared."

"What were you scared of? Me?"

"You *laughing* at me."

"I wouldn't laugh."

I thought of my chapped, runny nose . . . my shaggy hair and straggly sneakers . . . my broken inventions and broken friendships. "How could you not laugh at a big, hulky guy trying to act sensitive, romantic?"

"I'm *not* laughing."

"I know."

"So what do you want to tell me?"

"Everything!" I stretched out my arms, my hands pressing flat against the pyramid to soak in her warmth. "How I dream about you every night . . . how you're the first thing I think of when I wake up in the morning. Who needs an alarm clock when your name is the sweet bell that rings within me all day: *Hayley, Hayley, Hayley* . . ."

"What else?" she whispered.

"I want to tell you how even the smallest things about you stick in my mind. Like the way your chin tips when you're angry or defiant. How your Squint of Suspicion dares every-one to 'fess up—or move on. And your hair . . ."

"My *hair*?"

I laughed. "Last Memorial Day, May thirtieth, you got a new haircut, remember? You hated it. You swore you wouldn't remove your Gadabout cap for a year. But when I saw you . . ." I closed my eyes, smiling at the memory. "It's like after someone takes your picture using a camera flash. You know how everywhere you look you see only splashes of blinding white? Your hair was that flash. And for at least an hour I saw only splashes of blond . . ."

"Last *May*? But how did you—"

"And now, even in the dark, I see that splash again, Hayley. *Hayley!* You're a brilliant sun in some rare, distant galaxy. And I'm a tiny planet orbiting you, gazing at you, glowing in your reflected brilliance for a million millennia. That's all right for now. It's all I need. There's just one other thing I want—"

"A . . . kiss?"

"What?"

I jolted from my trance. The coarse concrete scraped my back. "No! I can't. *We* can't—"

"I just wondered what it'd be like. It would be . . . my first."

Mine too.

I closed my eyes again and saw Hayley's face and my head whirled in an orbit of words until—

And what is the first kiss
I'd give to you?
A secret blurted
without words—
The cautious dot

over the i *of* Risk—
A whispered "Yes!"
to a wished-for question—
An X to mark the treasure
on love's unfolding map—
My autograph on our story
yet unwritten.

When the last syllable had floated into the sky, I realized, to my shock, that the words, the poem, had come from me.

I heard a creaky sigh. Or maybe it was the creak of a windmill vane. Or the front gates . . .

"Hayley? Hayley! Are you out here?"

Hayley yelped in stark white panic, *"It's. My. Dad!"*

"Eep!" I scrambled to my feet.

"Hide!" Hayley ordered.

In two leaps I launched myself across the path and through the tiny window of the Windmill, landing on my shoulder with a painful *oooof.*

Yuck. I'd hidden in the Windmill once before (that's another story), but I'd forgotten its aroma of mummified hot dogs, stale cat pee, and dust.

I buried my nose in the collar of my shirt and tried not to sneeze.

"Hayley!" Mr. Barker called again. "Are you out here?"

I heard a scrabbling from the Pyramid . . . the crunch of gravel . . . the jingle of pocket coins.

"Yes, Daddy! Over here!"

Heart thudding, I peeked through the window.

A flashlight beam swept past my face.

I ducked.

"There you are, Peach! What are you doing out here this time of night? I went to fix a snack and—"

"I'm sorry I worried you, Daddy." Hayley's words trembled. "I woke up too, and realized I—I'd forgotten to lock Gadabout's gates. Then I heard a noise. I thought raccoons were rummaging through the Snack Shack trash cans again."

"It's pitch-black out here! Why didn't you turn on the lights?"

"I didn't think—I mean, it's such a beautiful evening . . ."

"Chilly, is what it is. You're shivering! Let's go inside. You should've put on that pretty new sweatshirt you bought with Goldie. It does wonders for your eyes—even in the dark." I could hear the teasing smile in Mr. Barker's voice.

"The sweatshirt! I got hot and took it off. I left it in the Snack Shack. I'll get it. Meet you outside the gates, okay?"

"Here, take the flashlight."

I heard the fading crunch of footsteps . . . the squeak of the Windmill . . . a moat frog gargling.

Then a whisper: *"Cullen! Cullen, where are you?"*

I didn't answer. I took sips of breath and hoped Hayley couldn't hear the battle drums of my heart.

"If you're still here, Cullen, wait ten minutes before you leave, okay? I'll leave the gates unlocked so you can get out."

I still didn't answer.

"*I hope to see you again someday. I still have so much to tell you. Maybe when I'm older—*"

"Let's go, Hayley!" Mr. Barker called. "It's late!"

Hayley's last, sad whisper pierced the night air—and my heart. "*Aloha, Cullen.*"

I lifted my head and watched the flashlight beam bob up the path.

Chapter Twenty-four

"Where on earth did I put my car keys?" Mom mumbled the next afternoon as she rifled through her gargantuan purse.

I checked my watch. 1:33 p.m. Joonbi's party had started at 1:00. Because of Mom, I was late. As usual.

If only I could be late enough to miss the entire party. After last night, I didn't feel much like celebrating. Or seeing Hayley. Or anyone else, for that matter.

"I should just stay home," I said aloud.

"Nonsense, I'll find them!" Mom dumped her purse contents onto the kitchen table.

"But my knee really hurts," I said, hobbling a bit for effect. "Maybe it's broken." I told Mom I'd injured it yesterday afternoon at hapkido. Actually, I'd banged it last night while diving through the Windmill's window.

Mom laughed. "You've been hanging around Mr. Hypochondriac too long. Your knee is *bruised*—not an acceptable excuse for bailing on a party at the last minute."

"What is, then?" I asked.

"Death. And perhaps bleeding from the eyes. Ah-ha!" Mom dangled her keys like a noisy wind chime. She swept the remaining detritus into her purse. "Got your towel and Joonbi's gift? Then let's roll!"

"I have tons of homework due on Monday," I said, trailing her to the garage. "Isn't homework an acceptable excuse?"

"Not today it isn't. Today you're going to *socialize*. School's been in session almost two weeks, and you haven't spent time with any of your friends."

Maybe because all my friends bug me, I thought, slamming the car door. *And vice-versa.*

Twenty-five minutes later, Mom nosed Dad's Cad into the packed parking lot of the Lemon County Country Club.

"I'll never find a spot, let alone one big enough for this boat," Mom said. "What's going on? Are all these people here for Joonbi's party?"

"Probably," I said. "She's famous." Then I noticed a banner hanging above the Club's entrance.

VARSITY GOLF TOURNEY TODAY!
LEMON COUNTY LEAGUE WELCOMES
PATRICK HENRY AND
THOMAS PAINE HIGH SCHOOLS

"That explains it," Mom said. "Hop out, sweetie. I'll be back at four. Slather that chapped nose with sunblock, stop looking like you're on your way to an execution, and *have fun!*"

Dad's Cad careened away.

A uniformed guy offered a starched greeting and opened

213

the club's massive doors for me with a flourish. When I asked him how to find the pool, his white-gloved hand pointed *that-a-way*.

My flip-flops sank into thick rich carpet as I hurried through the lobby. Another uniformed guy opened another set of massive doors that led to a cobblestone patio overlooking the velvety-green sea of golf course. Club members sat admiring the view, drinking from tall, frosty glasses. I followed the cobblestones along a meandering path. From behind a prickly hedge came the shrieks and splashings of toddlers.

A diving board towered above me. Tied at the top was an immense cluster of balloons in electric stomach-turning magenta and bird-poop-yellow colors. The balloons yanked against their strings in a vain attempt to escape.

Joonbi met me at the gate. She wore a swimsuit that matched her shell-pink manicure—and a look of desperation in her red-rimmed eyes.

"I'm sorry I'm so late," I said, holding out her gift. "Happy birth—"

"Steve!" She pinched my arm. Her ponytail quivered. "I was afraid you weren't coming! Truth!"

"My mom is Time Impaired, remember?" Then I realized she'd been crying. "Hey, what's wrong?"

"My party is a Grade A Disaster!" She launched into a soliloquy, the usual lilt in her voice squashed flat, as if steamrollered. "I've had an awful stomachache since breakfast. I don't know if it was the cheese omelet or seeing those . . . those wretched decorations! I begged Umma to let me have a party *for once* that didn't include my sisters. She agreed, but then let *them* do all the decorating! Steve, they chose the dorkiest, most putrid stuff, just to humiliate me! And your friends, they're not talking to each other or swimming or eating or anything! I can't bear two more hours of this. Truth!"

I scanned the pool area. "Where are the rest of the guests? Aren't any of your other friends here yet?"

"I just moved here! I don't have any other friends! Just you—and yours."

"What about the students from Hapkido Family Fitness? The ones mobbing you for your autograph and stuff?"

"Fans aren't friends, Steve. *Please help!*" She towed me across the hot cement to an area shaded by wide umbrellas and arranged with chairs, lounges, and a cooler filled with iced drinks. A teak table nearby was laden with untouched bowls of chips, dips, and platters of fruit and veggies.

In the center of a larger table, surrounded by gifts, sprawled a massive sheet cake slathered in bird-poop-yellow frosting with clumps of electric-magenta sugar roses. More indigestion-causing balloons cascaded in grape-like bunches from the hedge. Plates and cups, featuring cartoons of frolicking kittens exclaimed: *WHEEEEEE! NOW YOU ARE 3!* Someone had drawn the numeral 1 in black marker in front of the 3 to create a crude 13.

"I hate my sisters," Joonbi said.

I felt a sudden wash of empathy for Hiccup—and gratitude to my parents for thirteen years of blissful only-child status.

"Hi guys," I said, barely noticing Hiccup, Goldie, Pierre . . . Where was . . . ?

There.

Hayley sat munching a carrot stick. Dark circles rimmed her eyes. She wiggled the carrot at me and offered a pale smile.

My legs locked. My knees quivered like Jell-O.

"Wow," I said, my eyes blinded by her splash of blond hair, the flash of her steel-blue swimsuit. "You look . . ."

"What?" Her SOS challenged.

"Ready for a swim," I finished lamely.

Another pale smile. "Later. I just ate a carrot."

"Yeah, me too. I mean, I think I'll try one!" I reached for the platter, almost stepping on Ace's foot. He lay on a towel between Hayley's chair and the water's edge.

"Watch it," he muttered from beneath a large sombrero.

Was his pinky toe touching the leg of Hayley's chair?

"*Sneeze! Dah*-ling!"

Goldie wore a gold lamé bikini, saucer-sized glitzy sunglasses, and a glossy tan she obviously obtained from a jar. She beckoned from where she reclined in an OPSP: Optimal Pool-Spying Position.

"This party"—she pouted—"is *so* not fun!"

"Why don't you try having some, then?" Ace said.

Goldie leaned to tip him into the water.

"Don't even think about it," he intoned.

She jerked back and continued her pout. "I was led to believe this was an *exclusive* club. But I have yet to see *one single celebrity*."

Joonbi's eyes pleaded with mine.

"So!" I blurted, shedding my T-shirt, tossing my towel on a vacant chair. "I'm ready for that swim now! Who's with me? Doesn't the pool look refreshing?" I gestured like a game show host at the glittering water. It lapped in a lagoon of pale aqua ripples.

"Oh, puh-*leeze*," Goldie said. "This swimsuit is not for *swimming*. It's not even water-resistant!"

Hayley snorted.

"Hector, how about you?" I asked politely. "Want to take a dip?"

He stiffened. One side of his face was covered in a weird, blistery rash. "It is unwise for a patient with *hic!* shingles to engage in water activities," he replied. "In addition, have you forgotten that chlorine causes an unsightly inflammation of my ep*hic!*dermis? How imbecilic of me! Of course you've *hic!* forgotten. We have only known each other *ten years*!"

"Uh, right," I said, trying not to rise to his bait, trying not to regret my decision about the book contracts. "Pierre, is your epidermis sea-worthy?"

"Eye zink not." He pointed to an armband fashioned out of black electrical tape. "Eye am, 'ow you say, pining."

"Pining?" Goldie said. "What are you, a tree?"

"Eye am mourning zee loss of my senses." Pierre whisked off his beret and held it against his bare chest in the vicinity of his heart. "What a fool eye wuz, falling for zee likes of July! But zen, as a wize French poet once said: '*Afflicted by love's madness, all are blind.*'"

"He wasn't French," Ace's hat murmured.

"Who wasn't?" Goldie asked.

"Sextus Propertius. The Roman poet."

"Ace!" Hayley said. "You've been reading love poems?"

He shrugged. But *two* of his toes were now touching her chair . . .

"Cake!" I shouted, and lunged for the box of birthday candles, "accidentally" trodding on the toes touching Hayley's chair. "Time to eat cake!"

"Eez zat what zat eez," Pierre said with a sneer.

Joonbi started to cry. "I know, I know! The cake is horrible—and so is my party. Truth!" She dropped onto a lounge, swiping at tears with the corner of a fluffy beach towel. "Go ahead. Leave if you want. I'll understand! You can call your parents to pick you up. There's a phone in the snack bar."

"No need!" Goldie dug into a sequined beach bag. "I've got my cell!"

Hayley shook her head vehemently, the golf ball earrings swinging. Her chin tilted and her words were defiant: "*None* of us want to go home, Joonbi."

Goldie's mouth popped open, fish-like, but Hayley kicked her in the beach bag and the mouth closed again.

"And we all love pink cake," Hayley continued. *"Don't we?"*

Hiccup hic-spluttered. I could tell he was conflicted between saying *yes* to ease Joonbi's pain and *no* to eating frosting made with partially hydrogenated oils and Red Dye No. 2.

"Pink flavor is my favorite!" he finally said. "May I have the honor *hic!* of cutting the first slice for the Birthday Girl?"

"No, thanks," Joonbi said. A tear slid down her cheek and onto her trembling lips. "I have a stomachache."

"You are still *hic!* ill?" Hic asked. "Your physician has provided no relief?"

"Let's talk about something else, Hector. Nobody wants to hear about my health problems."

"*I* do. What was your physician's *hic!* diagnosis?"

"You really want to hear about this? Truth?"

"Tru*hic!*uth," he answered.

"Okay." Joonbi swiped at her eyes again. "Well, first my doc suspected an ulcer."

"Discounted after a course of ant*hic!*biotics, yes?"

"Yes! How did you know?"

Hic smiled. "Go *hic!* on."

"Then he thought I had a condition called IBS."

"Yes, yes. Irritable Bowel *hic!* Syndrome."

"You know what IBS is?" Joonbi asked, impressed.

Hiccup hic-shrugged. "It's prevalent in our *hic!-hic!* hectic society. Even Tony Sandoval, the school *hic!* nurse at Jefferson, has been afflicted with it."

Ace sat up abruptly. His sombrero tumbled into the pool.

He peered at Hic over the top of his sunglasses, then stood, stretched, and sauntered to mutter something in Hic's ear.

"Are you *hic!* positive?" Hiccup asked.

Ace tossed him a *you-dare-to-doubt-me?* expression.

Hic's blistered face brightened. "Excuse me *hic!-hic!* a moment."

He bolted to the snack bar.

I dispatched a silent *What-did-you-tell-him?* to Ace.

He shrugged, sauntered back to his towel, and lay down again.

Moments later Hic returned, a newfound confidence in his walk and words.

He cleared his throat. "Tell me more about your intestinal condition, Joonbi," he said, snatching Goldie's notepad and pen from her hands.

"Hey!" she cried, but he paid no attention.

"So then," Joonbi went on, "Umma got me an appointment with a gastroenterologist, who decided it wasn't IBS, after all."

"He has also ruled out colitis, pancreatitis, appendicitis, and diverticulitis?"

"That's right!"

"Mm-hm. Mm-hm." Hiccup jotted a few notes. "Allow me to research this. I'll get back to you posthaste."

"Surelee," Pierre said, "zee doctor 'as already left no 'eye-tis' unturned?"

With an exaggerated yawn, Goldie reached for her cell phone again.

"Presents!" I suggested. "Joonbi, do you want to open your presents?"

"Ooo, *yes!*" Goldie squealed, the cell phone forgotten. "You'll *adore* mine. Open it first!" She dangled a tiny mesh bag with silken drawstrings.

Joonbi peeked inside. "A gift certificate from the Primp and Preen Day Spa. For a complete makeover! Ha, this isn't a hint, is it?

"Why, *yes,*" Goldie said. "Yes, it is."

"Open mine next," said Hayley.

Joonbi tore open the thin box. "Another gift certificate! This one's for four free rounds at Gadabout Golf. That's the place your family owns, right? Cool!"

"*Pfff!*" Goldie pfffed.

"Thanks, Hayley," Joonbi said. "I've never played mini-golf before. Is it hard?"

"Some of Gadabout's holes are tricky, especially the Volcano. But I'd be happy to give you a few pointers."

Joonbi ripped into the rest of her gifts. There was a French-Korean cookbook from Pierre ("Wis not a single reci-pee containing see-weed!" he boasted); a birthday card from Ace that read *No Presents Except My Presence*; a hapkido belt holder from me and—

Joonbi gasp-yipped. "Thank you, thank you, Steve!" She pulled me into a strangling hug. "But I thought you weren't going to write another one!"

"Another what?" I said, trying to detangle and de-strangle myself.

221

Hiccup cleared his throat. "Actually, Stephen had nothing to do with what's in that box. *I* wrote it."

"You wrote what?" I asked.

"The book."

"What book?"

"That book."

"*This* book!" From within layers of delicate tissue, Joonbi lifted a small, stapled booklet with a blue construction paper cover.

Hic nodded. Then, ears pinking, he discovered his immense feet to be of immense interest.

"What did he write?" Hayley asked.

All five of us peered over Joonbi's shoulder. She cradled the booklet in the palms of both hands.

Aloud, Ace read: *"101 Ways to Bug Your Brothers and Sisters. For Joonbi Park. Written and illustrated by Hector Denardo."*

Chapter Twenty-five

"I'm glad *someone* understands the *orthodontic* importance of a book like this!" Goldie said, her eyes shooting me harpoons.

"I think you mean *mastodonic,* Goldie," I said.

"What*ever.*" She slipped her sunglasses to the top of her head to read Hiccup's pamphlet over Joonbi's shoulder. "Hiccup, this list is an absolute *scream!* Number twelve is to *die* for. Number seventeen is to *double-decker die* for!"

"*Oh-hoh-hoh-hoh-HO!*" Pierre agreed, laughing through his nose, his pining apparently at an end. "Feest zee eyes on numbaire twenty-zree! My leetle brothaire will finally get eez comeuppityance!" He kissed Hiccup on both cheeks. "Eye saloot you, mon ami!"

"Interesting," Ace observed. "He was never your friend *before.*"

Joonbi flung her arms around Hiccup, grinning impishly and squeezing him so hard he burped. The air smelled momentarily like salad dressing.

"This is the most hilarious thing I've ever read!" she said. "It's even funnier than *Bug Your Parents.* Thank you, Hector.

I feel so much better! Even my stomach doesn't hurt as bad. Truth!"

"You are most welcome," Hic replied with a solemn bow. But he could barely conceal the grin tugging at his lips.

"I smell a *best seller*!" Goldie said. "Hiccup, I hope you plan to sell this book *immediately* to the Ridiculous Reads Publishing Company—unlike *someone else* who shall remain *nameless*."

Gosh, could she mean little ol' me?

"My desire, first and foremost, was to write this book for Joonbi," Hic admitted. "But perhaps I should consider selling it."

Whoa. Had I heard that right?

"*Oooo*, you'll be *famous*!" Goldie said.

"Notoreeeous!" Pierre agreed.

"You'll have a grand, flatulent lifestyle!"

"*Affluent* lifestyle," I corrected absently, still sort of shocked by Hic's words.

"What*ever*."

"But Steve," said Ace. "This is your idea."

"It is and it isn't."

"But the idea of writing a book about bugging—"

"Ideas can't be copyrighted," I said, trying to ignore the pang of—what?—in my chest. "And I don't have any siblings. It wouldn't make sense for me to write that list. So Hiccup can do whatever he likes."

Hic avoided my eyes but responded with another bow.

"Zen, tray magnifique! Eet shall be so!" Pierre clutched his rib cage, gasping in paroxysms of glee. "*Oh-hoh-hoh!* Read numbaire eighty-two! Eet. Eez. Too. Much!"

While Ace, Goldie, and Pierre clustered closer to Hic and Joonbi, Hayley motioned for me to join her at the other side of the pool.

"I can't believe you're not furious with Hector," she said.

"Naw. Just . . . disappointed."

"Disappointed?" She fixed me with an intense SOS. "Stephen J. Wyatt, tell me the truth. Why did you turn down that four-book contract?"

A shadow fell across us from behind. "I want to know too," Ace said.

"I'll tell *you* if you tell *me*."

He straightened his sunglasses. "Tell you what?"

"Forget the innocent act, Ace. What did you whisper to Hic that made him rush off to the snack bar?"

He shrugged. "Not much. Just to ask the waiter for a tablespoon of . . . balsamic vinegar."

"Balsamic vin—?" Then I remembered. "When Hic rejoined us, he wasn't hicking anymore, was he? Tony's cure— it works! But Ace, how did you know . . . ?"

A smile jerked his lips—then vanished.

"You!" I began. "*You* were outside the nurse's office that day when Hayley pretended to have the hiccups! You *and* Goldie overheard Tony talking about the vinegar! You led Goldie away from the door, *didn't you?*"

He shrugged again, but I knew I was right.

"You like Hiccup, don't you, Ace," Hayley said.

Another shrug. "Always have."

Hayley hid a smile and nudged me. "The contract . . . ?"

"Okay, okay," I said. "But both of you have to promise never to breathe a word of this to anyone."

Hayley crossed her heart.

Ace mimed sticking a needle in his eye.

I took a breath. "I said no to the publisher because he wanted to publish my books without Hiccup's illustrations."

Hayley gasped. "Why didn't you tell Hic?"

"We're not exactly, uh, speaking these days."

"But he is—was—your best friend! He wouldn't want you to turn down that kind of opportunity because of him."

"That's the other reason I didn't say anything." I sat at the pool's edge, dangling my feet in the water. "It's been Hiccup's dream to get his cartoons published. How could I tell him the publisher thinks his art is no good? Especially when I think it is. I mean, he worked hard helping me research *101 Ways to Bug Your Parents*. And his cartoons, they enhanced the list, made it funnier."

Hayley sat to dangle her feet too, her sun-warmed arm touching mine, prickling the hairs there.

Ace moved to join us.

"You like Hiccup, don't you, Steve," Hayley said.

"Always have." I splashed her with my foot.

She laughed and splashed back.

Ace froze. His dark brows arced as if he was seeing something, seeing *us* for the first time. Without a word, he turned and headed for the high dive.

Hayley watched him go, then bent to twiddle her fingers in the water. "By the way," she murmured, her lips hidden by the curled C of her hair. "Now that Ace is gone, I can tell you. You won't need to forward e-mails from Cullen anymore."

I couldn't look at her. "How come?"

"He—we—decided it was best not to write each other anymore."

I swallowed. "I'm sorry, Hayley. I know you really liked—him."

"Yeah, well, thanks for being such a good friend. I never would've learned what an amazing writer Cullen is, what an amazing person Cullen is, if it wasn't for you."

"Yeah," I said.

Goldie let out a shrill whistle. One arm waved like a palm tree in a hurricane as she pointed to the high dive.

Hayley squinted into the glare and I shielded my eyes as we watched Ace scale the steep metal rungs of the high dive. Up, up, up he went. When he reached the top, he parted the mass of balloons, sauntered the length of the board, bounced thrice with wide circular arm motions, and then—

—launched into a perfect jackknife dive.

When he hit the water, it barely splashed. He surfaced two seconds later, sunglasses still in place.

Goldie, Hiccup, Pierre, and Joonbi clapped, hooted, and whistled.

"Did you know he could do that?" I asked. "I didn't know he could do that!"

"There's a lot about Ace we don't know," Hayley said.

Huh. There's a lot about a lot of people you don't know . . .

She squinted again at the high dive. "Those are the ugliest balloons ever. If I were Joonbi, I'd hate my sisters too!"

"Maybe we should get rid of them for her. The balloons, not her sisters."

Hayley leaped to her feet. "Great idea. Race you to the top!" She shot up the ladder, a steel-blue rocket aiming for the stars.

I made it as far as the second rung. High altitudes cause my stuffed nose to pound. "Can you untie them?" I called. "Or do you need scissors?"

"I'll just pop them! Oh, Stephen, you've got to come up here! The view is amazing! I can see Hiccup and Joonbi— they're sitting together, talking! And I can see the tennis courts and the lawn bowling area and the riding stables and the golf course and—"

She faltered. Stuttered.

"What?" I said, inching to the third rung. "What else do you see?"

Then I heard it.

The squeal. That serrated, girly-girl squeal:

"I SEE CULLEN!"

Chapter Twenty-six

Hayley streaked down the ladder, practically landing on my head. "Cullen's on the golf course!" she said. "He's playing golf!"

Varsity Tournament Today . . . Lemon County Welcomes . . .

"Where?" I asked.

"I just told you! On the golf course! There!" She pointed beyond the hedge. "He's with the goons and another team. There's a huge crowd!"

Patrick Henry and Thomas Paine High Schools!

Oh no.

OH NO.

I grabbed Hayley's hand. "What are you going to do?"

"I want to watch him play. I want talk to him. For real this time, face-to-face!"

"But I thought you two decided—"

She shook off my hand. Sped away.

I sped after her at warp speed, slip-sliding on the wet concrete.

The lifeguard blew a whistle. "Walk, please!" she hollered. *"WALK!"*

"Yeah, fine, no problem!" I slowed to a speedy stroll until some guy accidentally distracted the lifeguard by canon-balling atop two preschoolers.

I kicked into warp again. "Hayley, wait!"

She was yanking on shorts and shirt over her bathing suit . . . stuffing her feet into sneakers . . .

Another whistle blast.

Goldie's ESP (Extra-Snoopy Perception) bristled to attention. "Is there a fire? A celebrity sighting? What's going on?" she demanded.

"Nothing!" Hayley said. "I just saw—a friend. I need to talk to him."

"*Him?* You mean he's a *he*? A *guy*?" Goldie snatched her notepad from the table. "That means only one thing: *Cullen Fu Handsome!*"

Hayley flung open the gate, tore along the path.

"This is a bad, *bad* idea," I said, catching her at last.

"Why?"

"Because . . . because . . ." I floundered for a plausible explanation. "You might fluster him! Ruin his concentration!"

"I'm not an idiot." Hayley dodged two elderly ladies in tennis togs. "I just want to watch him play. I won't talk to him till *after* the tournament."

I heard a stampede behind me. Hic, Pierre, Ace, and Joonbi were charging down the golf cart path, Goldie in the lead.

"They're playing the eighteenth hole," Joonbi said. "That means the tourney's almost over. Which team are we rooting for?"

"Zee burgundee boyz," Pierre said.

Hayley had reached the crowd. "I can't see anything from back here!" She snaked in between onlookers, ducking an elbow here, a camera bag there.

I serpentined in her wake, Goldie & Co. in tow.

"Ooo, it *is* him!" Goldie squealed. "Cullen Fu Handsome!"

"Shhhhhhhhh!"

A cluster of spectators glared at us, fingers to their lips.

"Sorry," Hayley whispered. "Sneeze, can you see Cullen? Did he take his shot yet?"

The crowd burst into polite applause.

Hiccup stretched on tiptoes. "He just sunk his putt."

Hayley danced a little jig. *"Yes!"*

I peered around a she-bear of a woman wearing a sun visor, and caught a glimpse of Cullen as he plucked his ball from the hole. He waved it at the crowd. They burst into applause again. She-bear and Hayley clapped hardest of all.

"Who's winning?" Hayley asked her. "Do you know Cullen Fu Hanson's score?"

The woman turned. She was a dead ringer for Cullen, only prettier and less muscley. And sans the triangle goatee.

Auntie!

"You know my Cullen?" Auntie asked, smiling.

Hayley nodded. "Is he your son?"

"Nephew." Auntie's voice swelled with pride. "He pau now. Shot under par today. Da team captain, he go next. To win, he need to sink dis short putt. Den we go to state championship. Piece of cake, eh? Hush, now. Here he come."

Marcos the Moke.

My stomach squirmed. I hadn't been this close to him since that day at Lickety-Split Chick.

He selected a club from his bag, gave a thumbs-up to the crowd, and strutted onto the green. His ball lay about three feet from the hole.

Piece of cake, indeed. I'd sunk a million shots like this at Gadabout. There was no way Marcos could miss—even blindfolded.

He made a big production anyway, to keep the crowd in suspense and himself in the spotlight. First he hunched, eyeing the hole while stroking his chin. Next he placed his club on the ground to measure the miniscule distance. Then he removed his cap to scratch his scarecrow hair and stroked his chin again.

"If he licks his finger and checks the wind direction," Hayley muttered, "I'm going to scream."

"You're so tall, Hector," Joonbi whispered. "Can you tell me what's happening? I can't see a thing!"

"There is ample space right here," Hiccup said. He took her hand and helped her wedge into the spot directly in front of me.

The inky tuft of her ponytail tickled my nose.

"Uh, Joonbi, could you move to your left just a tad?"

Marcos stood over the ball, club grasped in his hands.

I scrubbed at my nose. "Joonbi, your pontytail—"

Marcos wiggled his butt. Glanced at the hole. Glanced at the ball. Hole, ball, hole, ball . . .

The crowd held a collective breath.

Another butt wiggle.

Another fierce nose tickle.

And then—

I tried to hold back. Honest, I did. I pinched my nostrils and sucked in a breath so hard that I almost absorbed Joonbi's entire head, but as Marcos attempted to tap the ball—

"AHHHHH-*CHOOOOOEY!*"

Marcos twitched.

The ball arced—

and rolled past the hole.

Half the crowd released a collective moan. The other half clapped, cheered, and shook hands with the team from Thomas Paine High.

Marcos's face paled. Then it darkened to cherry punch . . . roasted eggplant . . . black death . . .

He let out a roar.

"I recognize that sneeze! *Where is he? Where is that snot-nosed punk!*"

"Eep!" I tried to edge backward, but my legs turned rubbery like overcooked spaghetti.

I saw a club sweep high—and charge.

People squealed, shouted, scattered . . .

"YOU ARE SO DEAD!" Marcos screamed.

Chapter Twenty-seven

Run! my brain ordered my legs. *Run—or die!*

The next thing I remember, I was dangling from a thick tree limb, heart pounding, chest heaving, my hands and ankles clutching for dear life. Marcos raged below, cussing, grunting, flailing with his club to whomp me like I was a human piñata.

"Mr. Mathias!" a voice shouted.

Marcos swung and missed again. He bellowed in frustration.

I hugged the limb tighter, the bark scraping my cheek.

"Mr. Mathias, *stop right now.*"

"No!"

"Put the club down. You're embarrassing yourself! You're embarrassing our team. You're disgracing Patrick Henry High."

"I don't care!" Marcos stabbed at me with a finger. "This punk cost me the game, Coach! He ruined my chance at the championship! If he hadn't sneezed, I would've sunk that shot. He messed with me on purpose! He's a sneaky, snotty, conniving—"

"That's enough." The coach's tone left no room for nego-
tiation. "Leave him alone and come with me. *Now.*"

Marcos spat a curse word, flung his club to the grass, and
stormed toward the clubhouse.

"You okay, kiddo?" the coach asked, peering at me upside
down. "Did he hurt you?"

I gulped. Licked my lips. Croaked: "I'm—okay."

"Do you need help getting out of that tree?"

"Yep." My hands and feet felt permanently bonded to the
limb.

Something brushed the tips of my straggly hair.

"Relax your feet, Stephen," Hayley advised, gently touching my head again. "Uncross your ankles. Then relax your
legs."

I did as I was told.

"Relax da fingers," Cullen added. "First one. Den da others. No worries. I got you, *menehune.*"

I let go.

His massive arms caught me around the waist, eased me
to the ground, steadying me as the blood rushed to my head.

"You aw right?" he asked.

"Yeah." I took a dizzy step. "Thanks."

"Yes, thank you, *Cullen . . .*" Hayley said, her voice filled
with Sigh.

No-oh-no. Panic washed over me again. Hayley and Cullen
were standing mere molecules away from each other!

"Time to leave, Hayley," I said, yanking her arm.

"Ow. Let go."

The coach patted my shoulder. "I'm sorry about Mr. Mathias, kiddo. Inexcusable behavior. Inexcusable." He shook his head. "Mr. Hanson, excellent game. You played very well. We'll talk later. I need to make sure Marcos doesn't leave the country club before he and I have a little chat."

The coach left.

I yanked at Hayley again. "Time to—"

But Joonbi, Hiccup, and the rest of the gang clamored around me.

"Are your muscles and tendons sprained or sore?" Hic asked, his face pale, frightened. "I insist you receive immediate medical attention! And it would behoove you to remember RICE: Rest, Ice, Compression, and Elevation." He patted my shoulder, my arm, my back, my shoulder again.

"I'm okay, Hic. Really."

"I'm so embarrassed," Joonbi said, hanging her head. "All my years of training, and I did nothing! When that guy charged at you, I should've taken him down. But he looked crazy and he came at you so fast! Father will be disappointed in me."

"Sparring in the safety of a *dojang* is far different from an authentically dangerous situation such as this," Hiccup assured her. "None of us realized Marcos's intent, nor his insanity, until too late."

Joonbi beamed a grateful smile.

"What a *super-duper scoop*!" Goldie yelped, scribbling into her notepad. "I can see the headline now: *Golf Tourney Lost by a Nose! Team Captain Goes Bananas; Tries to Bludgeon Brainy Bugging Boy!*"

"Yeah, about that," I said to Cullen. "I'm really, really sorry about the sneeze. I feel awful. I can't believe it. I lost the game for your team! I—I don't know what to say. The championship . . . your scholarship!"

"Yeah, das one big bummahs, man." He made a face. Twirled his club. Gazed out at the eighteenth hole and sighed. "But . . . not your fault, brah. Part of da game is grace under pressure. Sneezes happen. Mistakes happen. Either you learn from dem, try fo' stay focused despite dem—can or no can. Marcos—he no can."

I shuddered. "I can't ever go back to my classes at Patrick Henry, can I? Marcos will kill me. I mean, you warned me not to humiliate him again—"

Cullen shook his head. "Dat moke wen humiliate himself."

"But he blames *me*."

"No worries, brah. Coach will deal. Marcos no can lay one hand on you. If he try, everyone goin' know eets him, eh?"

"I guess."

Cullen draped a heavy arm across my shoulders. "Come meet Auntie. All of you. She got one cooler full of Lappert's ice cream in da trunk of da car. Kauai pie flavor. So *ono*. Wen grind some last night and it da kine wenbrok da mout!"

"I need a translator on aisle three!" Goldie said. She

nudged Ace and whispered, "But he *is* a *dreamsicle*, isn't he? No wonder Hayley is hopelessly lost in Crushville."

Ace stuffed his sunglasses into a pocket. "Hayley likes . . . Cullen?"

"Well, *duh*."

"I thought . . ."

"*Hmph!* Don't you *ever* read my columns?"

"Not if I can help it." He glanced at Hayley, plucked a pine needle from his shirt, and sauntered up the hill.

"There is still the matter of Joonbi's birthday cake," Hiccup said. "If I understand Cullen's tropical terminology, I believe it would taste immensely ono with Auntie's ice cream."

"That's a great idea, Hector!" Joonbi said. "My sisters 'forgot' to buy ice cream for my party, but we've got millions of spoons. Let's show Auntie where to bring the cooler." She took Hiccup's hand, buzzing him back to the pool.

Everyone else started to follow. Except . . .

"Cullen!" Hayley said. "Can I . . . may I talk to you a second?"

My head swirled. My legs felt rubbery again. "No!"

"Of course she can!" Goldie singsonged, stopping to lick her fingers and flip to a fresh page of her notepad.

Hayley snorted. *"Privately."*

Goldie turned on her heel, pebbles spraying. "*Hmph!* Like I won't find out eventually," she muttered. "I always get my . . . *information*." She stomped away.

"Wat's da haps?" Cullen asked Hayley, looking polite but confused. "Uh, wot your name again?"

Hayley smiled. "You don't have to pretend, Cull. Steve knows all about us, remember?"

Cullen fingered his shark-tooth necklace and glanced at me for help.

Hot panic roiled in my stomach, raced into my throat. "Hayley," I choked. "Don't!"

But she did.

"I couldn't let things end like they did last night, Cullen. Not without you hearing how I feel too . . ."

"Last night?"

". . . especially after all the amazing things you said, the amazing things you wrote in your letters!"

"Ha? Lettas? Eh, I need fo' go now. Da ice cream stay melting . . ."

"But—"

I stepped between them. "Let him go, Hayley," I said. "He doesn't know what you're talking about."

"Of course he does. He's just pretending—"

"Auntie and da keiki stay waiting," Cullen said to me. "Aloha!" He shambled off.

Hayley moved to go after him.

"Don't." My voice cracked. "He really doesn't know."

"What do you mean?"

I squirmed. "It's almost four o'clock. My mom will be here any minute. Your dad too. I promise I'll explain everything later."

Hayley crossed her arms and shot me an SOS that rattled my soul. "You'd better explain now."

I shoved my hands into my pockets. My Gadabout keys stabbed the fingers of my right hand. I clutched at them, staring at the pebbles on the path.

"Stephen J. Wyatt."

I lifted my head. Stared deep into her eyes. Took a deep breath and said: "Cullen didn't write any of those e-mails, Hayley."

"That's ridiculous. Of course he—"

"No. He didn't."

"Then who did?"

"I did."

"No."

"I *did*."

"*No.*"

"And last night . . . at the Pyramid. That was me too."

"*No.*"

"It's true."

"*No!*"

I recited: "And what is the first kiss/I'd give to you?/A secret blurted/without words—/The cautious dot/over the *i* of *Risk . . .*"

Hayley's breath caught. Her cheeks reddened. Her hands clenched into fists.

I stood expecting, deserving, to hear her yell, scream, tear my ears off.

"Why did you do it," she said, her voice flat. "We're best friends. We care about each other. Why would you want to hurt me, make a fool out of me? Did you think it was funny? Was this your idea of a joke?"

"No, oh, no! Everything I wrote, everything I said last night was—is—true. It's just not how Cullen feels. It's how . . . I feel."

The blue of Hayley's eyes blanched with shock—and disbelief.

"It's *true*," I repeated.

She shook her head. "Then why pretend—?"

"Because Cullen didn't like you!" I confessed. "He barely remembered who you were! I just couldn't bring myself to tell you that. I didn't want you to feel what I—I mean, I didn't want you to get hurt. I wanted to save you from that. I wanted to protect you."

She snorted. "I told you before: *I. Don't. Need. Protecting*."

She turned her back on me and didn't speak for a long time. I didn't either. What else could I say?

After a couple of minutes—or a couple of hours—Hayley faced me again. She held out her hand.

A sigh burst from my chest. I moved to take her hand in mine.

She wrenched away. "Your Gadabout keys. I want them."

"What—?"

"I can't trust you anymore. I don't want you working for Daddy and me anymore. If you ever step one foot on Gadabout's property, I'll call the cops. That's not a threat, it's a promise. Got it?"

In a painful daze, I pulled the keys from my pocket. Dropped them into her open palm.

"Hayley—"

"Don't call me," she said. "Don't e-mail me. And if you see me at school, don't speak to me."

Tears pricked my eyes. "For how long?" I asked.

"For. Ever," Hayley answered.

Chapter Twenty-eight

"Are you sure you won't come with us to the movies?" Mom asked that night after dinner as she rummaged through her gargantuan purse for the car keys.

It was the third time she'd asked me. The third time I'd shaken my head.

"It's not like you to turn down a Monty Python marathon. Are you running a fever?" She touched my forehead with the back of her hand. "You've been awfully quiet."

"I've got . . . homework on my mind, Mom." Not entirely true. I just didn't want to explain why I didn't feel like laughing at funny movies.

Would I *ever* feel like laughing again?

Mom switched tactics, dangling a bribe like her rediscovered keys: "We'll get ice cream afterward . . ."

"Woman, if you eat any more ice cream during this pregnancy," Dad said, "you're going to give birth to a chocolate sundae."

"Oh, piffle." Mom tossed the keys on the counter, stuffed a squishy lumbar pillow into her purse, tugged at her stretched-to-the-limits *Spamalot* T-shirt, and kissed me on the cheek. "We'll be home around one a.m. Finish your homework, don't open the door to strangers, and please, *please* don't test any inflammatory experiments. Coming, David?" She waddled out to the garage.

"G'night, son," Dad said with a little wave.

"Uh, Dad? Aren't you forgetting something?" I plucked the car keys from the counter and held them out.

He snatched them with a wry smile. "Last chance to join us . . ."

I gave him a Look.

"Okay, okay. Just thought you might want to take your mind off a few pesky issues, like to lie . . . or not to lie."

"Not anymore."

"Did you tell your . . . friend the truth?"

"Yep."

"Good for you! How'd it go?"

I could feel my lips twist into a shrug. "About how I expected."

"I'm sorry to hear that."

Mom laid into the horn.

"Do you want me to stay so we can talk?" Dad asked. "I don't mind. I've already seen *The Holy Grail* a hundred and forty-seven times."

"No, thanks." Then, because I knew he really wanted to help me somehow, I said: "But would you bring me some ice cream?"

"What flavor?"

"Pistachio and strawberry."

"Will do!"

Mom laid into the horn again.

"Coming, Barbara, coming!" Dad said, hustling to the garage. "Honestly, woman, we're only forty-five minutes late!"

Four hours later, I lay flat on my back, fully clothed, staring at the ceiling—just as I had for the last four hours.

No, I hadn't thought about homework. I hadn't thought about anything. My brain felt barren. Benumbed.

The phone jangled and I jumped, one flailing arm knocking the Nice Alarm to the floor. The second hand broke off.

"GOLF TEES!" I shouted.

The phone jangled again. I snatched the receiver and shouted: "WHAT!"

Silence.

Then: *"Menehune?"*

"Cullen?" I flopped back down on the bed. "I didn't mean to scream at you, but I—"

"Eh, brah! Listen up already. No get much time."

Something strange and urgent in Cullen's voice wrenched my stomach. "Why are you whispering? I can barely hear you."

"I calling fo' warn you."

My neck prickled with chicken skin. "Warn me about—?"

"Marcos and his braddahs. I hear dem talkin' stink."

"What do you mean?"

"Dey plan fo' get back at you. Make plenty pilikia. Tonight."

I lurched to my feet. "They're coming after me? *Here? Now?* But my parents aren't home. I'm alone! Cullen, you said I was safe, that Marcos wouldn't try—"

I heard muffled voices through the receiver. Then scuffling, scraping sounds, like Cullen had stuffed his cell phone into a back pocket.

"Cull? Cullen!"

"Sorry. Had to hide da phone. Listen, menehune. Marcos, he one pupule—crazy—moke. But he not stupid. He not going hurt you. I tink da buggah going make pilikia at Gadabout. Warn da squint-eye girl, eh? Your ku'uipo."

"Hayley's not my—"

"No matter. Warn her. Gotta go."

"Cullen, can't you help me stop them?

"No can risk it. Eh, c'mon, wikiwiki time. Hurry!"

The call disconnected.

Hands shaking, I punched Hayley's number.

My heart th-thumped through two rings, three, four . . .

Hayley, answer the phone, Hayley!

Five rings. Six . . .

"Hello?"

"Hayleyit'smedon'thangup!"

She hung up.

I hit redial.

"Hayley, *please* don't hang—"

She hung.

I hit redial again.

"This is an emergency!" I screeched when she answered.

246

"If you won't to talk to me, fine! At least put your dad on!"

"Daddy's not here, he's on a date," Hayley said. "I'm hanging up now *for the last time.* Don't call again. I won't answer."

Click.

I slammed down the phone.

Fine, just fine.

Why am I trying to warn her, anyway? I thought as I paced the room. *Hayley doesn't need my protection. She's said so, more than once. Let Marcos and his goons do whatever they want. I've been terminated. Banished. I'm an ex-employee. Gadabout isn't my problem anymore . . .*

I flung myself into my desk chair. Flicked on my computer. Picked the Nice Alarm off the floor.

Forget her. It's not your job to be her hero. Concentrate on your homework, your inventions now. Stop. Thinking. About. Her.

But I couldn't.

When I stared at my computer screen, or at the broken alarm cradled in my hands, or even when I closed my eyes, all I could see was *Her:* Hayley as she looked that late afternoon when she climbed atop the North Pole and stood like Joan of Arc—straight and proud and beautiful in her determination to protect Gadabout.

Okay, so maybe she wore cut-off jeans and a steel-blue tee instead of armor. And maybe fighting for her dad's mini-golf course with the dyspeptic moat frogs and a Tower of Pisa that drooped instead of leaned wasn't as heroic as defending France.

But Hayley never did stuff to be a hero. She did stuff for

the same reason she'd stuck by me when I got inventors' block . . . and scolded me for purposely bugging my teachers in seventh grade . . . and nagged me till I agreed to take morning classes at Patrick Henry High, even though all I really wanted was to hang out at Jefferson Middle with her and Hic.

The reason?

Because it was right.

I raced to the garage, grabbed my bike, and pedaled into the night.

When I reached Gadabout Golf, all seemed normal.

Too normal.

Quiet.

Too quiet.

I stashed my bike in the bushes. Dashed the dark stairs to the Barkers' loft. As usual, the porch light was burned out. Over my heart pounding in my ears, I could just barely hear the muted music and laughter of a late-night TV show.

I rapped on the door.

No answer.

I rapped harder.

Someone lowered the TV volume . . . padded across the wood floor . . .

"Daddy? Did you lock yourself out?" A cold blue eye peered at me through the peephole. "Oh, it's *you.* Go away."

"Let me in! It's important!"

"Go away."

"Cullen warned me to warn you! He thinks Marcos and the goons are coming to make trouble at Gadabout. *Tonight!*"

She snorted. "Why would they do that?"

"Because they know we are—we *were*—friends. Cullen says they can't hurt me without casting suspicion on themselves. So they're going to hurt something I love instead: Gadabout."

"They wouldn't dare. Daddy swore if he saw them here again he'd call the cops!"

"They're not expecting to get caught, Hayley. They don't know I know! They don't know that Cullen and I became friends when—"

"When you were *pretending* to help me? *Pretending* to be *him*?"

I winced. I couldn't blame her for not believing me. After all, I'd done nothing but lie to her for the last two weeks . . .

I heard a faint crash of metal on concrete. The crash came from somewhere on the course.

I thumped the door with my fist and hoarse-whispered: *"Did you hear that? Someone's on the greens!"*

"It's raccoons. A family of 'em," Hayley explained, but her voice betrayed a hint of uncertainty. "They've been rooting around the trash cans for an hour. Go home, Stephen. Your ploy to get me to talk to you won't work."

Another metallic crash. Then the shatter of breaking glass.

"That's not raccoons, Hayley! Call the cops. Hurry!"

"What?"

"Do it! Call 911! Do it *now!*"

I turned and leaped down the stairs, three at a time, and sprinted across the gravel parking lot to the gates. Hayley had my Gadabout keys, but I didn't need them. The lock and chain had been cut.

I pushed open the gate and slipped inside, creep-running in the dark along the familiar path to the office. That lock had been cut too. The door stood ajar.

I pushed it open with my knuckles. Peered into the blackness. The still air smelled faintly of peppermint.

I didn't go in. I knew what I'd find: chairs overturned, golf clubs snapped. Pencils, score cards, and papers strewn across the floor. Crude graffiti scrawled across the walls.

I backed away. Turned at the sound of a heavy groan like that of an ancient rotting redwood dying, falling.

Then—a tremendous splash.

It had come from the direction of Hole #17. Except, there was no seventeen any longer: only a black hole in the night where the Leaning Tower of Pisa should be.

I crept-ran again, trying to tippy-toe across crunchy gravel, trying to ignore what I sensed in the darkness: broken vanes dangling from the Windmill . . . the splintered masts of the Pirate Ship . . . flattened tombstones at the Haunted Cemetery.

I came to a halt at King Arthur's Moat. Gawked at a huge bulk submerged in the murk and mud.

Marcos and his goons had toppled the Leaning Tower of Pisa.

I felt hot. Anger pricked my eyes, my neck, my arms. My fists clenched.

I had to stop them. But how? And where were they now . . . ?

Muffled laughter. A machete-like sound, hacking a trail through—

The Bungled Jungle.

I stepped off the path and took the shortcut I knew so well: through the eerie shadows of the Enchanted Forest, skirting past Little Red Riding Hood, huffing and puffing past the Big Bad Wolf, then scaling the mossy knoll to the edge of the swamp to sneak up behind the biggest, baddest wolf of them all: Marcos the Moke.

Chapter Twenty-nine

"Marcos!" I hollered. "Stop. *Stop now.*"

He whirled—and laughed when he saw me.

"Look who it is, the Snot-nosed Kid!" He lolled against his putter, calm and casual, as if ready for a relaxing game of pee-wee golf. Only the clench of his hands and the sweat trickling from his temples gave his anger away. "So! Once again you're sticking your nose where it *snot* ought to be."

"That sounds like my schnoz, all right." I tried to glimpse the damage around me—shredded palm fronds, a toucan hacked in half—without taking my eyes off him. "Where are your goons tonight, Marcos?"

"Asnooze in their roost. Chickens, all three of them. Decided to keep their noses clean. July didn't show either. Now that's a surprise. This was *her* idea." He shrugged. "No matter. How'd you know I'd be here?"

I shrugged too. "Lucky guess."

"You lie, snot-head. Cullen snitched, didn't he? He'll pay through the nose. I've left enough evidence here to finger him and only him. And with his criminal record—"

"What—what kind of evidence?" I wanted to keep him

talking so he wouldn't wreck anything else; wanted to keep him talking until the police got there. *Oh, Hayley, I hope you called the police!*

"That would be telling, wouldn't it?" Marcos bent to pick up another club. "In stereo!" he cried, and lashed out with both arms, slashing more palm fronds, hacking another toucan to feathery bits. He laughed and lashed again so hard that one putter flew from his hand, landing at my feet. With the remaining club, he splintered a grass hut.

"Cut it out!" I shouted.

"What if I don't 'cut it out'?" he taunted, panting. "You gonna fight me, Little Big Nose? Yeah? You and who else?"

"Me." Hayley strode from the dark to stand at my side.

"How sweet," Marcos jeered. "Beauty and the Beak!"

"Me." Ace appeared too, plucking a feather from his shirt.

"And I." A tall figure loomed behind Ace.

Hiccup!

A grizzly-size shadow emerged from within a tangle of ferns. "Ho!" said Cullen, arms crossed. "Me too, brah."

A police siren wailed in the distance.

"And *them,*" Hayley added with a tight smile.

Marcos's face purpled. He pointed his putter at me—and lunged.

I grabbed the putter that lay at my feet. Struck it to the left to block his attack. His club flew from his hands. He roared and bent to retrieve it, his gaze meeting mine with a frightening fury. With my club I hooked the back of his ankle—and yanked.

Marcos tumbled backward into the Swamp.

Two inches of tepid green slime seeped over his body. His head lay captured within the mossy grin of Crikey the Crocodile.

He struggled and thrashed and howled. "I'm *drowning!* Get me out of here!"

The air filled with the smell of rotting algae, Trix cereal that's been soaked in rotting algae—and peppermint.

The sirens drew closer.

Marcos thrashed again. "Brat!" he screamed. "Twerp! Snot-nosed punk—!"

I waded into the Swamp. Stood over him, club swept high.

He shrank, eyes widening with fear.

I *whooshed* the putter through the air. But at the last second, with the measured control I'd learned in hapkido, I stopped, the club hovering just above Marcos's face. And then—

—I beeped him on the nose.

"Stephen J. Wyatt," I said, "at your service."

Two hours later, the police had come and gone, taking our statements and Marcos with them.

"What will happen to him, Daddy?" Hayley asked.

Mr. Barker, who'd arrived not long after the cops, rubbed a weary hand through his curls. "There's a lot of damage," he answered with a sigh. He surveyed Gadabout from where the six of us stood atop the North Pole. "Several thousand dollars' worth, at least. Marcos is eighteen, so he'll be charged as an adult. That means he'll face jail time."

"And what," I asked, my throat dry, "will happen to Gad-about?"

Mr. Barker rubbed his head again. "We've no choice. We'll have to close completely to make repairs. It could take months. I don't know what we'll do about the Tower of Pisa. It's a total loss."

"I can help!" I said. "I can design a new Pisa for you in my CAD class. And with the right tools, I bet I can fix the stuff Marcos smashed. I'll work every Saturday and Sunday, Mr. Barker. And every holiday. And—"

"It would be an honor for me to assist, as well," Hic-cup broke in with a hapkido-ish bow. "Provided it is in a mosquito-free environment, of course."

"Yo, I'm in too," Ace said. He pinched an invisible mos-quito from Hiccup's shirt and flicked it to the ground.

"Don't know much 'bout *jungle ball*," Cullen said, fingering his shark-tooth necklace. "But my dad, he da kine carpenter. Back in small kid time, I learn my way round a hammer and saw."

"Thank you, all of you," Mr. Barker said. "I'm overwhelmed by your generosity." He pulled me into a rough hug.

I glanced at Hayley. She was wiping her eyes with the hem of her shirt. Not a blouse. A regular old *T-shirt*.

"It's late," her dad continued, "so we'll finish discuss-ing this tomorrow. Right now, you should all be home, in bed. Steve, I'll call your parents, yes? They must be back from the movies by now and worried sick about you. Where's your bike? I'll throw it in the back of my truck and take you home. Hiccup, Ace, how did you two get here?"

"We also arrived via bicycle," Hic said. "I pedaled; Ace rode on the handle bars."

I almost laughed.

Mr. Barker stifled a smile. "Fine, that's fine. Your bike can go in the truck too. Cullen? Do you need a lift?"

"No tanks. I got Auntie's car."

Mr. Barker hugged me again. "Thanks for coming to warn us, Steve," he said. "All of you. If you hadn't been here, who knows how much more damage Marcos would've done." He ruffled my hair, then headed for the parking lot. I'd never heard him walk without jingling his pocket change.

"I go too, *menehune*." Cull slapped me on the back, almost dislocating my spine. "See you tomorrow. No, *tonight*. Dinner at six sharp. No be late—or I eat all Auntie's *huli huli* chicken myself, eh?"

"Thanks for coming, Cull." I held out my hand. "You took a big risk."

My hand disappeared within his paw. "Naw. Bigger risk if I stay home."

"What do you mean?"

But he only smiled, his straight teeth gleaming white as the North Pole's snow. "Shaka," he said to Hayley and lumbered away.

"I. Am. So. Mortified," she said with an intense blush. "Mortified that he knows that I believed—that he—that we—" She blushed harder. "Oh, *golf tees!*"

"Yeah, about that." I gulped. "I'm really, really sorry."

She didn't, wouldn't look at me. She turned to Ace and Hic instead. "What I want to know is: What are *you* guys doing here? Don't take me wrong. I'm glad you came. But if Cullen didn't call you, how did you *know* to come? How did you know what Marcos was going to do? I mean, even Goldie didn't know, and she's the snoop with the scoop!"

"Ace appeared without warning on my doorstep," Hic explained. "He insisted we must make haste to Gadabout to assist you; that my hapkido skills could be useful." He frowned. "But Ace, how did *you* know Hayley needed our assistance?"

A recollection zinged my brain. *"July!"*

Hic's frown deepened. "Sneeze, the current month is *September*. The stress of this evening has obviously affected your cognizance. If you are receptive to alleviating the problem, I can provide you with a few memory-enhancing exercises, or a mnemonic device or two that would—"

"Hiccup, I meant *July Smith*. The Queen of the Clubs. Pierre's *Juliette*. Ace's sister. Am I right?"

Ace shrugged. "I overheard her making plans with Marcos on the phone. I wasn't sure she was serious. So I did the only thing I could do." He blew on the nails of his left hand, then polished them on his shirt.

"Which was . . . ?" I prodded.

"Locked her in her room."

Hayley, Hic, and I burst out laughing.

"She must be expectorating with fury!" Hiccup said, pleased.

"Don't you think it's time you let her out?" Hayley asked.

Ace shrugged. Gazed at the stars as if they were the numerals on a clock. "No." He sauntered off toward Mr. Barker's truck.

"I should assist with the bicycles," Hic said. "Steve. *Sneeze.* I am enormously relieved and . . . pleased you are uninjured."

I coughed at an odd lump in my throat. "Does this mean . . . we are friends again?"

He shoved his hands into his pockets. Hunched from his great new height to look me straight in the eye. "Friends can get mad at each other, sometimes bug each other, right?"

"Right."

"Then—I never *wasn't* your friend, Sneeze."

We both blinked. Nodded. Grinned.

"Man hug!" he cried, and pounced, crushing me, slapping my back so hard I almost coughed up a lung.

"Ow! Get off me!" I half laughed, half gasped.

"Boys!" called Mr. Barker. "Let's go!"

Hic hustled to the truck.

"Steve'll be there in a second, Daddy!" Hayley hollered. Then she faced me, fists on her hips, the SOS on red alert.

Eep.

"Why did you come tonight?" she demanded. "I fired you! I told you I never wanted to hear or see or talk to you ever again! So why did you bother to warn me about Marcos? He could've killed you, you know."

"I know," I said. "But at the time, I didn't think about that.

It didn't occur to me at all. And if it had, I would've come anyway, because . . ."

My voice trailed off. But gazing into those beautiful ice-cream-cold blue eyes, breathing in the fresh peach scent of that skin, my words continued inside my head:

Because it was right . . . because it was worth the risk . . . and because . . .

I closed my eyes and thought of:

Pierre: "disguising" himself with a ridiculous moosetache; buying carwash donuts; slaving away at Lickety-Split Chick, a place he hated more than pork rinds . . .

Hector: speaking in monosyllables, hicking in polysyllables, accusing his best-ever friend of being a traitor . . .

Ace: *reading*. Reading *textbooks*. And *Roman love poems*. And silently playing the role of guard dog . . .

Hayley: shopping with Goldie; squealing like a girly girl in equally squeal-ly clothes; believing that a gorgeous guy *surely* had gorgeous brains to match . . .

And me: pretending to be someone else because I didn't believe the someone I was would ever, could ever, be enough.

"Because," I said aloud with a grin, "sometimes love makes you do crazy things."

Epilogue

"Stephen J. Watt: You're not peeking, are you?"

Hayley's guiding hand became a boa constrictor squeeze.

"You're kidding, right?"

"Are. You. Peeking." Her SOS seared through my blindfold.

"*Ow!* Okay!" I laughed, rubbing my arm. "Yes, Hayley, I'm peeking!"

"What can you see?" she demanded.

"Not much. Just feet. So I know Goldie's here . . . and Ace and Pierre and Hector and . . . Oh! I'd recognize those shell-pink toes anywhere. Hi, Joonbi!"

She gave a lilting laugh. "You recognize my toes? Truth?"

I nodded. I could also see that she and Hiccup were holding hands.

Pierre noticed too. "May wee! 'Ave you two no 'eart? Take zis deesplay of P, D, and A outside. Eet reminds me, wis much pain, of Juliette!"

I could hear Goldie roll her eyes. "Oh, like you ever held July's hand!"

"Eye did! Eet eez zee truth!"

"Pffff!"

"Eye 'ave been eensulted! Eye challenge you to zee duel!"

"Give me that club, Pierre," Hayley said. "You know rule number one at Gadabout."

"I saw them hold hands once," Ace put in.

"You see?" Pierre's words were puffed with pride and vindication. "Please to give Goldee zee details, Ace!"

I imagined Ace's shrug. "It was a Friday. July was forced to touch his hand when she passed him a customer's bag of French fries."

"I hope you did not partake of those potatoes, Pierre," Hiccup said with a chuckle. "It is a known fact that digesting foods high in fat and salt contribute to an increased prevalence of—"

I smiled beneath my blindfold. Ah, some things never changed. While others . . . ? Well, a lot had happened in the month since Marcos the Moke vandalized Gadabout. Such as:

After round-the-clock research, Hiccup discovered the cause of Joonbi's stomachaches: a rare disorder called Eocinophilic Gastroenteritis. EG has no cure, but after Joonbi's doctor confirmed Hic's diagnosis, she was given a prescription for a new-on-the-market drug—and is feeling much better. Joonbi and Hic are now an "item" and spend every moment possible together, honing their hapkido skills and comparing notes on how to annoy their older siblings.

The editor in chief of Ridiculous Reads changed his mind

about Hiccup's illustrations. Or, rather, the editor's mind was changed *for* him. Seems the publisher and sales department thought Hic's illustrations were buggably hilarious with loads of kid appeal. So, RR made me and Hiccup an offer—and we signed on the dotted line. Keep your eyes peeled for *101 Ways to Bug Your Parents, Teachers, Friends, and Siblings*, coming soon to a gift store near you!

As for Hayley and me, well, there's only so much apologizing a guy can do. So I'd hung back, giving her space, giving her time, hoping that one day she'd come to trust me again, want to be friends again. Although, secretly, I was starting to think, starting to fear, neither would ever happen.

So I almost fell over when the phone rang that afternoon.

"Stephen!" Hayley said in her businesslike tone. "It's an emergency. Get to Gadabout. *Now*."

I dropped the receiver, clipped on my tool belt, hollered a hasty good-bye to Mom and Dad, and sped off on my bike. Now, twenty minutes later, I stood, blindfolded, inside Gadabout's musty office for the first time since the ransacking.

"Wait a sec," I said with an SOS (Squinch of Suspicion). "This isn't another surprise party for me, is it?"

Hayley snorted. "No, but it *is* a surprise! Okay, everyone, on the count of three. One . . . two . . ."

She whisked off the blindfold.

I blinked in the bright light—and gasped.

Hayley, Hiccup, Joonbi, Goldie, Ace, and Pierre stood shoulder to shoulder behind a large table. And spread across the table, sprawled a model of . . .

"*Gadabout Golf!*" I whispered.

"A *new and improved* Gadabout Golf," Hayley corrected. "Not only did Daddy get enough insurance money to repair the damage Marcos did—but to do a few major renovations as well."

I traced my finger along the miniature gravel paths . . . the teeny-tiny vanes of the Windmill . . . the powdered-sugar snow of the North Pole . . .

"Wow," I said. "It looks—"

Hayley's SOS zeroed in on my face. "It looks what?"

"Great!"

"Huh. You mean it didn't used to look great?"

"No. Yes! I mean, soon it'll be a greater great."

I touched a turret of King Arthur's Castle . . . saluted the skull-and-crossbones flag on the Pirate Ship . . . ran a hand down the sugar-cube-sized coarse blocks of the Great Pyramid . . .

"Why haven't you said anything about hole seventeen?" Hayley asked with mock innocence.

I searched for Pisa but couldn't find it. "I did the drawings in CAD. I gave them to your dad, but I don't see the tower anywhere. What happened? Were my calculations wrong? Did you have to—"

Then I gaped. Gawked. Almost cried.

Where Pisa had once leaned, there now hunched, like a boxy toad, a tiny replica of . . .

The Nice Alarm.

I beheld it for a long moment—or maybe it was an hour—before I noticed Hayley, smiling into my eyes.

"I told you it would get built," she said. "No. Matter. What."

"For thousands to enjoy," I whispered.

Goldie frowned. "It's an *alarm clock*. How does it work for mini-golf?"

"Give us a few months and we'll happily demonstrate," Hayley said. "But first, what do you think?"

Pierre removed his beret and placed it over his heart. "Well, eet eez not zee Eiffel Tower, 'owever—"

"Not *you*!" Goldie whapped him with her notebook.

"Steve . . . ?" Hayley coaxed.

I didn't need to answer. She already knew. Just like she always knew when something with me was Just. Exactly. Right.

I smiled back into Hayley's eyes and said to her—because there was only her:

"It's love at first sight."

101
WAYS TO BUG YOUR FRIENDS and ENEMIES

by Stephen J. Wyatt & Hector Denardo
illustrated by Hector Denardo

WARNING!

The authors wish it to be known that this list was created for entertainment purposes only. It is not for instruction nor is it intended to encourage you to purposely irritate your friends and/or enemies. If you are lame-o enough to attempt any of the suggestions, you do so

AT YOUR OWN RISK.

1. Sneeze all over their birthday cake so only you can eat it.
2. Steal their One True Love.
3. Write letters or e-mails to them impersonating their One True Love.
4. Gossip about them behind their back. Extra points if you submit the gossip to the school newspaper.
5. Tell him he has a unibrow.
6. Tell *her* she has a unibrow.
7. Tell him his fly is undone when you're in the middle of a big crowd of girls.
8. When you notice she has a new hairstyle, blurt: "Eww! What happened to your hair?!"
9. Show pictures of them that they hate to the person they have a crush on.
10. Don't sit next to them in class or on the bus.
11. Sit behind them in class and tap them repeatedly on the shoulder. Alternate with repeatedly kicking the back of their chair.
12. Hum or whistle under your breath when they're trying to concentrate.
13. When your class is having a slide show or PowerPoint presentation, jump up and say: "I have a question!" and block their view.
14. When the teacher asks a question, raise your hand and say: "My friend knows the answer!"

15. When a teacher asks for a volunteer, point at your friend. Extra points if you can get everyone else in class to point at your friend too.

16. Ask if you can copy their homework and/or borrow their class notes because you were too busy spending the day at a nearby amusement park.

17. Brag about your latest A.

18. Brag about your latest A even if you know they got a D or an F.

19. Never study for tests, but get A's anyway.

20. Be a teacher's pet.

21. Take the last good meal in the cafeteria so they're forced to eat Chef's Surprise.

22. Snitch food off their plate when they're not looking. (Extra points if they are looking.)

23. Have so many after-school activities that you don't have free time to hang out with them.

24. If they forgot to bring their lunch money, offer to loan them some of yours. Make them wait while you search for ten minutes, then say: "Oops! Sorry! I guess I don't have any money after all."

25. When you see them in the hall, keep stepping in front of them so they can't pass you.

26. Draw weird creatures or cutesy stuff on their binders, folders, or book covers.

27. Don't invite them to your birthday party.

28. Forget their birthday.

29. Forget what she gave you for your birthday and re-gift it to her on her birthday.

30. Tell them that the Tooth Fairy, Easter Bunny, and Santa Claus do not exist.

31. Tell them the Tooth Fairy gives you $20 a tooth when you know they only get $1.00.

32. Pull pranks on them on April Fools' Day.

33. Decide you're too old for trick-or-treating before they are.

34. If they call you when you're busy, say you'll call them right back. Then forget.

35. Give them the silent treatment.

36. Repeat everything they say.

37. Repeat everything they say.

38. Use chat-speak (LOL, OMG, BFF, etc.) in everyday conversation.

39. Send them chain letters. (Extra points if the chain letter promises them ten years of bad luck if they break the chain.)

40. Don't tell them when you're angry with them.

41. If they ask you what you're angry about, say: "I shouldn't have to tell you!"

42. Use sarcasm. Always.

43. Interrupt them when they're trying to talk.

44. Leave weird messages on their answering machine or voicemail.

45. Blurt out the punch line to a joke they're telling.

46. If they pass notes to you in class, don't write back.

47. When you're on vacation, don't send them postcards.

48. Run off as soon as they start talking about their problems.

49. Run off as soon as they ask you about your problems.

50. Keep pushing them to talk about their problems even when they've said "I don't want to talk about it!"

51. Imitate them.

52. Do bad imitations of them.

53. Click SEND on their e-mails before they're ready to send them.

54. Pick them last to be on your team. Sigh heavily and say: "I guess I choose _____." Extra points if you act like you're doing them a huge favor.

55. Don't pick them to be on your team.

56. When they're getting ready to kick, hit, throw, bat, catch, or spike a ball, shout: "Don't mess up!"

57. Show up late. Everywhere. For everything.

58. Promise to do something with them or go somewhere with them. Then forget.

59. Always bring your annoying little brother or sister along.

60. Ride so fast on your bike that you make them eat your dust.

61. When they ask what you want to do, say: "I don't know. What do YOU want to do?" When they respond, "I don't know, what do YOU want to do?" repeat the same thing back to them.

62. Never let them play the games they want to play or watch the TV shows they want to watch.

63. Get scared in the middle of a scary movie at the theater and say you have to go home. NOW.

64. Pretend to come over to hang out with them when you're really only spying on their cute older sibling.

65. Pay more attention to their cat or dog than you do to them.

66. Pay more attention to their parents than you do to them.

67. Never invite them over to your house.

68. When they spend the night, make them sleep on the floor.

69. During a sleepover, fall asleep early when you know they like to stay up late.

70. During a sleepover, wake them up early even if you know they like to sleep in late. Extra points if you poke them or put the dog/cat on their head.

71. Read their diary or journal without their permission.

72. Share what you read in their diary or journal with your other friends. Or their parents.

73. When you're going someplace in the car together, open your window and let the freezing and/or stifling hot air come in.

74. Listen to your iPod instead of to them.

75. Sing aloud to a song playing on your iPod. Extra points if you sing off-key.

76. Follow them around and narrate everything they're doing.

77. Laugh at everything they say.
78. Tell them how much fun you had when hanging out with someone they dislike.
79. When there are three of you hanging out together, make sure two of you gang up on the other one.
80. Tease them about their latest secret crush.
81. Get a crush on their mother or father.
82. Blab to everyone you know who their secret crush is.
83. Blab to their secret crush that your friend has a secret crush on them.
84. Spend more time writing notes to your One True Love than you do with your best friend.
85. Yak on and on and on about your crush and how cute he is, how wonderful he is, how fun he is, until your friend is ready to barf.
86. Race off somewhere as soon as they start yakking about their crush.
87. Sing: "(name) and (name), sitting in a tree, K-I-S-S-I-N-G! First comes love. Then comes marriage. Then comes a baby in the baby carriage!"
88. If you have braces, slurp your food really loud to get it unstuck.
89. Eat crunchy snacks when they're trying to concentrate.
90. Burp in their ear. Loudly.
91. When you're hanging out together for a whole day, get hungry when they're full and tell them you're full when they're hungry.

92. Beg them for part of their lunch. If they say no, whimper and give them the "puppy eye."

93. Smell their hair.

94. Give them stupid nicknames.

95. Name their furniture.

96. Sing the "Oscar Meyer Wiener" song, the "Meow Mix" song, or other songs they despise.

97. Make jokes about people who still sleep with stuffed animals or "blankies," completely forgetting that they still do too.

98. Squeal in a loud, glass-shattering way whenever you're excited about something

99. Move away. One point if it's to a new neighborhood; ten points if it's out of state.

100. Do everything on this list—on purpose!

101. Do everything on this list—TWICE.

A Glossary of Cullen Fu Hanson's
Pidgin Hawaiian English
(Note: Italicized words are part of the Hawaiian language)

Ada (AH-dah): Other

Aloha (Ah-LOW-ha): Hello, good-bye. It can also mean love and affection. See * on page 281

Aloha'oe: (Ah-LOW-ha oh-EE): Greetings, farewell

Ali'i (ah-LEE-ee): Hawaiian royalty

Auntie (also spelled Aunty): Aunt

Bo-da-dem: Both of them

Boddah you? (usually: "Why, boddah you?"): Does this bother you? You got a problem with it?

Buggah: a guy

Bummahs: Bummer! What a drag, that's too bad

Brah: A good friend, buddy, pal

Braddah (also spelled bruddah): Brother, dude

Brok da mout: Broke the mouth; incredibly delicious

Buss up (usually "All buss up"): Broken, busted up, destroyed

Chance 'um: Take a chance, go for it

Chicken skin: Goose bumps

Cockaroach: To steal

Crash: Fall asleep

Da: The

Da cute (usually "Ho, da cute!"): Precious, just sooooooo cute!

DA HAPS: What's up? What's happening?

DA KINE: Similar to the word *watchamcallit*, although it can mean just about anything! Da kine can be a person, place, thing, verb, adjective, adverb, or even a phrase. The speaker and the listener, however, usually understand what is being referred to.

DAT: That

DEM: Them

DEN: Then

DEY: They

DIS: This

DOZEE: Those

'EM: Them

FO' REALS?: Really? Is that so? Are you kidding me?

GEEVUM: Give it. Can also mean "go for it!"

GRIND: To eat

GRINDS: Food

HALE (HAH-leh): House, home

HANABADDAH (HAH-nah-BAH-dah): Runny nose

HANG LOOSE: Take it easy

HAOLE (hah-OW-leh): A caucasian

HO!: An exclamation used at the start of a comment about something important

HOWZIT: How are you? What's going on? What's new?

HULI HULI (HOO-lee, HOO-lee): Barbecue

JUNIOR (JOON-yah): Nickname for one's son or a younger boy

KEIKI (KAY-kee): Kid, child, children

KINE: Kind of, sort of

KOA (KOH-ah): Courage, guts

KU'UIPO (koo-OO-EE-poh): My sweetheart

LICKENS: A spanking

LIKE, LIKE FO': want to, would like to

LIKE BEEF?: Do you want to fight me?

LOLO: Crazy, loopy, looney, absent-minded

MAHALO (mah-HA-low): Thank you

MENEHUNE (meh-neh-HOO-neh): The legendary little people of Hawaii

MO BETTAH: More better, it would be better if

MOKE (rhymes with Coke): A tough local guy, a lumbering bully

NO LIKE: Don't want to

NUFF ALREADY: That's enough!

OKOLE (oh-KOH-leh): Butt

ONO (OH-no): Delicious, tasty, yummy

NO CAN: I can't; it's impossible

PAU (pow): Done, finished

PILIKIA (pee-lee-KEE-yah): Trouble, problem

RAT BITE: A bad haircut

SHAKA: All right, cool (The word is usually accompanied with a hand gesture where the thumb and pinky finger are extended while the three middle fingers are curled. Sometimes the hand is wiggled back and forth for emphasis. Other meanings include: hang loose, hello, goodbye, take care, etc.)

SMALL KID TIME: When I was little; during childhood

Sistah: Sister; a friend who is also a girl or woman

Stay: Am, are, is

Stink Eye: Mean or dirty look

Supa: Super

Talk Stink: Talking badly about someone

Talk Story: Chat, yak, talk, gossip, shoot the breeze

Ting(s): Thing, things

Wahine (wah-HEE-nay): female, girl, woman

Wass up?: What's up? What happened? What did you do? What are you doing?

Wat's da scoops?: What's happening, what's up, what's going on?

Wen: Past tense of whatever comes after it. For example; "I wen go" means "I went"

Wit: With

Wot: What

Wikiwiki (WEE-kee-WEE-kee; usually "Make wikiwiki" or "wikiwiki time"): Fast, speedy, quick

*THE MEANING OF ALOHA:

"And wherever [the native Hawaiian] went he said 'Aloha' in meeting or in parting. 'Aloha' was a recognition of life in another. If there was life there was mana, goodness and wisdom, and if there was goodness and wisdom, there was a god-quality. One had to recognize the 'god of life' in another before saying 'Aloha,' but this was easy. Life was everywhere—in the trees, the flowers, the ocean, the fish, the birds, the pili grass, the rainbow, the rock—in all the world was life—was god—was Aloha. Aloha in its gaiety, joy, happiness, abundance. Because of Aloha, one gave without thought of return; because of Aloha, one had mana. Aloha had its own mana. It never left the giver but flowed freely and continuously between giver and receiver. 'Aloha' could not be thoughtlessly or indiscriminately spoken, for it carried its own power. No Hawaiian could greet another with 'Aloha' unless he felt it in his own heart. If he felt anger or hate in his heart he had to cleanse himself before he said 'Aloha.'"

—Queen Lili'uokalani
Hawaii's last reigning monarch (1891–1893)

Acknowledgments

My heartfelt thanks to . . .
Tori Caron, BFF (Best Fan Forever!),
for (mon dew!) zee "shipping" of Pierre and Juliette;
Bruce Hale and Janette Cross,
for their help with the Pidgin English
(and extra mucho mahalo to Bruce
for the expert boy's-eye view);
Mary Hershey,
my sweet-and-wise fAiRy gOdSiStEr,
who taught me the magic of A.F.I.N.;
Allwyn and Frances Fitzpatrick,
Santa Barbara Montessori School teachers extraordinaire,
for a most excellent education on adolescent crushes;
John M. Fox,
for the literary dopamine;
Craig Jaffurs,
who listened to each chapter and validated the
true-to-the-core bits by getting The Squirms;
Isaac Jaffurs
(who does not at all resemble Cullen nor the Goons),
for his tips regarding high school golf;
Patterson Jaffurs (son extraordinaire),

who taught me how to take Marcos down, hapkido-style;

Jess Garrison, my editor and cohort-in-comedy,

for helping me make a good story great

and for laughing at (almost) all my jokes;

my sweetie-of-an-agent, Ginger Knowlton,

for sticking by me for 20+ years;

and to Edmond Rostand, for writing *Cyrano de Bergerac*:

Best. Play. Ever.

Also, special thanks to my readers in Alaska,

Alberta (Canada),

California, Colorado, Florida, Greece, Indiana, Maine,

Minnesota, Missouri,

New Jersey, New York, North Carolina, Ohio,

Ontario (Canada), Pennsylvania, Rhode Island,

Seoul (Korea) and Texas

who suggested some of the 101 Ways

that appear in this book.